Terror Comes to Berwyn

By Edward S. Tonry

DEDICATION

This book is dedicated to you, the reader
in hopes that you may actually buy this book.
Don't laugh, it *could* happen.

Cover by Judy Bullard.

ISBN-13: 978-1-7326648-5-2

Unkempt Wombat Press

Chapter One

The Invisible Man Disappears

It was a Tuesday in late May, 2019, and Jack Sorenson was unhappy. The French news said 'Art Smuggler Arrested' and mentioned his name with his passport picture. Not his pseudonym, the name he told the public, the always anonymous "John Smith" but his real name, Jack Sorenson.

The BBC said 'Art Theft Foiled', again with his name and the same picture. CNN had been more over the top. 'The Man Behind the Arrest of Art Thieves' made it sound like he had saved the world. Exaggeration, but only to a degree. *They had, at least, been able to find my high school graduation picture. The benefit of being an American news network. At least they didn't use my ugly driver's license photo.* He turned off the television and looked at Marcy as she finished dressing. Seeing his brand-new fiance eased his gloomy mood.

"I'm famous now, love. I wanted to help the police, return a stolen painting, catch some art smugglers, and what did I get?" He smiled to show he was being facetious. "Fame. Publicity. Notoriety. My picture in the news! Me! The guy who's never wanted attention. Nobody knows my face. Well, no one knows both my face and my name. Now everyone does. I'm going to have to adapt."

"Oh, my, Jack! Is this a disaster? How can you do your little private favors for people if you're well known? *Can* you still do your work?"

"Do you mean, 'What am I going to do now? Who will want to use me now?'"

He looked at his reflection in the mirror, the same innocuous face he always saw, the same soft brown hair, with a little touch of gray now at the edge. He was tallish and had an average build. He never stood out in a crowd. Until now.

"No, darling, I don't think it's that bad. The headlines said that an art smuggler was arrested and that I helped arrest him. They did go on some about my mysterious occupation, especially CNN. They didn't really know anything about it, though. It's bad, but not a disaster."

"You're overlooking something, Jack," mentioned Marcy as she pushed him away from the mirror and began combing her bright reddish-orange hair. "You've spent a lifetime avoiding the press, and don't know how they can milk a story for days and days. I enjoy that when they feature one of my paintings, dragging the story out forever. You're different.

"This was yesterday's news and by today, all over the States, the newspapers, the news programs on TV, the whole internet will be full of this story, and your face will be smiling out of half of the photographs. Your name will be in every story, too. You live by anonymity, dear one. You've often told me that. What *will* you do now?

"If a man is paying off the building inspector, and you subtly drop an envelope in the inspector's pocket, the man and the inspector are both happy. And so are you because of your fee. But the inspector won't want to be seen anywhere near you now. Even this Paris news station said that you 'transfer funds for dubious purposes.' The Chicago papers will have the same stories about you, and they'll want more details. How could they not? Local boy makes good, and all that. Who is telling them all of this anyway? In any case, you're going to lose a lot of clients, aren't you?"

"Maybe, maybe not. I guess I should check my voicemail. Oh, no. Twenty messages. Wait, some are duplicates, but not enough. Well, it could have been worse. It may still be worse, some of my clients may not have wanted to call me.

"I should calm down. There's nothing I can do about any of this now. I can worry about it later, love. For now, let's go out for a decent breakfast. My world may have come tumbling down about my ears, but I'm still hungry."

A block away, looking out onto a sunlit May morning in Paris, the trees along the Seine all dressed up in their finest new leaves, a soft breeze shaking them just enough, the world looked better. Jack smiled wanly, but it was a smile. Marcy looked at him with concern, not really certain how much of what he had said was real, and how much was trying to reassure her.

"Is this really as serious a problem as I think, Jack, darling?" she asked after ordering her breakfast. "I know you like to work in the shadows, coming and going mysteriously. Surely all of your work is not, um, improper. Is that a discreet enough word?"

"Oh, yes, very discreet," replied Sorenson, "and, no, it is not all improper. I do have a lot of clients who pay people off, most of the twenty who called me. But the payoffs I deliver are from small time cheats, business men who would rather spend a thousand a month in payoffs, than four thousand a month in maintenance on their buildings, or the cleanliness of their kitchens, or the safety of their factories.

"If they pay out a thousand a month, I get a hundred a month for my fee. Twenty of them gone is only a loss of two thousand a month, and I can survive that. I'm more concerned about the men who haven't called yet. Some of them pay me much more. I'm sorry, my dear one, but I will have to make some phone calls this afternoon, and we will have to go back to Berwyn today, or tomorrow at latest. These men will not want to talk about our relationship on the phone, so I must see them in person."

"Um, Jack, ah," stumbled Marcy, "I don't know quite how to ask this. Let me be blunt. Does this change your question last night? It doesn't change my answer."

"Change my question?" asked Jack, surprised. "Nothing will ever change that question, Marcy. The only thing wrong with that question was that it took me so long to ask it. I have always wanted to marry you. I still want to marry you. If I was flat broke, I would *still* want to marry you. I'm glad that your answer is still the same. I knew it would be.

"But I won't be flat broke, living off my wife's earnings. I have some clients who will be surprised to know that Mr. Smith is really Mr. Sorenson, but they will still use me to move money for them. The men who use me to pay for their mistresses' apartments, the gamblers who don't want to be seen going to a bookie. They really don't care what my name is, or how well-known I might be. Ten percent of a big gambler's winnings can make up for an awful lot of unscrupulous businessmen. Especially if the gambler knows what he's doing, and most of mine do."

He waved at the waiter for some more coffee before continuing.

"What bothers me the most is that I am now known to the world. I have lived out of sight for so long that I'm not sure if I can live in the light of day. I have been invisible. Invisible to polite society. Invisible to those who would steal a gambler's winnings. Invisible to the police. And suddenly everyone can see me. It's a strange feeling.

"The Jack Sorenson who was invisible, not there at all, has now disappeared, and is visible to the entire world. Everyone can see this ordinary face, and recognize it instantly. People will say to their friends, 'What a nice head of brown hair he has,' and I can't stop them. I feel like a butterfly pinned to a card in a display case at the museum."

"Then it is a disaster. Oh, dear, I feel so sad about this for you."

"No, I still say it's not a disaster. I'm changing, too. And not just because of my new-found fame. I used to call everyone who wasn't a close friend 'Mr. Jones' or 'Mr. Brown' just to avoid offending them by being too casual. After we celebrated my proposal last night, I did a lot of thinking about us, and about myself.

"I find myself wanting to be less formal with people, even my clients. I feel like becoming more open to the world, because of you. I want to do this, even if I'm not sure how open I can be. I've been closed off from everyone for so long, it's going to be a challenge. And now I have to go back to salvage what I can of that old life, and repair it in a new mode. But it'll be good for me, and us."

"Jack, you made me unbelievably happy last night when you proposed," Marcy admitted. "I wanted to spend days here in Paris basking in your love in a city made for love. But we're not children, we're almost fifty, for God's sake. I know that we can't put off unpleasant tasks just because they interfere with our delights. We can always come back to Paris. They aren't going to close it down. If you need to get home right away to take care of business, then let's go."

"Not even a small quibble?" asked Jack, with a grin.

"Not even a very tiny quibble," replied Marcy.

"Then you are the most loving woman in the world," Jack declared. "And I humbly thank you for that. I owe you a honeymoon in Paris, at least, for that concession. Do you want some more coffee? No, then let's go back to the hotel and check flights home. If we're lucky, we'll have to wait until tomorrow to leave. That will give us one more day to enjoy each other here and now."

***

"I've called all those men who left messages for me," Sorenson told Marcy. "I told them to call me back tomorrow after five in the afternoon. Whichever flight we take should get us to Chicago by early afternoon. This is Tuesday, tomorrow is Wednesday, and I can arrange to meet these men on Thursday. I am truly sorry to have to cut this romantic trip so short. I was going to have to be home by Friday, anyway. The men who want me to deliver money to their mistresses want me to do it on the first of the month. June first is a Saturday, so that means paying them on Friday.

"We still have the rest of this afternoon before us. It is still Paris, and it is still Spring. Could two people in love ask for anything more in life?"

"No, not unless they are gluttons," agreed Marcy. "You let me choose our sightseeing program yesterday. May I impose on your good nature to suggest today's schedule, as well?"

"Impose away, dear," Jack answered.

"I would like to visit the Place des Vosges, and the Musee Carnavalet, in the Marais," suggested Marcy. "We've both seen them before, but it's been a long while. And they are both so much reminders that an older

Paris is still here, alive in the heart of the new Paris.   And for dinner, L'Incroyable.   I think I took you there once before, and you loved it."

"I remember it well," Jack said, "and it will be a fine finish to our visit. Well chosen, dear one."

***

"Mr. Sorenson!" "Mr. Sorenson!" "Mr. Sorenson!" "Mr. Sorenson!" The same words echoed from every throat in the crowd of reporters at O'Hare Airport. Sorenson had anticipated some attention, though not as much as this. The story had been released to the news media on Sunday when the arrests in Paris had been made. Sunday afternoon in Paris was early Sunday morning in Chicago, and here it was Wednesday afternoon. *Why hadn't the story faded into old news yet? Marcy was right.*

Twenty or thirty reporters and cameramen were waiting for him as he left the customs area. The usual small flock of friends and relatives welcoming home a traveler had been shoved aside by a demanding news media. One lone policeman kept the mass behind the security rope, with difficulty.

"Can we have a statement, Mr. Sorenson?"

"How do you feel about the arrest of these criminals, Mr. Sorenson?"

"What exactly do you do for a living, Mr. Sorenson?"

"Were you frightened during the shootout, Mr. Sorenson?"

"Please, ladies and gentlemen," Sorenson announced, raising his hand to hush the reporters, "I've only just returned from Paris, and would like to return to my home. If you want a full statement, please contact my press secretary. Thank you."

As he walked quickly away, there was a pause. Then he heard the belated cries of "Who's your press secretary?" By then he and Marcy were out of range, hurrying out of the terminal. Marcy laughed as they slipped away.

"Oh, Jack, that was great," she chuckled, "saying 'please contact my press secretary' so calmly just like that. It was so spot-on, as if you've been dealing with the press all your life. What do you suppose they will do?"

"They will try to follow us now," Jack informed her, "if we give them a chance. And I don't intend to do that. Then they will turn their vast investigative talents to learning my phone number and my home address. Which means that I have only gained a respite for today.

"Tomorrow I may be able to squeeze some money out of one of them for an exclusive interview. If I can, that will help next month's cash flow. And if I can't, that means the story is finally dying out. And maybe I can become invisible again."

***

Thursday's meetings with his clients had been frustrating for Sorenson. Six of the twenty calls he had received were second attempts to reach him, so there were only fourteen men to call back. Five of the men he had called had simply canceled his services, and he didn't have to see them. The other nine were intent on making his life difficult.

"How are you supposed to deliver a payoff secretly if everyone knows your face?"

"The guy you deliver to doesn't want me to use you any more – you're too well known now. What am I supposed to do?"

"This guy's afraid to have you come near him, have you got another way to give him the money?"

Hour after hour, all day long, Sorenson listened to the same complaints from his clients about how his new celebrity was going to ruin their attempts to pay officials off. He met with each man separately for as long as half an hour, in different cafes or bars, all within a small area. There was no good answer to the questions, and the men knew that and still refused to accept the fact.

"I'm sorry about having my face made public," Sorenson told each of them, "it wasn't something that I wanted. The story was big and the news media jumped all over it. They demand pictures, not just words, so they had to find a photo of me. They used it without my permission, without asking me, without telling me. Still they did use it, and we both have to face the consequences.

"If the man you are paying off does not want to deal with me, then you should pay him off directly yourself, or find someone else who can do it discreetly. I had a friend who could have taken over for me. Unfortunately, he died last year.

"I can try to devise a new method of delivering the envelopes. However, almost any way I do it, I'll have to be near the other man at some point. Leaving an envelope full of cash in a mailbox, slipped under a door, or tucked into his morning newspaper just means that someone else might accidentally find the money. That would not be desirable.

"I *am* experienced at this work, you know. I once dropped an envelope into a politician's pocket while he was being interviewed by a TV news camera crew. No one saw a thing. I know how to do this discreetly. That's why you pay me. That's why no one has ever found us out.

"I'm sorry; if your payoff target does not want to have me deliver the money, I can't see any other way than for me to stop delivering the money. I hate to lose the business, but if your payee is reluctant, I don't see any alternative."

The real problem was that the man being bought did not want to be seen in Sorenson's presence, since the world now knew he delivered money under "dubious" circumstances. Sorenson had accepted this fact, and the related fact that he would lose some clients. His clients, however, were having trouble accepting the fact. They wanted Sorenson to become invisible again, at once, and refused to believe that he couldn't.

They also couldn't accept the fact that it was the man receiving their money who was the cause of the problem. Sorenson realized that after a while, his notoriety would fade and he would become invisible once more. However, the payees could not see that happening. They only saw the

most famous fixer in Chicagoland handing them envelopes in the middle
of a public street, while waving a banner labeled "payoff".

Sorenson was happy to be done with Thursday when it finally ended.
Friday was much more pleasant, even if busier. He normally took care of
bringing money to the mistresses of rich men on the first of the month.
This June, though, was starting on a Saturday, which meant that a meeting
at the man's office to get the money would have to be done on Friday.

His new fame meant that every man had to comment on his surprise at
learning Sorenson's real name, followed by a discussion of his adventures
capturing the criminals. Four brief visits to pick up some envelopes
turned into four long social calls. And the mistresses were just as well
informed about Sorenson's recent exploits. And just as eager to hear all
the details. At least the landlords were content to simply record the
payment of their rent.

Chapter Two

Trouble in Little Mogadishu

"I'm tired of talking about this,"Abdullah slammed the table with his fist. The Thursday that was awkward for Sorenson wasn't going well for him either. "We *must* steal this money. We *are* going to do this. I've explained why. You've all agreed with me. I'm not Yahye, I won't threaten you. Still, I will *demand* that one of you do this. Who? Who will volunteer? Are you all cowards?"

Ten people were gathered in Abdullah's apartment in what the people of Minneapolis called the Cedar-Riverside neighborhood, but what they called Little Mogadishu.

They, like tens of thousands of Somalis, had fled their homes in tropical Africa for the unlikely refuge of frigid Minnesota. They formed close-knit neighborhoods, found work, built families. Some kept their ties to their friends and associates in Somalia, including the terrorists of al-Shabaab and their rivals, the various warlords. One of those warlords was Diric, chieftain of a large band of warriors. He thought this justified calling himself a warlord, even if he didn't control very much territory.

Abdullah led Diric's "warriors" in Minneapolis. He had been given a band of twenty tough fighters, their wives, younger siblings, and a few old parents. He was the boldest of them, appointed leader because of his daring. America was not Somalia, though. The police actually enforced the laws, and hunted down thieves. The easy robberies in Somalia were a thing of the past. Every theft, burglary, robbery here had to be planned carefully.

His band had shrunk over the last few years as some found jobs that paid better than crime, and others lost interest in helping maintain chaos in a country that was fading from their memories. Yahye, the leader of the terrorist al-Shabaab, and his men committed any crimes that came to their minds. Abdullah was more cautious, especially after his gang began to dissolve. He couldn't afford to have anyone in jail, so they only stole at night, from stores without security cameras. It didn't raise much money, but he was reluctant to be bolder.

Abdullah was the biggest of the Somalis in his band, almost six feet tall. He looked larger, with a heavily muscled build. He wasn't fat because he exercised to be ready for street fights. Those fights were getting less frequent because Yahye's men carried guns all the time now. He was willing to talk tough, even about killing, but he knew he wouldn't kill anyone, maybe not even someone as evil as Yahye.

"*Somebody* has to steal the money. It's not going to walk here by itself and say 'Take me, I am yours,' just like that. Diric needs that money for his army in Somalia. He's determined to become a real warlord, with power over other warlords. Maybe even the whole country. He needs that money, which means *we* need that money. Even more, he does not want al-Shabaab to have that money. Bilan, you told us they are trying to raise ten million dollars to send to al-Shabaab, is that right?"

Bilan looked into Abdullah's eyes boldly. She was tall, thin, with floral patterns painted in henna on her hands and reaching up past her wrists halfway to her elbow. She was bolder than the other women who worked for Diric in America, bold enough to take on their first and most daring task.

She had managed to get herself hired to clean Yahye's house. She went to him, begging for work as a fellow Somali, knowing he had no wife to clean for him. He believed her story of being alone and friendless in a strange country. So was he, if he had ever cared to admit it to himself. Within just a few months of arriving in Minneapolis, she was Abdullah's spy, deep in enemy territory.

Abdullah returned Bilan's gaze with a fierce intensity. He stroked the line of hair, hardly a beard, that ran along the edge of his jaw. *She is tough, and has to prove it by looking at me like this, as if she were a man. I let her because she is almost as hard as any of the men, and I need every fighter I can get, even if she is a woman. Diric had sent me with my two brothers, almost twenty other men, and a few wives. Hardly enough to confront al-Shabaab here, especially now when so many have left us. And Bilan is the only woman who dares take an active part in our mission.*

Diric needs us to raise money for his army. Even more, he ordered us to frustrate al-Shabaab's efforts to raise their own money. If he can't become stronger with American money, then crippling his enemy is his only option. If al-Shabaab has already raised ten million dollars, I must push this little band to steal that money any way they can.

"I was cleaning Yahye's house last week," explained Bilan, "and they were saying they only needed a little bit more. A little bit, ha! They still need one hundred thirty thousand dollars to make the ten million. They have been raising money from many people. It is now late in the month and too many people do not have any more money to give. They will have to wait until next month, at least. I have also heard them complain that the donations are getting smaller. They're talking about using force again to get money from our people."

"So, nine million, eight hundred seventy thousand dollars," observed Abdullah. "What fools! They insist on waiting until they have a nice, even ten million dollars. Al-Shabaab needs this money as much as Diric does, and they hold on to it to make a bigger, more impressive contribution. Still, it gives us time to take it from them. So. Who will do it?"

He looked around the room at his "warriors" and sighed. *Six men, three women. And two of the women will only do what they had done in Somalia, cooking and household chores. I need daring fighters to take on al-Shabaab in the streets, boldly, bravely. We were all brave enough when we came here, but life is so easy in America. We have all gotten soft. Even myself. I used to be bolder.*

The comfortable American furniture we are sitting on, the fast foods everywhere, the cars, it is hard to keep my people focused on helping Diric. The television shows us pictures of the fighting in Somalia, and it also shows us silly programs and phony reality. Cell phones are very useful, letting me contact anyone in an instant. They also distract us all, with games, casual calls, tweets. How can I inspire them?

"That's a lot of money, Abdullah," commented skinny little Ali, in his mid-teens and Abdullah's youngest brother. "How many bags will we need to carry it away? I'm brave enough, even though I'm the youngest here. And if I have to make many trips with my backpack, I may get caught. Then they will be alert for our next attempt."

"The money is in two big green suitcases," Bilan informed them. "I have seen them. They are kept in Yahye's private room. But there are only the two pieces, and they can be both be moved at once. They have rollers to make it easy to move them. You know how lazy Americans are."

"You must not do the theft, Ali," ordered Taifa, his middle brother, but as clean-shaven as Ali. "Our mother asked us to protect you here. In a year or two, you'll be old enough to take such risks, not now. Are there no alternatives, Abdullah? Must we steal the money? What if we just burned it up? That would keep it out of al-Shabaab's hands."

"Do you think that being a warlord is easy?" asked Abdullah, frustrated and angered by his middle brother's question. "Do you realize what it costs to maintain an army, even in Somalia? Weapons cost money, and no one sells them to us without making a great deal of money for themselves. Westerners complain about the arms dealers selling us cheap arms, but those arms are not cheap, not to us. Diric must have money for more weapons, and so must al-Shabaab. If we cannot get that money they have, we must at least make sure they don't have it either. Still, I would rather get the money for Diric. We can do this if we're brave enough.

"So. For the last time: which one of you will steal this money? You all claim to support Diric. You all say you love him and will do anything for him. Prove it. Do this *one* thing. Steal the money. I cannot do it because Yahye knows me. His men know me. I would be killed before I could get into his house."

"*I* will do this," declared Zahi. A pointed tuft of beard on his chin made his face seem to stick forward in an almost threatening way, even though he was almost as small and scrawny as Ali. Abdullah looked at him, considering whether Zahi could handle the theft. *He is married to Bilan, and I would have given her the job if she had volunteered. Zahi has never asked for a difficult task before. He does what he is told to do, without argument. He never does more than he is asked to do. Still, no one else has volunteered.*

Abdullah sighed, *it is so hard to inspire Diric's followers in America. Back in Somalia, Diric was there in front of them, and ready to reward their efforts. They had nothing, so anything they made fighting was welcome. But here, even poor people live like princes. What could move a man to risk his life here, when a comfortable life is available to everyone for little effort? Yahye and his men have their religion to drive them on. Islamic fanatics didn't need any other motives.*

"How will you do this?" asked Abdullah. " Yahye is not an easy man to rob. He has many men around him at all times, and they are very willing to kill. I will give you this job. However, first you must convince me that you can do it and succeed. I know you are brave enough, but you have never volunteered for anything before."

"Bilan, my wife, works as Yahye's cleaning lady," explained Zahi. "She is allowed in his house without question. I have sometimes been there, too, when she needed help. Yahye's men will not help a woman with her work, so they let me help her. They think I am weak and womanish because I do this, but I am not so weak as that. Since no one else has spoken up, I will do it. We can go into his house tomorrow, Friday. They will all be at the mosque and the house will be empty and unguarded. Who would dare rob Yahye? Every Somali in Minneapolis knows how violent he is. We each take a suitcase and flee with them."

"By Allah!" exclaimed Abdullah, "what a daring idea! Zahi, I have been wrong about you. I did not think you were daring enough for big jobs. I apologize for this. No, you are not weak. You are the bravest of us all. The rest of you should be ashamed because you were so reluctant to do this.. All except you, Ali.

"Zahi, when you have the money you must not bring it here. Yahye knows my face, he knows I work for Diric, but he only *suspects* I am here. Still, I have seen Xidig in this street, looking around. You must not lead them here. I have thought this out in preparation for the theft. Bring the money to the train station in St. Paul. We can leave the bags at the station as checked baggage. Ask someone there where they store the luggage. The station will charge us a small fee to store the bags, and will not inspect them. We can retrieve them later when we are ready to send the money to Diric. Can you do this?"

"Of course, I can," argued Zahi, somewhat miffed. "I have not often asked to do work for Diric, but I have always done any job you gave me and exceptionally well. I am quite capable of doing this theft, and of delivering the money wherever you want."

"Bilan, are you willing to help your husband?" asked Abdullah.

"Naturally, I will do everything I can to help him," answered Bilan. "I would have volunteered if he had not, and I will help him all the way. I am so proud of him now. You know well you can count on me."

"Then, go with Allah's blessing, and may all go well. When you have the money, call my phone, and we will meet you at the train station. Is everyone agreed on this plan? Good. Then return to your homes, and prepare for tomorrow."

Everyone except his brothers left the house and Abdullah sent Taifa and Ali to cook their dinner. He threw himself into an armchair and it shook under his weight. He looked into the kitchen at Taifa, his younger brother, a little smaller but also well muscled. He couldn't see Ali, their youngest brother, so eager to fight, so young and unaware of the dangers of fighting.

He wanted to be alone to think. *I am happy that Zahi asked to do this theft. He is finally doing his share of the real work here. Real work. Hah! My grandfather would be ashamed of me. Stealing money to send to Diric. What for? To make him a more powerful warlord, so he can challenge al-Shabaab as the biggest danger to peace in Somalia.*

I was glad when Diric chose me to lead this band on his behalf. A position of importance, a chance to prove myself worthy to be one of his inner circle, to help rule the new Somalia he was going to create. The ashes of the old Somalia, more likely. So much more fighting back home, so many more dead. And the fighting goes on here. We fight Yahye and his men as if we were in Somalia. Thank Allah that no one has died here. The Americans have been tolerant but they do not like murders.

He went into the kitchen and pulled a banana from a bunch. Stripping the skin back, he walked back to his chair and ate the fruit.

Should we keep on doing this? Should I keep on? What is in it for me? I will not become one of Diric's inner circle. I am here and he is far away, making new friends. I worry about Taifa and especially Ali. Ali is so young and does not realize how deadly a game we are playing at. I should take him away from this. Still, where would we go? How can I renege on my promise to Diric? What about my promise to our mother? This is too hard a question. I can't answer it just now.

***

"I was surprised to hear you volunteer to steal the money." Bilan opened the door. "You have not been so dedicated to Diric as many of the others, nor so enthusiastic about doing work for him. You do what you're told to do, without complaint. Yet you do not seem eager to help. The others haven't noticed, they think you're just shy, not as daring as they are. But I know you, and how daring you can be. Why show your courage now?"

They sat down on the worn out sofa in their simple room. The white paint on the walls was flaking off in places, showing several different shades of white, cream, and beige underneath. Zahi looked intently at his wife.

"Bilan, my wife, my love, my very life, I care about you so very much. And I have seen how you are becoming afraid of spying on Yahye. You fear what will happen if he learns you work for Diric. And I have also seen that you are reluctant to work for Diric as well. Ever since your uncle wrote and told us what Diric's men had done to your parents, you have been less eager to help him.

"Before that letter, you would have volunteered without any hesitation. Now, I had to volunteer first to get you to help. I know what is going through your mind. I have heard you at night, crying for your mother and father. Bilan, we are both becoming disillusioned with warlords and fighting. We must get away from all of this. And ten million dollars will help us get very far away from al-Shabaab and Diric both."

"You want to take the money for us!" shrieked Bilan. "How can we get away with that? Abdullah will be enraged. He talks about how willing Yahye is to kill, but Abdullah is just as willing. He will come after us for taking the money for ourselves. And Yahye will also pursue us. It doesn't matter which one finds us, either will kill us."

"They can only kill us if they can find us," countered Zahi, "and they will not find us. Yahye and his men will be at the mosque for hours, and we can steal the money when they leave their house. We will have several hours before they know they have been robbed. And Abdullah will wait for our phone call to meet us at the station. He will wait for hours as well. We can get very far away from here in those hours."

"Oh, Zahi, can it really be as easy as that?" asked Bilan. "Where should we go? Can we go someplace warm? I am so tired of the weather here in Minnesota. Cold, snow, there seems no end to it."

"I am still thinking about this, someplace warm, yes, definitely," replied Zahi. "Until Abdullah asked for a volunteer, I had not thought we had any chance to get away from this life. You said I was daring, and maybe I am daring. Yet you know I am not a very brave man. I am ashamed to be so weak. But I saw the possibility at once of freeing ourselves, of going somewhere else and living as we want to live. I had to wait, in case one of the others would speak up, and because I was still thinking out my plan.

"See this American magazine called *People*? It has a story about an art theft and this brave man named Jack Sorenson who helped catch the thieves and who also returned a million dollars to his client. Only a very honest man would do that. Such a man as that could help us escape. It says he moves money around the world for people. He can take us and the money wherever we want to go."

"Can we go home to Somalia?" asked Bilan. "My parents are dead, but yours are still alive. We can share our new wealth with them. Surely, some part of the country is not at war."

"Somalia is always at war, every part of it," Zahi answered. "And both Yahye and Abdullah will think we will try to return to our homes there. Elsewhere in Africa may be a good choice. Many Somalis have moved to Kenya, though al-Shabaab has agents there, too. There are other places where we will not stand out, and be able to live well on this money.

"We could go to Nigeria, a place many Americans have heard of. I hear them talking about Nigerian princes and how rich they are. We will be rich and should live like princes, too. This Mr. Sorenson can bring us to a safe refuge there."

"We must have our passports if we wish to leave the country," objected Bilan. "We put them in that box at the bank, to keep them safe from thieves. And the bank is closed now. We must go there tomorrow, too. Where does this man live? Is he here in Minneapolis?"

"No, he lives in a place called Berwyn. It is somewhere near Chicago. I will look it up on our laptop computer now."

"Have some dates, Zahi."

"Thank you. Ah, here it is. So far away from us, so many highways and roads between here and there. I will print out the directions the computer gives and we will be able to find our way to this Berwyn, and safety."

***

Yahye's house on the side street was always kept locked. It was a small bungalow, with a porch and some shrubs planted by a former occupant. There was always someone to answer the door if a visitor came by. On Fridays, though, when they all went to the mosque, the house was empty, protected by the locked door and, even more, the reputation of the owner.

Officially, Yahye was just another Somali refugee, but his neighbors, and all the Somalis in Minneapolis, knew he was the local leader of the terrorist group al-Shabaab. They all knew he was a man to whom mercy was an unknown quality, who would kill anyone for any reason.

This Friday, Zahi and Bilan brought the key Yahye had given Bilan so she could come and clean at her convenience. The lock clicked open and Bilan slipped in quietly while Zahi brought the vacuum up the stairs. She listened to see if anyone was still in the house, and was startled to hear sounds from the back.

"Who's there?" asked Yahye, weakly. "Is someone there?"

"Yes, Yahye, it is me, Bilan. I came to clean while you were at the mosque," she said as she looked into the room. His head was propped up on a pillow and his right arm was outside the blanket, with a gun near his hand. His eyes were half closed and looked almost dead. The skin on his face looked abnormally pale and the scar on his forehead was darker than normal. Two large green suitcases stood on end by the back wall.

"Not today, woman. I am ill and do not want to be disturbed. Don't come tomorrow either. I am meeting with my men, and I don't want an outsider listening, even you whom I trust. We will be going to Xidig's wedding on Monday. Come then. I am not sure I will be well by then, but if I am here, I should be able to tolerate your cleaning then."

"Yes, Yahye, I understand," Bilan replied. "May Allah make you well soon."

Good, the woman has gone. He resettled himself on his pillows. *It's bad enough to be ill without having her fussing about the house, cleaning, making noise with that machine. What was wrong with a broom? I need quiet to think. We have to find more money to send back home. Cawil isn't one of the most important leaders, but he has their ear. He wants us to send him ten million dollars. I don't dare offend him.*

Hamza can rob more stores. The police are trying to find proof that we are robbing these people, but they have nothing yet. I wish Mahmoud were healthier, he's very loyal to me. But his leg is still too weak from that old wound, it won't heal properly. He thinks it may be broken, but he can walk on it. He may be right, he limps badly and he wouldn't try to avoid his duty.

The others are doing what I order, but it's not enough. Hamza wants to rob some banks. He says there is more money in a bank than in a store. True, but the police are more concerned about banks. Some American robbed a bank two months ago and the police were searching hard for him until they found him. Bashiir robbed an evil liquor store the same day, and no one looked for him.

But how else can I find another hundred thousand dollars? Bashiir took five thousand from that den of evil, but at that rate we would have to rob more than twenty, thirty stores to get all we need. Too many. A bank could give us ten thousand, maybe twenty thousand dollars all at once. I must think this through. Allah help me! I'm so ill, I cannot think properly.

***

"Yahye is still here," Bilan told Zahi as they left. "He says he is ill, but he looks too healthy to try robbing. He has a gun and will not hesitate to kill us if we touch the suitcases. And they are right there in his room. He wants me to come back Monday to clean, even if he is still ill then."

"If he is still inside, how can we steal the money?" asked Zahi. "If he is there, he will see us take the money, and shoot us."

"Maybe he will be asleep if he is ill," replied Bilan. "He looked very tired today. If he is sleeping we will have no trouble."

"That is true, Bilan, and it gives me an idea. There are drugs to make a person sleep. We can use them on him, and then taking the money will be easy."

"What kind of drugs, Zahi? Do you know about these things? Where can we get them?"

"I do not know, Bilan. Abdullah may know. He wants us to steal the money and will help us. He won't know until later that he is helping us to steal the money for ourselves alone. We need to tell him, anyway, that we can't get the money until Monday."

***

"You were supposed to call me when you had the money," growled Abdullah with irritation. "You were supposed to bring it to the train station, not here. Can you do nothing right?"

"Yahye was still there, watching his suitcases," stated Bilan, "with a gun next to him. He didn't go to the mosque because he was ill. He told me to come back on Monday. They're going to Xidig's wedding then, and the house will be empty."

"However, he might still be sick and stay home," added Zahi, "so I thought we could use some drug to put him to sleep. Do you know of some drug that will make him sleep quickly? Can we get such a drug?"

"Ah, Zahi, why have you not showed such admirable ideas in the past?" asked Abdullah with approval. "Knocking Yahye out is a very good plan. When he is sleeping, you can kill him, and steal the money. That will deal two serious blows to their organization. I like this idea very much.

"We have until Monday morning. That gives me some time to find such a drug. Come by here early Monday, and I will give it to you. Then the rest of the plan can continue as before – bring the money to the train station Monday afternoon. This is very good work, both of you."

***

"Taifa, I want you to steal some ether for me from a hospital," ordered Abdullah. "Zahi has come up with a plan to steal the money even if Yahye is home. He wants to knock him out with ether and steal the suitcases when Yahye is asleep. He can kill him at the same time, which will make our work much easier."

"Americans don't use ether in hospitals anymore," countered Taifa. "I can get something even better. You know I work for the animal doctor near here. They operate on animals just like hospitals do on people. The doctor told me ether is too dangerous, very likely to catch fire he said. So they use a drug called Sevoflurane. It works very fast and is very safe to use. I know where it is kept and can steal some from work without any trouble."

***

"Take this bottle, Zahi, it will put Yahye to sleep at once," advised Abdullah Monday morning. "Taifa, tell them how to use this drug."

"At the animal clinic where I work we use Sevoflurane, which works quickly. I stole this bottle over the weekend. Put some of the liquid on a cloth and hold it to Yahye's face. Make him breathe it in deeply. He will be asleep in seconds. Make sure he breathes in enough to make him sleep a long time. Don't breathe it yourself, or you'll fall asleep too."

"Then you can kill Yahye and steal the money," continued Abdullah. "I will be waiting for your call."

***

Bilan and Zahi entered the house quietly. There was no sound today. They looked quickly around the few rooms in the small house and sighed in relief. No one was there, as they had planned. The living room was clean, thanks to Bilan's frequent visits, but cluttered with handguns, knives, small pots, tools, and many other items Yahye's men used often. The walls were covered with large woven hangings, brought with them from Somalia, a reminder of home. A banner with an Arabic prayer hung on one wall.

Yahye's room was messier, perhaps because he had been too ill to keep it clean himself. The two big green suitcases were standing against a wall. Zahi lifted them both onto the bed and unzipped them. Raising the flaps, he and Bilan looked in wonder at the bundles of money, a mass of cash packed tightly into the cases. A moment of disbelieving awe, and then they closed the cases up again and brought them out to their car.

The suitcases were large and barely fit side by side in the trunk of their Chevy Malibu. They spent time trying to squeeze them in with their own luggage. Lying side by side, or atop of each other, the pieces would not fit into the trunk. They pulled their luggage out and placed it on the back seat of the car. Then they replaced the green suitcases easily in the now empty trunk. They hadn't been watching their surroundings until Bilan lifted the last suitcase into the trunk.

"Zahi, they are coming home already!" she yelled and jumped into the car. Zahi slammed the trunk closed, got in, and started the car. They sped away as fast as they could. In his rear view mirror Zahi could see the other Somalis getting out of their cars and looking in their direction. One car was following them.

***

"Who was that?" asked Xidig.

"Probably just Bilan and her weak husband," remarked Yahye. "I told them they should clean today while we were at your wedding. If they have left, then they are finished here, and we can continue our celebration here without interference from them.

"That man was very rude to tell you to move your wedding party. We were not making so much noise, just good, proper wedding music. Being a policeman may protect him from my wrath for now. Still, he should not treat us this way. We can make as much noise *here* as we want.

"I have a wedding present here for you and your bride," Yahye told Xidig, walking into his room. "I forgot to bring it earlier. You will like it very much, I think."

He stopped in the doorway in shock. The suitcases weren't in the corner any longer. His face paled, then darkened in rage. He turned to the wedding party and shouted at them.

"Mahmoud, we have been robbed," he yelled. "The suitcases are gone. Those dogs of cleaners must have stolen the money! We must find it at once! How long is it since we saw them drive away?

"Barely a minute," replied Mahmoud. "They can't have gotten far away yet."

Yahye picked up a knife from a table and threw it at the wall, where it stuck and quivered. His scarred face was dark with anger, his eyes glared. He had looked sickly at the wedding, but now he seemed to be a bellowing lion.

"Wait, here is Hamza calling me. Hamza says he saw them loading the suitcases into their car as he drove up. Yes, yes, Hamza, keep following them, we will come after you. Do not lose sight of them! How fortunate we came home when we did! He and Bashiir are following them onto the big highways. The I-94, he says, going south. Where are my men?

Where are the others? Why have a large gang of men when none are here when they are needed?"

"They are still packing up the food from the wedding to bring it here," answered Mahmoud.

"Food! This is more important! Why aren't they here yet? Xidig, take your car and follow Hamza. I will call Hamza to let him know you are coming to help him and Bashiir. I know Zahi's car; it is silver with a big dent in the rear side. Look for it."

"But, it's my wedding day," began Xidig in protest.

"Yes, I know it is your wedding day, Xidig. This is more important than a wedding. If we do not recover that money, Cawil will send men here to kill us all. So let your wife weep at home for a day or two until we find the money. Better that than have her become a widow. I will give you this one kindness, you may take your own car. So when you find the money, you may come home to her at once.

"Go now, and keep me informed. Mahmoud and I will stay here. I am feeling tired again from my illness."

The rest of the wedding party stood dumbfounded as Xidig left. The bride cried on her mother's shoulder. Her father fumed, silently, knowing Yahye's temper, *What sort of wedding is this?* Xidig sped up the street, heading for the highway. The wedding party sat around unhappily waiting for Yahye's permission to leave, but he had forgotten about them. He went onto the porch, sat on a bench, and brooded.

***

"Where do we go now, Zahi? They are chasing us! I think it is Hamza in that car. He will kill us."

"We will go south, because that is what the map shows. We must get as far from Minneapolis as possible as fast as we can. We should just drive very fast for a long time. Maybe we can lose them. America is a very big country and they will not know where we have gone. We must first get onto the road called I-94."

"There is the sign for that big highway, I-94, Zahi. I can still see Hamza behind us. Drive faster! If the police stop us, Hamza will be afraid of them and will have to drive past us, and we can lose him then. What does a speeding ticket matter if it helps us get away?"

***

After an hour, the bride's father gathered his courage and went out to speak to Yahye.

"Sir, you have sent Xidig off on an important errand," he mentioned politely. "I gather that he will be gone overnight. I understand your concern over your own matters, and approve of your using Xidig's help. However, I was wondering if the rest of us might be allowed to go home now. My wife and daughter are quite upset by all this. They do not understand, as I do, that a man must obey his duty."

The question took Yahye's eyes off the road just as a car came up the street.

Abdullah looked at the house. "Oh, no, Yahye is still here. Keep driving, don't let him see us. He's not dead. Did Zahi fail? Or was he afraid to kill someone?"

"Maybe Zahi and Bilan did manage to steal the money, but Yahye woke up already," guessed Taifa. "Maybe they didn't give him the drug properly. Maybe he was at the wedding after all, and has returned home to find his money gone."

"Maybe. Maybe. Maybe. That would be bad for Zahi and Bilan," groused Abdullah. "I told them they should kill Yahye when they had the chance. We must try to find them and hope they have the suitcases. Call Ali, and have him wait at the train station, in case they go there as they're supposed to.

"Still, if Yahye is here, they may not have stolen the money. If they had, he would be leading his men in the search for them. He would not be just sitting on his porch talking to some old man."

***

"I don't know where they are," Ali announced as he entered his house. "They never came to the train station."

"We drove all over Minneapolis and saw no sign of Zahi and Bilan, or Yahye's men," Taifa described their efforts. "They should have been searching for them as hard as we were. When we went to Yahye's house earlier, he was talking to someone. I think I have seen him before. It might be the father of the woman Xidig was marrying today. But if Yahye went to the wedding, Zahi and Bilan should have stolen the money and brought it to us."

"It is possible that Yahye and his men have found Zahi and Bilan," considered Abdullah. "They may not want to kill them in his house, so they are doing it somewhere more private."

"Yahye might let Hamza do the killing, but he would be there to watch," argued Taifa.

"Oh, please, don't talk that way," complained Ali, throwing himself full-length on the sofa. "I like those two. I would hate to see them killed by that monster Yahye. Maybe they left the city and the others are following them."

"If they stole the money early enough, Yahye would not be able to follow them," noted Abdullah. "All we can hope for is we just kept missing both parties."

"I guess so," admitted Ali. "They should have called us by now, even if they were being chased. They both have cell phones, and only one can drive the car. Why haven't we heard from them? Maybe we should go out and look for them again."

"Go where?" asked Abdullah. He got up from his chair and walked around the room. "We have been everywhere we can think of they might go. Bilan's cousin, her friend who works at the market, his friend who is a mechanic. No one has seen them since Friday, at least. That was three days ago No one has heard from them. They have disappeared. The only good news is that Yahye is at home and not watching them being killed."

"So we just wait?" asked Taifa.

"We just wait," sighed Abdullah, frustrated.

***

A long day of high-speed driving is very tiring for people who are not accustomed to it. The directions they had printed out were very good, and Bilan never misread them, and Zahi never missed a turn. However, six hours in a car is a long trip for people used to bus rides in Minneapolis, or staying home in Somalia. They had had a short break for gas and lunch south of Madison, Wisconsin. They hadn't noticed the other car that waited until they got back on the highway.

"We can't take them here, Bashiir," warned Hamza. "There are two state police cars in that parking lot. And they aren't having donuts in the cafe, they are talking to those other men. They would stop us in an instant if we attacked Zahi and his wife. We must wait for another opportunity. While they eat, we can fill up our gas tank too at that other gas station."

"Your car is too slow, Hamza," complained Bashiir. "We could have forced them off the road if we could have caught up with them. We were lucky to see them pulling off here, they were so far ahead of us."

"I bought the car because it would carry a lot of us, not for speed. I did not expect to engage in road races in Minneapolis. If they think they are safe and slow down, we will still have a chance to capture them and get the money. Call Xidig and tell him where we are."

The trip felt even longer when Zahi and Bilan got to their destination and learned from Bilan's cell phone that Berwyn has no hotels within the city limits. They were shocked – even if they never stayed in hotels, they knew about them and assumed they were everywhere in America. Bilan looked at her cell phone in dismay.

"Are you certain, Bilan?" asked Zahi. "Surely there must be some hotels in so large a city as this."

"No, not a single one. There are many hotels in the area, but I do not where Oak Park, Riverside, Cicero are. They are all just strange names which mean nothing to me. There is a policeman parked up ahead. Park behind him and ask him. He will know a close hotel because he lives here."

The policeman gave him directions to the Bide-a-Wee Motel in Oak Park, just north of Berwyn. They got lost momentarily and found, instead, the Restful Hotel in Oak Park. It was small, and not expensive. They had lived in a very basic apartment in Minneapolis, and this hotel room looked at least as nice, maybe even better. It wasn't the one the friendly policeman had told them about, they just came upon it first and decided it would do just fine.

"We are not in Berwyn," Zahi told his wife, "but we are not far from it."

"Will we be safe here?

"Yes, Bilan. No one followed us, or we would have seen them. No one knows we are here."

"Good," answered Bilan. "We do not know where this man lives, so tomorrow we must try to find him. He is famous, his picture is in this magazine, they write stories about him and his famous deeds. Everyone should know where to find him. Uncle Mohammed killed a wild hyena and everyone in our village knew him because of that, even people in other villages."

"Yes, except our village was very small compared to these American cities," observed Zahi. "We have driven the length of our village many times over, just today searching for this hotel. In such large places, even great fame might be unknown among so many people. The magazine has the names of other people involved in this story. Maybe they will know where to find Mr. Sorenson."

***

Hamza and Bashiir had the same problem as their prey, no hotels in Berwyn.

"I can see Bilan; she's looking at her cell phone," indicated Hamza, pulling off to the side of the street, "just as we are. She isn't finding a hotel either, I'll bet. Look, Zahi's talking to that policeman. He must be asking about a hotel.   We will ask the policemen the same question. Then we can capture them tonight in their room."

Zahi drove off, just making it through the light as it turned red. Hamza and Bashiir pulled into the space he had left. Hamza got out of his car and approached the police car.

"Excuse me, sir," he began politely, "those were my friends who just spoke to you. I missed following him through this light. I don't have a cell phone and I'm afraid I might lose sight of him. Could you tell me where you sent him, please?"

Unlike Zahi, Hamza did not get lost, and took a room at the Bide-a-Wee.

"I did not see their car in the lot here," Hamza told the others. "Maybe he has parked nearby instead. We must check every room here tonight after Xidig joins us. If we do not find them here, then in the morning we must start searching for them. Tonight, think about ways we can find them."

Chapter Three

The Nigerian Prince

"I'm sorry, but Inspector Radcliffe isn't here just now. I'm her partner, Detective Sergeant Mahoney, may I help you?"

"Oh, yes, please, sir." Zahi showed Mahoney his magazine. "You are in the story, too. Very good. We have read of this man Mr. Jack Sorenson who saved the famous painting and returned the ransom money. So very brave, and *honest*, too. My wife and I would very much like to meet him. Can you tell us where he lives, please? The story does not give this information."

"Hmmm, I'm not sure if … well, wait here a minute," apologized Mahoney. "I'll have to check to see if I have his address."

I know where he lives well enough, thought Mahoney as he walked back to his cubicle. *On the other hand, should I be giving his address to every stranger who walks into the station house? He has spoken about taking precautions against possible enemies. And I don't know if he really has serious enemies, and who they might be if he does.*

"Hello, Mr. Sorenson," Mahoney greeted Jack as he answered his phone. "Your fame has spread. I have a couple of your fans here who would like to meet you. They want your address and I don't know if I should give it to them. Do you want to see them? I kid about their being fans. They mentioned the return of the ransom and your honesty almost in the same breath. They may want to hire you."

"Thank you, Detective Sergeant Mahoney," answered Sorenson. "I don't mind meeting possible new clients, but never at my apartment. I wouldn't mind, though, if you were kind enough to give them my phone number. I appreciate your delicacy about this. You're really starting to like me, aren't you? Such a pleasant change. Thank you."

Sorenson heard Mahoney snort in derision as he hung up.

Going back out to the police station lobby, Mahoney told the waiting couple, "I can't find his address right now, but here's his phone number. You can call him up and arrange to meet him. Is there anything else you need?"

"Oh, no, sir. Thank you very much, sir."

"No, well, good day."

***

A week of unwanted publicity had changed Sorenson's life somewhat. Several of his clients had fired him for being too well known now. A few had changed their minds and rehired him, asking him to be extra careful and discreet in future. A couple of other men had called to ask if he would handle delivering the rent for their mistresses' apartments.

"My wife gave me the third degree over an entry in my checkbook," the man might say. "She wanted to know why I was paying a landlord when our mortgage was paid in full. I made up an almost convincing story to put her off. I'm just glad it was a new check register and she didn't see all the old payments."

Sorenson also turned down a man who wanted him to transport five very large suitcases filled with money to Colombia, letting the man know in no uncertain terms that he did not work for the drug trade, no matter how profitable it might be.

So Tuesday morning's call had seemed to be just another potential new client, attracted by the unexpected discovery of a new occupation, one that might be useful. The caller spoke good English, with an accent that Sorenson couldn't place.

"Mr. Jack Sorenson, sir, my name is Zahi Smith. I and my wife are immigrants to this country from Nigeria. We read about how you saved that valuable painting from being stolen, and how you returned a million dollars to the man who was your client. You are obviously a very honest man, and we need such a man. May we come to see you today to discuss a matter of great urgency to us?"

"Certainly, I am always open to new clients," admitted Sorenson, "however, I do not have an office. I work from my home, and do not see my clients there. Most of my clients want to keep their affairs private, so, to protect them, I prefer to meet them in public places. A coffee shop, a bar, a park bench. Or, we could meet at your home."

"We would not like to be seen in public," cautioned Zahi. "We have a room at the Restful Hotel in Oak Park. It is room fourteen, on the first floor. If you could please come now, we would be very grateful."

"I can be there in about half an hour."

He got into his car, just back from his mechanic's loving attention, and drove to Oak Park. The car was running fine, and the repaired body work looked as good as new. *Maybe I can keep it a few years longer,* he thought, *it is still a delight to drive.*

The hotel was plain on the outside, looking more like an apartment building. The parking lot was big, empty except for one car at the moment. Sorenson parked near the other car, a silver late model Chevy Malibu with a dented quarter panel. It was parked opposite the entrance to the hotel. This gave him the opportunity to walk past the Malibu and check its license plate. He entered the empty lobby and walked down a corridor marked "Rooms 1 to 16". He knocked on the door of number fourteen.

"Ah, Mr. Sorenson, sir," remarked the small black man who opened the door. "I recognized you from your picture in the *People* Magazine. Please come in. I am Zahi Smith, and this is my wife Bilan. Please sit down, please."

"Thank you, I'm pleased to meet you," replied Sorenson, shaking their hands and seating himself. "Before we begin, just to save time, I will tell you that I do not ever do money transfers for the drug trade, or the sex slave trade. There are other transfers I will not do, but these are absolutely forbidden. So, perhaps you could tell me just what you do want me to do for you."

"I am a prince in my home country of Nigeria," revealed Zahi, with pride. "I have been forced into exile by my enemies, however, and I am having trouble returning to my homeland and my proper place. I have acquired a large sum of money, one million American dollars, which will help me return home. I need help to move it to Nigeria. I hear that moving such a large amount of cash is discouraged, or even illegal. Can you help us ship this money to Nigeria?"

"Possibly," guessed Sorenson, thinking back a few years. *Walters wanted me to move twenty grand to England to bet on some big race. Too bad the deal fell through. That would have been a good payday. What were the rules? Forms, permission from both governments…*

"It's not illegal to ship a million dollars overseas," Sorenson informed them, "but anything over ten thousand dollars must be declared to the government. A form must be filed, explaining the purpose of the transfer. If the explanation is accepted, the transfer is allowed. If you have a plausible explanation to offer, you don't really need me to do this."

"Oh, it is so difficult for us," interjected Bilan, waving her hands around in agitation. The sleeves of her blouse floated around as she waved her hands and Sorenson noted the dark floral designs painted on her hands, reaching well above her wrists. "This five million dollars is what we need to get back to our home, and we cannot afford to lose it. And we have enemies who are searching for us and the money. We do not want them to get this money. If they find us with the money, they will kill us immediately. However, if we do not seem to have the money with us, they will wait until we have it. So, if you take the money to Nigeria for us, we will be safe, and so will the money."

Sorenson sat in thought for a minute, looking around the room casually. He noted the two large green suitcases near the closet, and the two smaller ones beside them. *The larger pieces could easily each hold five million dollars, if it was in hundreds. Maybe it's in smaller bills. Is it one million, or five million? Maybe there's more. Maybe I need to check them out first.*

"Would you like some tea, sir?" Bilan asked. "It's bottled, I'm afraid, but almost as nice as fresh tea."

"That would be very nice, thank you." Sorenson opened the bottle she offered him and took a drink.

"I might be able to do this for you," cautioned Sorenson, "though it may have to be done in several stages. You want to move the money to another country, and this requires permission from the American government and from the foreign government. It *is* possible to get permission. The larger the amount of money, the more carefully each government will consider your request. They do not want to let drug dealers launder their profits, or terrorists ship money to buy guns. The longer each takes to approve your request, the longer you will have to stay here.

"This leads to a new first stage. Not taking you and the money to Africa, instead, into hiding within the United States. I can easily bring you away from here without your enemies knowing where you have gone. A drive down a long straight highway will expose anyone following us. When there is no one behind us, we change our direction and go to Aurora, a city near here.

"We can take a train there and go to, say, Des Moines, Iowa. From there we can fly to any part of this country you want. I can add more jumps to make it harder for your enemies to find you, if you want. I think this will suffice against most foes. If you were interested in remaining in America, I would even help you set up bank accounts for your money and buy a house. I can even help you get new identities.

"This is the only way I can guarantee your safety. The governmental approvals may take days, or even weeks, to get. If you are in danger, you should go into hiding. If you will not do this, I can't offer you any promise of protection."

Sorenson took another drink of tea and set the bottle on a nearby table.

"Going to Africa may take a lot of preparation, and this will let you live safely while you wait. Besides the matter of getting permission to move the money, there is also the possibility of corruption in Africa. Americans can also be greedy and dishonest. However, I know how to threaten corrupt officials here. In Africa, those officials run everything, are less easily threatened, so we must hope we have an honest man to deal with. A bribe might work, although this requires delicacy.

"Anyway, I need some information from you first. I need to know exactly how much money is to be transferred. There are expenses in moving such large sums of money, even legally.   You will have to pay those expenses, not me. My fee is ten percent of the total to be moved, and I *will* check. And I don't like to be cheated out of my proper fee.

"I also need to know precisely where to deliver the money. I assume you don't want me to fly to Lagos and drop the money in the airport lobby. I would like an address in Nigeria, or you could meet me at the airport and take possession there.

"I would also like to know how the money is packaged now. A larger package is more awkward to handle, but easier to ship actually. Several small packages are easier to deal with individually,; numerous packages are more work to transport.

"And I will need your statement of the purpose for the transfer, for the government form. The same information can be given to both governments, since Nigeria must also approve the import of the money. Without that, the transfer will be much more difficult. With the approved form, the transfer is legal; without approval, the transfer will be illegal. I do not want to be arrested on your behalf, and I am quite prepared to turn you over to the police to save myself. I don't want you to misapprehend this.

"I will also need to make certain arrangements of my own for this trip. I have some commitments which I must take care of, or delay. When would you like to move the money?"

"We hoped to do it immediately," admitted Zahi. "Time is crucial to us. Our enemies nearly killed us recently because they knew we had the money with us. Can we go today?"

"No," objected Sorenson. "I said I have certain things to do before I can leave. Tomorrow would be fine if you are willing in going into hiding in America. If you don't want to hide here, I will still come by tomorrow to get your statement for the government forms."

"That will have to do," agreed Bilan. "Your questions, yes, we have several million dollars, we can count it tonight to give you a correct number tomorrow. The money is in those two large suitcases, there. We can give you an address tomorrow, as well. And the information you need for the government forms. We will be ready tomorrow, or whenever you can go."

"All right," Sorenson finished his tea, "I think that is all I need from you right now. I have your phone number, expect to hear from me tomorrow, even if I can't leave until later. Good day."

Sorenson walked back to his car, looking at the license plate on the only other car in the lot once more. He memorized it this time. *I'm going to have to check these two people out very carefully, because something is definitely wrong here.*

* * *

Sorenson spent some time at his computer, checking and re-checking things. He wasn't happy with what he found. *The license plate is from Minnesota. That's a problem, because there aren't a lot of Nigerians in Minnesota. However, there are a lot of Somalis there, and these two look a lot more like Somalis than they look like Nigerians.*

And is there one million in cash, or five million, or several uncounted millions? They didn't say anything, but they looked nervous when I mentioned reporting the money to the government. I wonder what lie they will tell to justify the transfer. If it's a good convincing lie, there will be no trouble. I wish I knew if they could tell a good convincing lie. They haven't so far.

Nigerian prince, indeed! Who does he think he is trying to fool? Well, he's an immigrant, and maybe he doesn't know how many Americans have been spammed, and even scammed, by Nigerian princes. He's not a prince, Nigerian, Somali, or otherwise. Maybe I should just tell them "No" and be done with it.

Zahi and Bilan Smith. Using my own fake name on me. Quite natural. They've learned that much about American culture, anyway. My email to Donny at the DMV may give me a real name to go with the license plate. I'll have to wait for his reply.

Five million, if I can legally transfer it, pays me a fee of five hundred thousand dollars. Now, that's impressive, more than I've ever made on one job. More than I usually make in a year. It will easily take the place of any number of small payoffs. Careful, Jack, don't let greed cloud your judgment. For one thing, I haven't seen any money yet. Is it real?

If I can't transfer it legally, do I still want to try to move it? Is it even legitimate money? Watch out for that greed! I can probably find a way to ship it out in some other container. Getting it out of the States is only half the problem. I have to get it into Nigeria, or wherever they really want it sent, without running foul of the local customs agents.

Nigeria has the same rule for importing cash that we have for exporting it. It has to be declared. If the declaration form is rejected here, I don't have to ship the money out, and I can just return it to the "Smiths." In Nigeria, though, a failed declaration may result in the money being confiscated outright. That's a problem even with a legal transfer from here.

He went down to the police station, and asked to speak to Detective Sergeant Mahoney.

"Well, Mr. Sorenson, what are you doing here today?" asked Mahoney with a laugh. "You only show up here if there's been some crime committed and I'm working on it. And I don't have any big cases on just now. So, what's the occasion?"

"Good afternoon, Sergeant," smiled Sorenson. "It's good to see you again, too. Today's visit is just a precaution. I have a possible client who wants me to move a very large amount of money out of the country. It's probably the one to whom you gave my number this morning. I recognize the risks of this being a money laundering operation, and I'm insisting they provide the Federal customs authorities a good reason for the export.

"I'm also concerned about the money being hot. Have there been any very large, multi-million dollar large, robberies in the Chicago area recently? Or in Minnesota? That's where my potential client is from."

"Multi-million? Wow, you are coming up in the world," exclaimed Mahoney. "I know we haven't had that big a robbery around northern Illinois. Let me check online for Minnesota.

He rocked back in his swivel chair, waiting for the screen to change. He gave Sorenson a discreet glance, trying to figure out what he was really up to.

"No, nothing anywhere near that large a job. Are you going to do this, anyway? And how did you get involved?"

"It pays to advertise, I guess," grumbled Sorenson, ruefully. "All this publicity over the art thieves has made me momentarily famous. I hate it, though it has attracted some new clients. It's good to know the money isn't from a bank or armored car heist. I'm still not sure I'll take the job. Thanks for your help and time."

I can see lots of difficulties with this job, even with the huge fee in the offing. The more I think about it, the less I like it. I should sleep on the idea, and see how I feel in the morning. I can always tell them I won't do it.

Chapter Four

"No" Was Not the Answer We Wanted

Xidig was frustrated. Hamza had told him to find Zahi, but gave him no idea of where to look. He wanted to get back to his bride, and he knew he couldn't return without finding the money. "Search" Hamza had said. Hamza and Bashiir were looking too, but Chicago and its suburbs was much larger than Minneapolis.

Zahi was supposed to be at this hotel, the Bide-a-Wee. That was where the policeman sent them, Hamza said. Well, they aren't here, are they? Hamza was sometimes too impetuous. He didn't always take time to think things out. He only liked planning when it led to action. What could have happened to prevent their being here? So many strange streets, maybe they got lost. Maybe if I look for another hotel near here, I'll find them. My cell phone will show me hotels near here. Here's one not too far from here. Restful Hotel. I'll start looking there.

***

"I saw Xidig just now," cried Zahi in a panic, an hour after Sorenson had left, "and he saw me. He called someone on his phone. Hamza or maybe Yahye must be here as well. They will come for us very soon, so we must leave at once. Pack our bags while I put the money in the car. Quickly, Bilan, quickly!"

As they got into their car, Zahi spotted Xidig again, at the east end of the parking lot. He was standing next to his car, trying to look inconspicuous while he waited for his friends to arrive. Zahi took advantage of this to leave by the west end of the lot, and turn north. At the next corner, he turned west again, and then south. By the time Xidig had gotten into his car and followed, he had lost sight of his intended victims.

"They saw me, and they ran away," confessed Xidig on his phone again, "I thought you would get here faster, but they left in a hurry. They still have the money. I did see Zahi put the two big green cases into his trunk. They came out again right away and left too fast for me to see where they went."

"Fool! All you had to do was to find them and keep an eye on them!" roared Hamza. "You said yourself you were lucky to have found them today. How much more lucky will we have to be to find them again? You should not have let them get away. I am not a patient man, Xidig. You know that. Don't wait for us to get there – start looking for them at once!"

***

"We have been driving too randomly, Zahi," cautioned Bilan, "where are we? Where are we going? I know we want to lose Hamza and the others, still, we should not get lost ourselves."

"I know, Bilan, I wanted to be certain they were not following us. Xidig saw me putting the green suitcases into the trunk. We need to replace them with different cases. Then we can leave the green ones someplace and they will go after the empty cases. Ah, here is a Wal-Mart store, just like in Minneapolis. They sell everything. We can get new cases here."

As Zahi paid for the new luggage, Bilan spoke to a woman at the help desk.

"My husband and I are new to the area, just visiting, and we need to find an inexpensive hotel. Do you know of one near here?"

"Oh, yes, dearie," said the clerk, "just go west down this street, Roosevelt Road, about a mile or two. There's a Travel Inn, they're pretty cheap, and decent enough for the price. Have a good vacation."

"There is a hotel west of here," Bilan told Zahi as they got into their car. "The woman said it was just a mile or two. We should see it as we go along. Oh, there it is, I almost missed the sign. Turn here, Zahi, right here!"

They asked for, and got, a first floor room in the motel. They parked by the door to their room, and Zahi was pleased that the car next to theirs was also silver.   They brought all their luggage inside with them, taking two trips to handle all the bags. It was starting to get dark outside.

"Before we do anything with the money," Zahi told Bilan, "I want to change the license plates on our car. I took Illinois plates from a car when we stopped for lunch. Xidig knows what the car looks like, but there are many silver cars in America. He will look for one with Minnesota license plates. That may be how he found us today. If I change the plates, he will not recognize our car. I will be back in a few minutes."

When he returned, Bilan had opened all four of their new suitcases and was starting to unload the money from the two large green cases into them. Yahye's gang had packaged the money into convenient bundles which made it easier to transfer it.   It still took an awful lot of bundles to make almost ten million dollars.

He helped her move the money, and after an hour the money was finally transferred neatly into the four black cases. They put the new bags into the closet, with old ones just outside of it. They sighed, tired after their work, and an evening of terror driven flight. They went to a nearby fast food place to get some supper and then went to sleep.

***

On Wednesday morning Sorenson found a reply to his email to Donny at the DMV.   The car was registered to Zahi Smith after all. *Fake all the way. No, not really fake, that* is *his name. It's just as good as fake though. This job is not getting better looking with time. Better to just call them up and give them the bad news.*

No one answered his call. The voicemail inbox was too full to take any more messages. He tried twice more in the morning without getting through. Just before noon, he drove over to the hotel. The parking lot was empty. He went into the hotel and rang a small bell at the registration counter. A woman came out of a back room and asked if he wanted a room.

"No, I'm looking for one of your guests," replied Sorenson. "Mr. Zahi Smith, in room fourteen. I saw him yesterday about some work he wanted

me to do for him. I came back to talk to him some more about it, but he's
not answering his phone."

"Oh, right, Mr. 'Smith', like I believed that one," the woman said with a
smile. "He checked out last night."

"Did he say where he was going?" asked Sorenson.

"No, I wasn't on duty last night," admitted the woman, "we never bother
to ask anyway, and most people don't tell us."

"Well, thank you for that information, anyway. I guess he didn't want me
to do his work after all. Good day."

Sorenson went out into the parking lot and stopped. He looked at the
building, and counted the ground floor windows. Room fourteen should
be next to that end. He walked over and looked in the window. The
curtains were drawn back, displaying a room waiting for a new guest. The
bed was made, there were no suitcases in sight, no trace of any former
guest.

*I wonder where he went, and why. Was he afraid of his enemies again?
It's theoretically possible that these enemies kidnapped him last night,
taking all his belongings, checking him out, and stealing his car. Well, in
theory, maybe, but not in the real world. Someone would have heard
something. Well, I didn't want the job anyway. Now I don't have to take
it.*

Then his phone rang.

***

Zahi and Bilan slept late Thursday, exhausted from their recent travel and
frights. When they awoke, Zahi wondered why Sorenson hadn't called
them back yet. He looked at his phone and remembered he had shut it
down the night before. He turned it back on and checked his voicemail for
a call from Sorenson. Call after call came up, all from Abdullah, wanting
to know where he was, was he safe, and did he have the money. He
cleared them all and called Sorenson.

"Mr. Sorenson, this is Zahi Smith. I am sorry that you could not call me earlier. I had to turn off my phone, we were being chased by our enemies. I was afraid they could trace my phone number by some computer thing. We need to see you now, urgently. We are at the Travel Inn, room 21. It is on Roosevelt Road, somewhere west of Berwyn, I think."

"All right, I'll be there within half an hour," sighed Sorenson. *I'm not happy to have to see these two foreigners again. I want them out of my life; they almost shout "Danger!", not a thing I like. Still, I need to tell them I won't take their job, and courtesy requires that I tell them this face to face.* He left his wallet on his desk, and put his normal false identity wallet into his coat pocket.

He parked in the middle of the lot and went to room 21. There were two silver cars parked near it, very similar, one with a familiar dented rear quarter panel. Neither had Minnesota license plates. He considered the possible reasons, and knocked on the door.

"Ah, Mr. Sorenson, how good of you to come so quickly," Zahi greeted him. "Our enemies found us at our last hotel, and we had to leave in a hurry. I am sorry we could not tell you. This makes it all the more urgent that you help us move this money now, today if possible."

"If your enemies found you last night," asked Sorenson, sitting down, "do you want to go into hiding somewhere else in the States? As an alternative? I suggested this to you yesterday, and it will protect as long as you want. Forever, if you like."

"We would rather return to Nigeria," revealed Zahi. "We have the letter you told us to write, telling the officials why we are bringing this money to Nigeria. Is this all right?"

Sorenson, being polite, read the letter carefully. He thought about it a moment and said, "This is fine, as far as it goes. Bringing money in to build a school sounds good. However, it doesn't specify the amount of money. You will have to be very specific about that. You told me yesterday that you were going to count it. Have you done so?"

"Yes, we counted it last night," revealed Bilan, pointing to the two large green suitcases. "It is $9,870,000. So your fee would be nine hundred eighty-seven thousand dollars. Is that right?"

"Yes. Assuming I take the job, and I might not," declared Sorenson, looking at her as Zahi roamed around the room nervously. "This letter can be used to bring the money into Nigeria, also. So you will need a second copy for them. Each government will want its own copy, with the amount spelled out.

"We have to get the letter approved by the U.S. customs office before we can do anything else. We should also send a copy to Nigeria to get their approval before we leave. You don't want to show up at the Lagos airport and find you can't bring the money in. This will take some time. However, it is necessary to avoid any ...."

Sorenson was interrupted by a damp rag over his mouth. He breathed in a strange odor and thought, *I'm always being attacked from behind.* He was feeling woozy, but still conscious. He pushed the rag away from his mouth and turned to face Zahi. He punched the small man just hard enough to knock him down. He looked down at him and was about to say something when he felt a sharp blow to the back of his head. He slumped to the floor silently.

"Zahi! What have you done?" shrieked Bilan, holding the table lamp she had bashed Sorenson with. "We need his help to get the money out of the country! Why did you try to knock him out?"

"I do not think he is going to help us, Bilan! He keeps talking about getting approval from the government to export the money. Maybe the Americans will let us take the money out of the country. Maybe. But what is the sense of sending a letter to Nigeria? We are not going there, are we? We should not have told him that lie in the first place. We should have thought this through better earlier. And you know how corrupt the officials are back home. If they are told we have a lot of money, they will seize it for themselves. We have to sneak it into the country if we want to keep it.

"You have always been braver than me, Bilan. You never worried about Yahye learning who you really worked for when you went to clean his house. I could not do that. If we can get safely away with this money, we will never have to fear anything ever again. Until then, I am afraid. I hate to admit that to you, my wife, but you know what I am like.

"We still have the drug we were going to use on Yahye when we stole the money from him. Why not use it on this man? It would keep him unconscious for some time and we could still use him to hide the money for now. His wallet will have his identification, which will tell us where he lives. I will take his keys, go to his apartment, and hide the money there. If we do not have it then Hamza will be stalled. He will not kill us until he can find it – Yahye will not let him. Yahye controls them all. I will take the money to where Mr. Sorenson lives, and you stay with him and give him some of the drug if he starts to wake up."

"We can hide the money this way, Zahi. However, we still need his help to get it out of America. You should not have panicked, Zahi. I am sorry I helped you. Still, you are right about Hamza – this will keep him from killing us for the present. I will do this, though I think Mr. Sorenson will be unhappy about being knocked out. He won't help us at all, now."

"Let me have his wallet," ordered Zahi, "so I can learn where he lives. Here is his address. Hand me that piece of paper, please."

He scribbled a number on a piece of paper.

Oh, look, ha, ha, he uses Smith as an alias, too. I will be back as soon as I can."

Zahi checked the parking lot for Xidig, put the new black suitcases into his car, and drove into Berwyn. He stopped at a gas station and got directions to Sorenson's apartment. He pulled up to a rather run down, nondescript building. He went up to the second floor and opened the door with the key from Sorenson's pocket. The apartment was small, with only a cot and a desk. Some ledger books were stacked on the desk, alongside a large calculator, plugged into the wall.

How can he live here, with only a cot to sleep on? There is no kitchen, either. How strange. However, there is a closet here, and the bags can be hidden safely.

Zahi returned to his motel room carefully. He was certain he hadn't been followed from it, but he might have been seen on the streets. No one was following him now, and he kept his eyes on his rear view mirror to look for Hamza or his thugs. Convinced he had not been seen, he turned into the motel lot and parked.

When he entered the room, Sorenson was beginning to stir. Bilan had the bottle of Sevoflurane in her hand and was about to give him a dose. Zahi waved her to stop, then put Sorenson's keys back in his pocket.

"Let him wake up now, Bilan. I must apologize to him now, and try to persuade him to help us after all."

Sorenson came back to consciousness slowly, his head swimming with foggy thoughts. He opened his eyes, blinked, and saw the fuzzy faces of two black people. Memory began to work, and he put names to the faces, Zahi and Bilan. Two Somalis pretending to be Nigerian. A pair of possible clients. Clients who had a strange way of asking him to work for them. He sat up and tried to stand. Zahi helped him to get into a chair.

"I am very sorry about this, Mr. Sorenson," apologized Zahi. "My wife was afraid you might not help us, talking about getting government approval before doing anything for us. We need to move this money now, and we may not get the government's approval. We know how government officials steal from the people they are supposed to help. And even if they approve our request, it can take time. We do not have time, there are men trying to kill us. Please help us, I beg you."

"No, Mr. Smith," growled Sorenson angrily. "I was planning to tell you I wouldn't take your job anyway, and this just firms up my resolve. I don't believe your story. You might be in great danger; that is your problem, not mine. I don't trust you. I don't want to end up in an African prison for smuggling money into some third world country. No. Absolutely not. I'm leaving now, and there's no sense in your trying to make me change my mind."

He stood, swayed a bit, then walked carefully out the door. He got into his car and drove home. He was still feeling a little woozy. A moment's rest in the car settled his head enough to climb the steps to his apartment. Inside, he reached into his jacket for his fake ID wallet, and found that it had switched pockets somehow. There was little in it, and it was all still there.

Now, why did they need to look into my wallet? Nothing's missing, so there's no harm done. Too many strange days lately.

***

Sorenson went to Marcy's apartment for dinner that evening. As they ate he cleared his throat and began, sheepishly, telling about his day's excitement.

"There was a time, and not very long ago, when I would have not mentioned this to you," Sorenson told Marcy. "But I have made a serious commitment to you, and because of that I must tell you things. Things that I don't want to worry you with. Things that I don't want to embarrass myself with. Things that may not really be important, but which you must be told because I want us to be one.

"Forgive the melodrama. It's just a long introduction to a confession. I was not careful today. I was seeing a possible client, one whose job I had already decided not to take, and he knocked me out. He used chloroform or ether or some such thing, a soaked rag pressed to my mouth. It was irritating, but I pushed it away before it had any effect. Then his wife clobbered me from behind with something and I was out cold. I think they may have doped me with the drug while I was out, too. I came to rather woozy."

As he talked, a gray tabby cat came up to his chair and looked up at him. It cocked its head, licked its paw once, then jumped onto his lap. Sorenson smiled at it and began to pet its back.

"Hello, Lucy, here to offer some nice cat therapy to the poor wounded warrior? Very nice of you. I'm embarrassed about being taken down like that. I'm more embarrassed because I told you I would be more careful from now on. I'm sorry, very sorry, to have to make you worry about me. The only good news is that I have told them I would not work for them. Absolutely. Positively."

"My goodness!" exclaimed Marcy. "How are you feeling now, dear? Did you go to the emergency room? Are you sure you're all right? I am concerned, of course, about you being drugged and slugged, dearest. But I am even more surprised that you would tell me about it. You really are serious about sharing your life with me, aren't you? I will *never* tell you to give up your life, Jack, however, I do reserve the right to ask you to think about it, from time to time. Why did they knock you out?"

"They were afraid I wouldn't help them. And I wasn't going to, either. I was trying to break the news gently, but they caught on right away. The man used the dope from behind, then his wife hit me from behind when I turned to face him. Again. I really need to get an eye in the back of my head. I was only interested because the money was going to be substantial. They were talking about moving almost ten million dollars. That's almost a million as my fee. I'm not greedy; still, I can be tempted. However, even temptation has its limits, and I turned them down."

"I said you were foolish not to take the money the Noltes offered you," Marcy reminded him. "Nice big sums of money do not come anyone's way all that often. Not even for a successful go-between like you. Still, I'm glad you rejected this job. I don't like to think of you working with people who might hurt you. Are you sure they won't try to get at you again?"

"I was angry and told them I wouldn't ever take their job. Not at any price. I don't think they accepted my refusal, but if they call again, I will just repeat my refusal. They don't know where I live …."

"Wait. They looked at my wallet. It had been in my left inside coat pocket. When I got home, it was in the right inside coat pocket. Wait again, that was my Mr. Smith ID, with the address of the little room where I keep my records. I hardly ever go there. So if they show up there, they'll be out of luck. That's all right, they can't find me, then."

"Well, I'm glad of that," confessed Marcy. "I used to worry about you as a part-time thing, a hobby of sorts. Now I find that I'm worrying about you more seriously; it's part of my job as fiancee. I need to take care of you if you won't take care of yourself. Are you staying tonight? I can give you some very nice care."

"I know you can, and I appreciate the offer of constant care. However, I'm still feeling the effects of the drug, and I'm not sure how well I'd respond to your care tonight. I also have to think some things through. My life is changing, mostly for the better because of you, but other parts of the change are still in flux. I need to work out in my mind just what I need to change, what I want to change, and how I can make the changes. Don't fret about this, I will ask your input and approval for anything I decide. Tonight, I need to do this solo. I'm sorry, dear one."

"I understand, Jack, I've been in the same place at times. Long, deep thought, all by myself, undistracted by anyone or anything. I know you will tell me when you are ready. Go home and get a good night's sleep. I love you, darling."

***

It was not yet midnight when Zahi awoke in a panic. He had dreamed about their being captured, about Hamza torturing Bilan, killing her while making him watch. He was covered in sweat and breathing hard.

The American had offered us a way out, though not a trip to Africa and now he will not do anything for us. I am afraid to stay here where Yahye may find us. He will not find us in Africa. Even if he tells his masters about us, they will not find us. If we cannot get to Africa, we must have help here. Abdullah will help us. He is strict, a very tough man, but fair. He will be angry we have taken the money for ourselves, then he will forgive us because we called him for help. Maybe he will let us keep part of the money. Maybe I can be daring once more, and lie to him. Tell him there was less money than Bilan thought. We can keep one million for ourselves and still live well on that, somewhere safe. I should call Abdullah now.

"Zahi! Where are you?" asked Abdullah frantically. "We are so worried about you and Bilan. I have been calling you constantly. Did you manage to steal the money from Yahye? Did you get away safely? Why didn't you bring the money to the train station? No, that's not as important as knowing you are safe. Where are you now? Tell me and Taifa and I will come to bring you home safely."

"We are in a city called Broadview," Zahi informed him. "It is near Chicago. We are in a hotel called Travel Inn on Roosevelt Road. We wanted to keep the money for ourselves and we came here to meet a man in Berwyn. He works with the police so he is honest, and he can help us take the money someplace safe. But we have angered him and he will not help us now. Xidig is in a nearby town looking for us, and maybe Hamza. Maybe Yahye and his whole gang. I am scared. I have tried to be brave, and I am not that brave. Please come rescue us."

Chapter Five

The House

"How are you feeling this beautiful Thursday morning, Jack?" asked Marcy, standing in his doorway in a floral print dress. "Would you like to join me for breakfast at Katy's again?"

"I'm feeling much better this morning," he replied, giving her a kiss. "Especially for seeing you here looking just as beautiful as the morning. Katy's will be perfect, I'm amazingly hungry."

Katy's Diner was indeed perfect, an ideal spot for breakfast, or any other meal before the late afternoon, when it closed. It was an old-style diner handling breakfast and lunch customers. It had been remodeled several times over the years, but the friendliness never changed. The food was very good, the service was fast and excellent, and Katy treated her regular customers almost like family.

Jack opened the door for Marcy, who gave his courtesy a smile as a reward. They took their usual booth by the window where they could watch the passersby with ease. Jack ordered his normal omelet and lots of coffee. Marcy decided on French toast and sausages, with less coffee.

"We've talked about this before," began Sorenson, "and I always brushed away all of the worries, yours and mine. That's just silly on my part. Peterson's death did bother me. Getting shot really irritated me. Irritated! Hah! It scared me silly. Now I've been beaten over the head and drugged unconscious. You are worried, and you have a right to be worried. I'm finally ready to admit that I'm worried, as well.

"I can't really give up what I do for a living. It's too lucrative. And my skills have been developed with only one occupation in mind. Still, I can be more careful about the jobs I take. All the publicity I've had recently has scared away some of the guys making payoffs to pols. That means less income for me, and also less risk of arrest. I was being too greedy in trying to replace that income. I should have told the people who drugged me 'No' to begin with. There are other ways to get the same pay. Well, not hundreds of thousands, but my normal pay at least.

"A man called me last night, late. He plays in a big poker game at a private gambling club. He and his friends have to park a couple of blocks away and walk through a bad neighborhood to get there. They want to talk to me about how I might help them."

"If it's a bad neighborhood, how is this safer?" asked Marcy. "I know you do not like getting shot. I've heard you say so, yourself. And I know you do not carry a gun. How can you think this is a good idea?"

"Well, it's just talk right now," allowed Sorenson. "In fact, it's just talk about talk. We haven't met or discussed anything yet. Just talk. I won't make a decision without checking with you first."

"Oh, no, not that!" exclaimed Marcy. "I told you last night that I wouldn't make you give up your life. And that includes approving of what work you do. I trust you to be careful now. I can't ride herd on you, and don't want to. I will let you tell me what you are planning to do. I may, *maybe*, let you ask for my opinion about your plans. Maybe. Don't expect me to interfere. You want me to be my own person, standing on my own feet. I want you to be the same. Why do you think I'm crazy about you? You're a charming rogue, dashing, daring, devil-may-care. Who wants a tame, sedate rogue?"

"A rogue, huh?" asked Sorenson with a laugh, "I suppose that is the way I've envisioned myself, too. Don't worry, I won't become too tame. Just a little more concerned about my back. No one's ever attacked me from the front, only the back. I'm not that scary from the front, am I?"

"No, dearest, I think you are remarkably handsome from the front. But then, I'm prejudiced."

"And I'm happy that you are. So, I know you came by this morning to hear what I thought about over night, and now you know. I suspect you had some other motive as well. What did you have in mind?"

"You and I have made a serious commitment to get married, my love," answered Marcy. "It's June now, and what better, or more traditional, month to get married in? We have to arrange the wedding itself, in church or before a JP. We need to plan a reception for our friends and families – we don't dare cheat our parents out of attending. They have waited so long for this, with very little complaining. There are oodles of details in planning such things."

"Ah, well, I am ahead of you for once," admitted Jack. "Last month Melissa suggested that I should marry you. Mind you, my proposal was my own idea, and not due to prodding from her. She also said she would be happy to host the reception in the restaurant. She also said something about providing you with bridesmaids. I didn't take that to be a serious offer, though."

"Bridesmaids!" exclaimed Marcy, laughing loudly. "Oh, Jack, I doubt there's been a real maiden there in decades."

"You forget Angela," countered Jack. "Melissa would never let her daughter work there, any more than she worked there for her mother."

"True, I had forgotten her," agreed Marcy. "Still, she's part of management, isn't she? Anyway, I have no problem with using Melissa's restaurant for the reception. If we go with a JP for the wedding, we could do the ceremony in the lobby. Maybe we could do dinner there tonight and ask her.

"All those things, while important, can be settled fairly quickly. What I want to do today may be the start of a long search. We will need a house when we are married. I have a very nice apartment, with a good studio attached. You have a delightful apartment, charming and cozy. We have both spent the night, or a long weekend even, at each other's apartment. There's a difference between a weekend and forever.

"Your apartment does not have enough closet space for my clothes. My apartment does not have floor space in the bedroom for your dresser. Neither has space for us to be together without being on top of each other. That is fun, but once in a while we will both want to take a breath. And I am taking you at your word about being more open and social with people.

We will entertain and throw parties. And both of our apartments are too small for that.

"So I want to start looking for a house today. I remember my parents looking for a house in Arizona when they retired. It took them three months, and they didn't think they were being overly fussy. If we get married this month, I'd like to have a new place to move into after the honeymoon. All right, that's ambitious. Buying a house takes time, closing, lawyers, surveys. That's all the more reason to start looking now. Are you up for this today? Can I drag you through house after house all day long? Will you be bored, or get tired?"

"Marcy, this is wonderful," exclaimed Jack with joy. "I hadn't thought about this part of marriage, but you're right. We need a place for both of us together. Room for you to paint in, room for me to dither in, room for us to enjoy each other's company. Room for us to share with our friends. Parties. What a foreign concept to me, one I'm all in favor of it, if you're there. Where do we start?"

"My car is outside; we get in it and go see this realtor who sent me a flyer."

Twenty minutes later they were walking into a realty office on Cermak Avenue. A blonde woman seated at a desk rose up as they entered and came over to greet them. She was what her husband fondly called "zaftig" and she thought of as just plump, still, he liked her with a little extra padding in the right places. She was smartly dressed, and that helped make her feel slimmer.

"Good afternoon, I'm Diane Fielding, may I help you find a house today?"

"Good afternoon, I am Jack Sorenson, and this is my fiancee, Marcy Delancy. We are indeed interested in buying a house."

"Fiancee. Oh, what a beautiful word," murmured Marcy quietly, hugging Sorenson tightly.

"Do you have any idea of what kind of house you would like?" asked Diane. "Any particular part of town, a big house, or something small?

Main streets, side streets, near stores and shopping, close to public transportation? How many bedrooms?"

"Oh, Jack, we didn't think about any of these things," groaned Marcy. "What do you want, what should *we* want? No, let me start, because I know you won't complain about this. I'm an artist, and I need a large room with a northern exposure and lots of big windows. A north-facing sun room would do wonderfully."

"Sun rooms normally face the south," countered Diane, sitting down at her computer to start the search. "North facing rooms don't get as much direct sunlight."

"True, but an artist wants indirect light," explained Marcy. "Show us what you have, and I'll find a way to adjust. After that, well, a decent sized bedroom, a library for your books, Jack."

"And for yours, too," mentioned Jack. "For *our* books."

"Ooh, there's another beautiful word, *our*," cooed Marcy.

"Yes, dear one. We will want a large living room for entertaining guests. At least one, maybe two, guest rooms. A basement, because your wine cabinet should expand into a proper wine cellar, Marcy. A good kitchen, a two car garage because this is northern Illinois and even cars like to spend the winter indoors."

"What about price range?" asked Diane. "I've already narrowed the search down pretty well, but the prices are all over the scale. Are you looking for something affordable, or is price not so much of an issue?"

"What can we afford, dear?" asked Marcy. "We will be saving the costs of our two apartments, and that will likely cover a pretty high mortgage. We each have some money we can pool for a good down payment."

"I think we can go pretty high," suggested Sorenson. "I think we want comfort over affordability. Print out what you've got so far, and let us look them over."

While Diane got the listings printed off, he led Marcy off to one side and told her in a whisper, "I intend to drop all four of my apartments. That will make any mortgage fit into our budget easily."

"Four apartments?" asked Marcy, puzzled. "I know you had a backup apartment to hide out in. But four of them? Really?"

"There was a time when I felt in danger," explained Jack, "a thing which you have been worrying about lately yourself. I have a second hide-away place, very basic, and another where I keep my financial records and do my taxes. The boogeymen that bothered me then are gone now. I've kept the extra apartments because of inertia – I would have had to make a decision to make a change. Now I've made that decision, haven't I?"

"Here's a half dozen places that you might want to look at," indicated Diane, coming up to them with a sheaf of papers. "I suggest you look over the information while we drive to them. I always think one gets a better idea of a house in person, rather than just by looking at listing sheet."

The first house was too small. The rooms were cramped, and it lacked any charm or personality. The second house was beautiful, with good sized rooms and nice woodwork. However, the sun room faced east, not north. It would only be good as a painting studio in the afternoon.

The third house was an impressive brick structure, stretched out along the street with a small semi-circular portico leading into the house, with a little balcony above it. There were two rooms at the ends of the building, one on each floor, whose walls were all windows. On the first floor, this room was at the south end of the house. On the second floor, it was on the north end. The size of the rooms wasn't apparent from the front, but Marcy looked at them with expectation in her eyes.

"I once knew the architect for this house," declared Diane. "He was furious at the builder for the construction work. His plans had two sun rooms at the south end, one above the other. The contractor goofed and misread the blueprints. He turned them around and swapped north and south upstairs. I've seen the inside already, and it's still a very nice house."

They entered the house, stepping into a modest sized foyer, with a dining room to the left. Closing the front door, they went into the living room, with a large sun room beyond. Marcy's eyes went wide, then she frowned and groused, "This is the living room; I can't paint here! And it faces south. *Damn!*"

Then she looked up at the ceiling, murmured "The contractor!," and ran to the stairs in the foyer. Sorenson and Diane Fielding followed her more slowly, and found her in what the listing called a "playroom" beyond two bedrooms. It was just as large as the sun room downstairs, nineteen by ten, with the same tall windows filling the walls. And it faced north.

"Perfect, simply perfect," Marcy was repeating over and over. "Jack, this is the house. Absolutely. No question. Ms. Fielding, we'll take it."

"Uh, would you like to see the rest of the house?" asked Diane, uncertainly. "The bedrooms, the baths, the kitchen?"

"Take me through the whole house," interjected Sorenson. "She is in artist heaven right now, and will not see anything, anyway. And the rest of this house had better be just as perfect, because she does want to buy it."

When they returned twenty minutes later, Marcy met them in what was now and forevermore The Studio with a sheepish grin on her face.

"I guess I got carried away," she apologized. "It's just, this is really the perfect place for me to paint. Much better than what I have now. Better even than that atelier I had in Paris, though without the atmosphere. Is the rest of the house okay, Jack?"

"No, the rest of the house is not okay," complained Jack with mock gravity. "The rest of the house is just as marvelous to me as this one room is to you. The master bedroom has a balcony overlooking the street. We'll have to remember to put on robes before stepping out in the morning. It also has a very large walk in closet that will easily hold all of our clothes. And a very nice master bath.

"There's what Diane calls a 'tandem room' in front of the master bedroom. It's like a parlor or sitting room, just for us. We could use it as our library,

and office, and private space, all in one. The kitchen is long and spacious.
We could both work in it at the same time without getting in each other's
way.

"There's a nice breakfast nook, and a large family room at the north end of
the first floor. Then there's the basement, with an enormous rec room and
another big room the listing calls bedroom number four. It's even bigger
than the master bedroom, without the big closet or bath. Our wine cellar
goes in there.

"With the big living room and sun room combination, the family room,
and the rec room, there is enough space to entertain a small army. Try to
tear yourself away from this one perfect room, and come see all the other
perfect rooms."

Marcy went with him as Diane repeated her guided tour of the house. She
actually paid attention to everything, and added her praise to Jack's about
how delightful the whole house was. Finally, she sat on the stairs going
up, and took Jack's hands in hers. Diane recognized the sign of a serious
personal discussion coming on, and wandered off into the sun room. She
didn't mind the extra time she was spending over this house. She could
tell that every extra minute was leading to a definite sale, and a hefty
commission.

"Jack, I really love this house," gushed Marcy. "It's not just the studio, it's
the whole house. Everything about it is just so very right. But do you feel
the same as I do? I would hate to give it up, but if it doesn't please you, I
will. Can you live here?"

"Marcy, dearest," answered Jack, "I could live anywhere if you were
there. Don't worry, I love this house just as much as you do. There is a
nice feeling about this house, the size of the rooms, the layout of the floor
plan, the natural woodwork trim, the hardwood floors. There's only one
thing I have to ask of you, dear."

"What's that, Jack?"

"Don't ever again say that you'll give up something you love just to please
me. I told you once that I know what I am worth, and I am not worth that.

I want you for my wife, my lover, my companion, my dearest, deepest friend. I don't want you as my lackey, my yes-woman. *You* are worth more than that."

Diane gave them ten more minutes before tiptoeing back into the foyer. They broke their embrace, a little embarrassed, and smiled at her.

"Please, Ms. Fielding," said Marcy, "we very much want to make an offer on this house. Today. This minute. Well, as soon as we can get back to your office. I don't want to lose this house."

Back at the realty office, Diane printed off forms and Jack and Marcy filled them in. Names, current addresses, Social Security Numbers, how often they had climbed Mount Everest, every possible question the seller might need to know the answer to, in order to accept their offer to buy.

"Well, that's that," Diane congratulated them as she took Jack's check for the earnest money. "The offer is now official, and we should hear back from the seller's agent soon, probably tomorrow. I will keep in touch with you when I hear from him. Thank you for your visit. Good afternoon."

***

"Your banker is very friendly and accommodating," commented Marcy, as they left the bank for the drive to Melissa's. She turned down Oak Park Avenue and continued south past block after block of similar yet different bungalows, the trade mark of the purely residential city of Berwyn.

"It's not called the Friendly Bank for nothing. I have done business with them since I started working. They are used to my unconventional job and irregular deposits. They ask only the questions the government wants them to ask, and never look askance at my answers."

"Do you think we can handle the ten year mortgage payments? They are considerably higher than for a normal thirty year mortgage. I know we're trading in a lot of apartment rents, especially for you, still, how will this affect our cash flow? God, such an unromantic question!"

"Unromantic, but necessary darling. Your income depends on what paintings you sell every month. Mine depends on the sort of 'errands' I run every month. I have spare cash at the end of almost every month and even the drop in 'favors' to some clients is not going to hurt that much. A few new clients are possible, also driven by the notoriety that has cost me some clients.

"And we mustn't forget the one time bonuses. I received a check from the trustees of the Art Institute for $78,000. Their protocols don't let them offer a reward unless a painting is actually missing. Since the museum got the painting back before the trustees had even heard it had been stolen they couldn't offer a reward. However, they did pass the hat.

"There are sixty-eight trustees and ten other officers, all men with comfortable incomes. Each tossed a grand into the hat. I'm still waiting to hear how much of a reward the French government will pay me for the arrest of the smuggler and his client. That should be a nice sum too. Not bad for a few weeks work."

Marcy gave gave him a skeptical look from the corner of her eye.

"A few weeks work, and getting shot. It *is* very nice of them to offer you something when they didn't have to. I guess maybe we'll get by after all."

"No, they didn't have to, but they didn't want to look cheap. Prominent people like to think well of themselves, and being generous is one way to feel good. A reward from the museum treasury lets them feel good at someone else's expense. They *are* willing to open their own wallets to get the feeling if they have to.

"Now for dinner. You suggested Melissa's for dinner tonight so we could tell her about our impending marriage and discuss our reception with her. It will also be a good opportunity to celebrate buying this house."

"Haven't you already told her we're getting married?" asked Marcy. "I thought the two of you were as thick as thieves."

"We are good friends," replied Jack, "but we don't live in each other's back pockets. We've only been back from Paris a week, and that week has

been very busy for me. I have gone whole months without seeing Melissa.
Besides, this is an announcement that *we* should make together. I'm not
getting married all by myself. *We* are getting married."

"There's another one of those beautiful words, Jack," said Marcy. "You
are just so full of them today. And I thank you for that."

***

Marcy pulled into the parking lot by Melissa's and they went into the
building. The lobby was empty, though it was already almost six, which
meant the restaurant would not be crowded tonight. The bar was open and
busy, as usual. Jack and Marcy ignored both rooms and went straight to
the maitre d's podium.

"Paul," Jack asked the maitre d', "could we get a table in a dark corner,
please? And I'd appreciate it if you would let Melissa know that we are
here and would like to … Never mind. Here she comes now."

"Jack! Marcy! How good to see you both!" Melissa exclaimed. She
wore a black dress that emphasized her figure, pale white skin, and long
black hair. It clung nicely without being rude. "How are the two of you
doing? What's new? Catch any more art smugglers, Jack? Sorry, I'm just
kidding. You are becoming famous, you know. I could put up a sign
saying that Jack Sorenson eats here, double my prices, and really rake in
the bucks."

Jack chuckled, "Go ahead, notoriety may as well help you if it can't help
me. Anyway, we have some news for you. Marcy and I are going to get
married, just as soon as we can."

"Why, that's marvelous, Jack!" cried Melissa with joy. "Congratulations
to both of you. Oh, Marcy, I am so happy for you. And for you, Jack.
What are you doing pointing at the back corner? Come on, we'll use my
private room and celebrate properly, on me. Paul, send Pierre in."

Pierre had come, taken their orders, and disappeared quietly. As he went
out, a sleek tawny cat sauntered in, looked around, and hopped onto
Melissa's lap.

"Hello, there, Kitty," purred Melissa. "Silly name, isn't it. One of the girls thought we should have a cat, because this is a 'cat house.' That was silly, too. The girls like having a pet around for the slow times, and she does keep the mice out of the kitchen."

Jack and Marcy told Melissa all about their adventure in Paris, both the police and the meals. Marcy described the proposal elatedly. Jack talked about his dismay at becoming famous. They both raved over the house they were buying, all in between courses.

"A very long time ago," began Jack, "oh, it must be all of two weeks, I reckon, you offered to throw the wedding reception here if I married Marcy. Is that offer still good? I won't let you do it for free, you've got a business to run, after all. And this *is* the best restaurant in Berwyn. If we get a JP, can we do the wedding in the lobby?"

"Jack told me about your offer of bridesmaids, as well," added Marcy over coffee and brandy. "I think I might have to decline that bit. However, I would like to ask you to be one of my matrons of honor. You are Jack's friend more than mine, but we *are* friends. Jack counts you as one of his dearest friends, and you should be in the wedding party because of that. You can't be best man, so matron of honor is second best."

"I'd be honored, Marcy," answered Melissa. "I'm not Jack's friend more than yours, I've just known him longer. I've been looking forward to the two of you getting married for years. Now it finally happens! What date have you picked for the wedding? I will clear my calendar of everything to make room for you. Wedding and reception. I insist on both!"

"Marcy says June is the perfect month for a wedding," commented Sorenson. "And I think she's right. We haven't actually talked about a specific date, though. We have to let our friends and relatives have time to get over the shock. What about June 30, dear? It's a Sunday, but Saturdays are out – all the JPs will be busy with other weddings. And it's still June."

"That's wonderful, Jack. Three weeks will give us time to plan, and for our parents to come in. Is that good for you, Melissa?"

"I said I'd clear my calendar, and a Sunday makes it easier. That will be perfect. You should come in next week during the day and talk to Zoltan about the food for the reception. This is going to be so great! And you're buying a house, too! What wonders!"

"Well, we need a house for all of my stuff, and all of his stuff," confessed Marcy. "We found a truly gorgeous house that has everything we could possibly think of in it, including a wonderful studio for me. And so we made on offer on it."

"We're going to take a ten year mortgage if we can," Jack divulged. "I have a regular history of deposits with my bank, and a good relation with my banker, so I don't think the irregular nature of my occupation will matter."

"A ten year mortgage makes for a very high monthly payment," objected Melissa. "Are you sure you want to go with that short a term?"

"For reasons that you know a little bit about," explained Sorenson, "I currently rent four separate apartments, two large and expensive, two small and cheap. I no longer need them. Marcy rents only one apartment, but it *is* a nice one. So we are going to save the rents on five apartments, and put that money toward the mortgage payment on one house. We actually come out ahead, even figuring in the property taxes."

"Get used to that, Marcy," chuckled Melissa, "Jack always calculates every single thing he does. He's the shrewdest man alive, and never does anything on a whim."

"He did one thing on a whim, I think," suggested Marcy. "I know he didn't calculate anything about it. That's why I said 'Yes'."

Chapter Six

The Murder

"We must move again today, Bilan," announced Zahi when they awoke Thursday morning. "I do not want to spend more than one night in any one place until we are sure we are safe. The man at the desk told me of two other inexpensive hotels near a place called a zoo. He says they exhibit wild animals there. America is very strange.

"I have a confession to make to you, Bilan. Last night I awoke very frightened. I was worried about you and how vicious Yahye is and how he would kill you. I could not bear to think about that and I called Abdullah to come rescue us. Maybe I should have been braver. You know I am not that brave. I am afraid now that Abdullah will punish us. He will not kill us, but his punishments can be harsh. I do not know if I should tell him we are moving. If Mr. Sorenson will not help us, we need Abdullah to protect us.

"We will call Mr. Sorenson later and tell him where we have gone, and ask him if he has changed his mind. He wants ten percent of our money to take it to Africa. Surely, if we tell him again how much we want to move, his greed will make him forgive our carelessness."

Zahi and Bilan put the two big green suitcases into the big trunk of the Malibu, then squeezed the two smaller bags with their clothes in beside them. The big green luggage was empty, but it still worked as a distraction to their enemies. Everything was packed tightly, all out of sight.

They drove to one of the motels near the zoo in Brookfield. When Zahi parked in the lot Bilan stopped him from getting out. She looked at him with something he had never seen in her, fear.

"Zahi, I am so afraid for us. Hamza and his men are after us and we have no one to help us. This Mr. Sorenson may not want to help us after we drugged him. Even if he is willing, he says it may be difficult to bring the money with us to Africa. We both know how corrupt all officials are there. Maybe we should forget Africa.

"Maybe we should just take the money, right now, and run away somewhere else in America as Mr. Sorenson suggested. Hamza does not know we are here at this motel. If we leave tonight, after it is dark, he will not see us and follow us the way he did in Minneapolis. We can go anywhere we want. This is a very big country, Zahi, and we can drive a long way from here. Then we can be safe."

"I understand what you are saying, Bilan. I feel the same fear. However, I feel out of place here. Even in Little Mogadishu I felt a stranger. So many Somalis all around us, and it still felt like a foreign place. I would feel more at home in Africa. That is why I want to try Mr. Sorenson one more time. Maybe if I apologize deeply enough, he will help us. Maybe if we offer him twenty percent of the money. We can easily live on eight million dollars. If he says 'no' again, I promise you we will do what you want. We will go off tonight and lose ourselves in this huge country."

***

Abdullah and Taifa arrived in Broadview just after eight in the morning, having driven hard all night from Minneapolis. They had left as soon as they could, but Abdullah had to give Ali instructions for the rest of his band. They drove as fast as the car would go, which made them run low on gas twice. And which caused the Wisconsin state police to pull them over twice to issue speeding tickets.

They were tired and irritable when they arrived, and it took them another hour to find the Travel Inn. Abdullah was outraged to find that Zahi and Bilan had already checked out. Abdullah considered his options: *We have the names of the two hotels the desk clerk had given them. That will make it easier to find them, at least. Now I'm too tired to drive any farther. We can stay here and sleep for a few hours before going to the other hotels. They will probably still be there.*

***

Bilan looked at the motel near the zoo and shivered. The clerk at the last motel had told them about it, but if Hamza was looking for them, the clerk might tell him, too. The other motel the clerk mentioned was just as dangerous. She checked her smart phone for the name of some other motel near them.

"Zahi, we should go somewhere else, somewhere no one knows we are going to. The clerk back there was friendly, but what if he is also friendly to Hamza, and tells him where we are. Here, look at this motel. It isn't far from here, but no one knows we will be there. Let's go there now."

They drove to the new motel and got a room. They went to a McDougal's next door for lunch, and spent the day talking, trying to decide what to do. Either Sorenson was going to help them now, or they would flee tonight. They kept debating whether they should leave now or later, and whether Sorenson could be appeased.

"Maybe we should ask that policeman if he has found Mr. Sorenson's address," suggested Bilan early that evening. "He told us he had it, just not at the moment. Maybe he has found it by now. That apartment you described cannot be where he really lives. We should find out where that is. He has not answered our calls today. Maybe we can talk to him in person again, tonight."

"That is a good idea," agreed Zahi. "We can go to the police station again and ask. And maybe they can tell us of another hotel for us to stay. If we are going to move every night, we need to know how to find as many hotels as possible."

They drove slowly through the unfamiliar streets until they were near the Berwyn police station. There was a parking lot right there, closed off. A large machine with huge rollers was passing over an expanse of fresh asphalt. The lot was being repaved. They left the car in a public lot two blocks from the station house, and walked back toward it.

***

"We've checked every motel near Berwyn," complained Bashiir, "and they're not at any of them. Where are we going now? We already know there are no motels or hotels in Berwyn."

"Despite that, I saw a listing on the Google for a hotel down this street," explained Xidig. "I didn't make a note of the address, but it's along here. I tried to find it again, and couldn't. I forgot how I found it the first time, but it is here somewhere. Just keep driving and we'll see a sign."

***

"They didn't move to either hotel, so where do we look now?" asked Taifa.

"I don't know, I really do not know," sighed Abdullah glumly. "Zahi said he came here to see a man who worked with the Berwyn police. Maybe if we go to their police station, we can find this man. He may tell us where they are."

Ten minutes later Abdullah gave a yell of surprise and pointed out a car some distance in front of them.

"That's Hamza's car! He is going the same way we are, so we can go to the police station and follow him at the same time. If he finds Zahi and Bilan, we will be here to rescue them. And if not, we can ask about them at the police station."

***

Zahi and Bilan crossed some railroad tracks and were walking down the sidewalk toward a large public swimming pool when a car went past them. They didn't notice the men in the car, but those men noticed them. Xidig turned the car into the pool's parking lot and sped to the exit at the other end close to where Zahi and his wife were. They arrived just as the couple were stepping onto the driveway.

Hamza and Bashiir jumped out of the car and grabbed Zahi and Bilan. The two fugitives struggled against their captors and screamed, then Xidig helped subdue them quickly before anyone around could do anything. Zahi and Bilan were thrown into the back of the car, and held down by Hamza and Bashiir. Xidig drove them away to the south.

"Where should we take them?" he asked Hamza.

"When we were looking for them this afternoon," remembered Hamza, "we passed a forest, right in the city. It was south and west of here, I think. Here, on this map, go west to this Harlem street, and south to the forest. It will be dark soon, and no one will be there. We can do what we want with these thieves."

As they drove away, they did not notice the car a block behind them, with two more Somalis paying close attention to everything they did.

"We were too far back to save them," confessed Abdullah. "That is my fault. What have I done? I was afraid they would see us if we were too close behind them. I knew they would try to seize Zahi and Bilan if they found them. We should have been closer. We might have been able to stop Hamza and rescue our friends. I was too worried about being seen too soon.

'Now is when we must not get too close to them, Taifa. They must not suspect we have come here from Minneapolis. We must get that money before they do. And now they have the thieves. They will torture them, I am sure, to make them say where the money is. Our only hope is to overhear them, and then get to the money first."

"I know this, Abdullah," remarked Taifa, "Diric would not have sent me with you if I was a fool. I will leave my headlights off as long as I can. It is still light enough to see where I am going. Ah, they are turning onto a busy street. That makes it easier for us to hide."

"Where are they going?" asked Abdullah. "Oh, there they are, going into this forest. Be careful following them into it. They stopped up ahead. Stop here and we will walk up to them and listen."

***

"We should have rushed them and saved our friends," moaned Taifa morosely as they drove back to their motel.

"With knives? Bashiir was holding a gun," countered Abdullah. "Xidig had a gun too. Hamza had a knife in his hand, but he almost always carries a gun. They all do. How could we have saved them? I am ashamed that I didn't try, but it would have been useless."

"Why did they kill the thieves, Abdullah?" asked Taifa. "The thieves did not tell them where the money is. Now no one knows. Such a stupid thing to do!"

"I think they made a mistake," considered Abdullah. "Hamza can get carried away. He is a fanatic who lives for al-Shabaab. His duty was to retrieve this money, Maybe his anger blinded him to that duty. He killed Zahi without thinking about it. Zahi was a small man, and not physically strong. Maybe he did not realize how hard he hit him."

"Why kill Bilan, as well?" asked Taifa. "She said she did not know where the money was. That Zahi took the money and hid it somewhere. And she didn't know where. However, if Zahi knew where the money was, so did she. This is almost certainly true. We know they were very close, and he would have told her everything he did. She is very brave; even so, she could have been forced to talk. Hamza knows how to do this. If he doesn't, I know that Xidig does."

"Did you not see what happened?" asked Abdullah. "He did not kill her, she killed herself. He held the knife in front of her face, threatening her. She threw her head back and then forward again, with all her might, and swung her body forward, also. She impaled her eye on his knife, driving it into her head. A very brave woman. Diric would have wanted her, and not just for his harem."

"It is late and I am tired. I am also frustrated that we have no way to find the money now. What are we to do, Abdullah?"

"Tomorrow we can look for their car," replied Abdullah. "Hamza and his men are cutting up the bodies and that will take them some time. They may leave them in the forest, or take them somewhere else. When they have finished, they will also be tired. And they will be angry with each other. They will not start looking any earlier than we will. Let us go to bed."

They returned to their motel and got into bed. However, Abdullah couldn't sleep. *What have I done? I sent Zahi and Bilan to their deaths. I only meant for them to steal the money from Yahye, it still led to their deaths. I am to blame as much as Hamza. What would my grandfather say about how I act now? What would the imam say? He doesn't support either side, and preaches peace in a peaceful new homeland. How peaceful am I making this home for us? How can I atone for their deaths? Will Allah ever forgive me?*

Chapter Seven

Finding the Bodies

Melissa's Hotel, as it was officially known, was a busy place at night. The bar was open all afternoon, and the evening hours saw a number of regulars who enjoyed the ambiance of old leather and walnut paneling. The restaurant was one of the best in a town noted for good dining, and reservations were always required. The hotel rooms were upstairs, beyond the velvet rope barrier across the grand staircase rising out of the lobby.

There was no regular registration desk at the head of the stairs, just a large lounge overlooking the lobby below. A corridor at the back of the lounge led to some rooms. There were many large, comfortable looking chairs, sofas, and love-seats scattered around the lounge. In the evening, they were mostly occupied by the residents of the hotel, and their visitors. The residents were all female, in their twenties or thirties, fairly attractive, and nicely dressed. Their visitors were almost exclusively male. Officially a hotel, it was, in fact, a brothel.

Melissa Maguire owned and managed the hotel, as had her mother Miriam before her, and her grandmother Ophelia before *her*. Her own daughter Angela, now twenty-three, had been learning how to manage the whole establishment for years. As had her son, Anthony, or Tony Jr., as the family called him. Her husband, Tony Russo, ran the pizzeria in town his son would take over eventually.

Angela, busy in law school, was also busy with her day job, running the restaurant and bar. She studied or went to class in the morning, then came home at eleven to open the businesses. Back to school at two for more classes until six, when the evening trade began to arrive. She studied her texts in the office while supervising a staff that needed little supervision. Although they did not open for business until just before noon, there was a lot of work to be done in the morning. Even the early morning, when the first supplies would be arriving.

It was convenient the family lived in a large, comfortable bungalow next door to the hotel. Angela just had to step out the back door of the house, walk down the alley to open the back door of the hotel, and find the dead bodies.

She was a tough twenty-three year old. She had been insulted often enough about her mother's occupation to have a thick skin. She had helped toss mean drunks out of the bar. She had helped toss unruly "visitors" from the hotel. None of that prepared her for finding two naked, mutilated bodies lying in the alley by the hotel's back door.

She screamed loudly.

***

Paul Radcliffe was the senior Detective Inspector on the Homicide Squad. His black hair was neither short nor long, carefully combed and parted. He wore a brown suit with a pale tan shirt. Almost six feet tall, and slender, he had a spring in his step most days. This morning his forty-odd years felt like a lot more. One of the perquisites of being the senior inspector on Homicide was that he got called in just as soon as a nasty murder was discovered. And his normal shift had only ended at midnight, six hours earlier.

By the time he had arrived in the alley, the area was crowded with policemen. Technicians from the crime lab were still photographing the scene and looking for possible trace evidence. One of them was climbing into one of the dumpsters behind the hotel, just in case some evidence had been tossed into it.

Two uniformed cops were keeping spectators away from the grisly spectacle, one of them directing a delivery truck to the front door of the hotel. Radcliffe's partner, Detective Sergeant Mike Feltz, was already interviewing a young woman, who was being comforted by a somewhat older woman.

"Good morning, Mike," Paul greeted his partner. "What have we got today? They only told me it was nasty. How bad is it?"

"Over there, under that tarp," pointed Feltz. "This is Angela Maguire, who discovered the bodies, sometime around six, and her mother, Melissa Maguire, who owns the, um, 'hotel.' This is Detective Inspector Paul Radcliffe, ladies. He will be in charge of the investigation. If you will excuse us for a few minutes, he will need to inspect the bodies."

Angela and Melissa has already seen the bodies and turned away to avoid seeing them again. Sergeant Feltz guided Radcliffe over to the covered bodies. Before lifting the tarp, he put his hand on Radcliffe's arm and warned him.

"This is really gruesome, sir," Feltz warned. "I've never seen anything like it. Their heads have been removed, and their hands. Not surgically, either. It looks like they were hacked off with an ax or a machete. And there seem to be signs of a beating, as well. Are you ready?"

"Yes, I've seen some pretty stomach-churning stuff in my day," commented Radcliffe. "I can stand it, no matter how bad it is. Lift the tarp."

Two medium brown bodies, one male, one female, were lying on their backs. The heads and hands were missing, as Feltz had said. There was very little blood on the ground, or on the bodies. Radcliffe felt his stomach twinge. With some difficulty he stopped its urge to do somersaults. He drew a deep breath and knelt next to the nearest body, the man, and began to examine the marks scattered over the torso and groin. He rose, and repeated the process with the female's body.

"Okay, cover them again," he ordered. "No need to upset everyone here by putting this on display. We'll have to get a detailed report from the medical examiner. Those marks do look like they were punched by a fairly strong man; I want an official statement about all of them. How far have you got interviewing the witness?"

"Not far, just name and address, really," admitted Feltz. "I was only marking time until you got here. I knew you would want to question her yourself. I didn't want to force her to remember that too many times."

"That's fine. Are there any other witnesses? It's early, but not that early. Did anyone else use this alley before she came out at six? Six is well after daybreak in June. Was anyone out and about early, jogging, putting out the trash, walking a dog? Not so much did they see the bodies and not report them, but did they see someone who might have been about to dump the bodies, or hurrying away? Get the boys going through the neighborhood, asking the questions.

"Ladies, may I ask you to come down to my office at the police station? I do need to talk to you, Miss Maguire, about how you found the bodies. It will be more comfortable there, and you won't have to look at them, even covered. Your mother may accompany you, if you wish."

"Thank you, Inspector," answered Melissa, "may I have a few minutes first? I have to give some brief instructions about the restaurant to my son. It won't take long."

***

"He calls this comfortable?" Angela asked her mother quietly, looking at the wooden chairs in Radcliffe's office.

"He didn't say 'comfortable,'" whispered Melissa, "he said 'more comfortable' as in more comfortable than standing in an alley. As a student lawyer, you should be more careful of catching nuances in speech. As a taxpayer, you should be happy that the city doesn't waste our money on nice furniture."

"Try the couch," suggested Sergeant Feltz, coming in with Radcliffe and apparently reading their minds. "It sags, but it's softer than the chairs. This is Officer Joyce Durkin, who will transcribe our interview. Let me just ask you to start with your own statement of what happened this morning, please."

"I went out about six this morning to open up the hotel," began Angela. "The deliveries for the restaurant begin to arrive around then, so one of us opens up the back door to the building. There's not really much to say. I went out, and there, right by the door, were two horrible dead bodies. That's it. I screamed, and ran back into our house. I guess I was still screaming because I didn't have to wake anyone up. We called the police. Squads and detectives and technicians arrived. You came, and here we are. That's really all I know."

"That's fine," indicated Radcliffe. "Let me poke around for details in this, if I may. Was the back door to the hotel open or closed?"

"Closed. I closed it last night after the restaurant shut down. Maybe eleven. No, twelve midnight, there were some diners lingering until eleven, and the staff took a little time to finish cleaning up. And I locked the door."

"Thank you. That was going to be my next question. I tried the door just now, and it is still locked. How many people have keys to that door?"

"My parents, my brother, and I do. And the pastry chef, he starts early making bread, sometimes before six. That's it."

"Do you really think someone who works at the hotel did this awful thing?" asked Melissa.

"No, I don't," admitted Radcliffe. "Most killers don't dump bodies near their homes, or anyplace connected to them. They don't want even a hint they might be involved in the murder. The one major exception is someone who has a grudge against you, or the hotel. Which is why I have to work through the list of all possible suspects.

"We have procedures and I have to follow them. Your family and your staff are almost certainly not involved in this crime. I must still clear you 'by the book' before I can start suspecting others. If I don't ask these questions, someone else will ask me why I didn't.

"Next stage. I need to find out who the victims are. Do you have any black employees? In the bar, in the restaurant, or in what we will politely call the hotel?"

"It *is* a real hotel, you know, with a license and everything," objected Melissa. "Yes, we do have black employees. Why wouldn't we? However, I don't think these were people who worked in any part of the hotel. It's hard to tell without," she shuddered "oh God, uh, without seeing their faces. We have a lot of Hispanics, some with darkish skin, working in the bar and the restaurant. One of our bartenders is black, but he's a bit heavy. The man in the alley looked very skinny.

"God, this is awful. Two of our cooks are also black females. And they are definitely heavier than the woman in the alley. And she was rather more flat chested than the women upstairs. I really don't think these people could be anyone who works for us, or resides in the hotel. We'll check on everyone, just to be sure."

"What about black, um, well, customers upstairs?" asked Radcliffe. "Could it be someone, um, stopping in for....? What euphemism do you prefer here?"

"That depends on whom I am talking to," explained Melissa. "At home or in the hotel, we might use one set of terms. In public, we might use a different set of terms. Talking to the police, even those who are not on the Vice Squad, I will be very discreet. I run a residency hotel for women. They sometimes have visitors. Period.

"Angela closed the restaurant and the bar around midnight last night, as she told you. I stayed up another hour to see the last visitors out. When I do this, I also check on the women residents, just to wish them a goodnight. I also check to make sure no visitors are hiding for some nefarious reason. There were no visitors still in the building at one in the morning."

"I was afraid of this,"groaned Radcliffe. "There was no pool of blood, so the victims were not killed where they were found. They had no apparent connection to the place they were found. There is no way to identify the victims. Well, that's my problem, not yours. I thank you for your kind assistance. Mike, give them your card. If you think of anything else, give him a call. Please follow Officer Durkin out, and she will print out your statements for you to sign."

***

"What's this car doing here, Joe?" asked Bill, sweeping more twigs, gravel, and odd junk into a neat pile. He and his partner were getting the parking lot ready for repaving. There were lots of bits of broken asphalt, candy wrappers, and used condoms from late night visitors. The lot was popular with lovers because it was out of sight of the police department two blocks away, and because it was as good as invisible between the city park and the railroad tracks.

"This lot is posted, 'No Parking – Closed for Repairs' very clearly. So why did someone leave his car here? Did they think Friday doesn't count?"

"Because the sign was knocked down," replied Joe, adding to his own pile. "I live down the street from here, and I noticed it when I was out jogging this morning. I put it back up; last night it wouldn't have been obvious."

"Well, call for a tow truck and get this thing moved to the impound lot," directed Bill. "The boss wants to get this re-paving project started right away, weekend or not. There are five diamonds in these two parks, softball season is about to start, and this is the only off-street parking near here. The grinders are coming this afternoon to start tearing up the surface, so let's get the place cleared out. They've got the re-paving bug. Yesterday the police station, this lot now. The sooner we get done here, the sooner we can go back to the office and goof off."

***

"I thought the big parking lot was where Zahi left his car," suggested Taifa, "can't be – it's closed down. Even though it is early those two Americans were already working on that lot. We laugh at their love of pleasure and leisure, and they are working as hard as any poor dirt farmer back home."

"Still, the car is not there, even if it should have been," grumbled Abdullah. "And it is not anywhere on any of these streets. We have been down every street for blocks around that pool where they were captured. Where could they have left their car? It is maddening!"

"And here comes Hamza and his men. They must have been at their prayers this morning before coming to look for the car. Well, we can leave them to look. They won't find it either."

***

"We captured them here, by this swimming pool," indicated Bashiir. "They were walking, so their car must be somewhere nearby."

"They are from a rural part of Somalia," countered Xidig, "and are used to walking long distances. They could have parked anywhere."

"True," admitted Hamza, "however, they would not have wanted to be far from the money. Bashiir is right, the car must be near here. Xidig, drive slowly so we can look at every car parked along the street. Remember, it is silver, and the license plate is from Minnesota, not Illinois. So it will be distinctive."

"What about this parking lot?" asked Xidig. "It is close by and large. Could they have parked in here?"

"Xidig, can you not read the sign?" complained Hamza. "This lot is closed for repair work. You can see the whole length of the lot, and there are no cars in it. There are only those two men working there. Drive down here, instead."

***

"Thank you for meeting us, Mr. Sorenson," greeted the short, portly man. "My name is Bill Edens, this is Tim Rogen, Albert Schwarz, and Jerry Randall. As I told you when I first contacted you, we play in a high stakes poker game at a private gambling club. We like the game. We like the other players. We like the club. We hate the neighborhood.

"The club has been there for years, and the owner isn't going to move it because of the neighborhood. The club has good camouflage, and doesn't get raided. Someplace else may not have these advantages. We've talked with him and we understand this. The location isn't a problem for him, he has plenty of security guards in the place. Our problem is, they can't walk us to our cars, and we can't park near the club.

"Anyone walking a couple of blocks in that part of Chicago is taking his life in his hands, even if he isn't carrying a bundle of cash. Going in isn't so bad, they may not spot him when he gets out of his car. But they watch the exits from the club like vultures. They figure everyone there wins big, and want to take it all. Tim's been robbed, Jerry's been chased. Albert and I have been lucky so far, still, it's really scary.

"We've tried cabs, and Uber and Lyft, and none of them like that part of town. We can sometimes offer a big enough tip to get a ride to the club. No one will come out to pick us up. So when we heard about you, we started to think you might be the answer to our problem. You deliver money for people. Maybe you'd deliver the people, too. We realize there'll be a fee of some sort. But knowing we won't be robbed makes a fee easy to think about.

"Are you well armed? Former Navy Seal? Martial arts expert? How do you fight your way through to deliver the money?"

"Hmmm. I don't," explained Sorenson. "I never go armed, for a number of reasons that I won't bother you with. I don't fight my way through gangs, I avoid them. Most of the time the money delivery is very prosaic. The landlord does not try to stop me from paying for a kept woman's apartment. A man receiving an immoral payment of some sort, does not object to my dropping an envelope into his pocket.

"You have an unusual problem, still it's not a unique one. You're going to Custom Synthetics, aren't you? I know the place fairly well. It used to be a real business, and the real owner, not the one you talked to, decided it was a perfect front for a private casino. It is hard to find someplace so well-disguised. And the neighborhood was still acceptable until the last few years.

"One solution would be for one of you to drop the others off at the door to the club, park his car, and walk back with empty pockets. Of course, the gang members won't know his pockets are empty, and they may not be happy to find they are.

"I can offer you a variation on this idea. You have already tried cabs and their ilk. That's the right and sensible idea. If a cabbie won't drive you there or pick you up, you need a more dependable driver. For the right fee, I can chauffeur you to the door, and pick you up later. The sidewalk in front is safe because of the guards. Does this sound acceptable to you?"

"Service right to the door, coming and going? That sounds good to me," declared Albert. "What sort of fee are you going to ask? We asked around about you, and people said you charged ten percent to move money. I would like to be safe, however, that seems a bit high of a cut to drive us there and home again."

"Yeah, we sometimes bring fifty grand or more, each," mentioned Jerry. "If we win big, we bring even more home. Ten percent of that from each of us is just too much. No offense meant."

"None taken," answered Sorenson. "Ten percent is my normal charge for making payments for people, especially people who are on the edge of the law. It includes a built-in margin for possible legal problems. I have a different fee for placing a bet for a gambler with a bookie. This is another different situation, so I think I will create a new fee, just for you gentlemen. How often do you go to the club?"

"Every Tuesday night," remarked Tim. "We try to get there about eight o'clock, and generally leave around midnight. We have day jobs and can't stay out all night. Does that fit your schedule?"

"Oh, yes, that's fine. I will charge you five hundred each for the round trip. Cash up front only. Two thousand for the four of you, fifteen hundred if it's only three of you. I would prefer to pick you up from one location, say Mr. Edens' house. You've already given me your addresses. I asked for them because I need to know who my potential clients are. I don't work with drug dealers, for instance. I think his house is the most convenient for you and for my driving you to the club and back.

"When you are ready to leave, or just before, call me and I will be at the door in about twenty minutes, depending on late night traffic. Stay inside until I show up at the curb. If you don't want to go to the club some night for any reason, just let me know before evening. And I will let you know if I will be unavailable on any specific night. For instance, I will be on my honeymoon the first two weeks of July, so you will be on your own then."

"Getting married, huh? Congratulations!" cheered Bill. "That's fine. We manage now, we'll manage for two weeks in July. Is that five hundred apiece fair for you? I know it's reasonable for us. How do you make ends meet at that price?"

"Gentlemen, really! Do the math! Please. Two thousand a week for, say, just fifty weeks a year works out to one hundred thousand dollars. And just for driving a few hours one night a week. I set my price seemingly low to tempt you to take it. My recent publicity has crimped my income a little. Lots of my clients don't want to work with someone in the spotlight. I could charge you less and still more than make up what I've already lost.

"And the price makes sense for you, since you are each, *each*, worrying about losing fifty thousand every week. Instead of my normal ten percent, you can think of this as a bargain one percent. You get to keep your money, you get peace of mind, and I get a nice fee every week. Do you want to do this? Starting next Tuesday?"

"My house at seven-thirty Tuesday night," agreed Bill Edens. "Cash up front. We'll be expecting you, Mr. Sorenson. I think it's going to be a pleasure to do business with you."

Chapter Eight

At the Morgue

"Where's Mike?" asked Paul Radcliffe as he came into his office Monday morning. He had had a long and frustrating weekend. Two murders at dawn on Friday to top off his regular week of work. No days off with two fresh victims, a lot of long hours, no chance to rest. The Missing Persons desk had no matches for either victim. The only slightly built black male who was missing had large tattoos on his upper arms. Homeless shelters weren't missing any regular visitors. Nor were women's shelters.

Two headless bodies meant two dead people with no faces. That meant no pictures to send to other cities missing persons bureaus. That meant no calls back saying "we have a possible match for you victim." And that meant frustration.

No hands, either. No hands meant no fingerprints. No fingerprints meant no search through AFIS, the Automated Fingerprint Identification System. It meant no comparison with databases of criminals, or immigrants, or military people. And that meant even more frustration.

And now his assistant and partner, Mike Feltz, was late to work. *I should cut him some slack, he's had as long and irritating weekend as I've had. We're used to a later shift, too, and he may be having trouble adjusting to mornings. Even so, where the hell is he?*

"Mike won't be here today" mentioned Detective Sergeant Sam Mahoney, walking past Radcliffe's office. "Or for a while, actually. He got run down last night crossing the street. Just a legitimate accident, not that that's any consolation to him. He's got a broken leg. Not too bad, but he's on medical leave for a while."

"Oh, hell," grumbled Radcliffe. "I need his help on this case. We haven't got enough detectives to go around and now this happens. Not that I blame him, but damn!"

"Oh, yeah, the headless body case," remembered Mahoney. "Phyllis told me about it this morning. She said you were grumpy all weekend over it."

"Oh, so my wife talks to you about my cases, does she?" asked Radcliffe, in mock indignation. "Just because we both work for the same police department, she thinks that's all right, does she? Harrumph!"

"Harrumph, yourself, dear," chuckled Phyllis Radcliffe, coming in with a grin. "As if we don't tell each other every detail of every case we each work on. That's OK. I'll make it up to you. I'm not busy with anything big, so why don't you borrow Sam. You don't mind, do you, Sam?"

"No, not at all," confessed Mahoney. "I'm already used to saying 'Yes, Inspector Radcliffe' so I'll fit right in. And Homicide will be a nice change from Major Crimes. Give me an hour to find Mike's notes and go through them to catch up with the case, and I'll be with you."

***

"We have searched the entire area near where the thieves were kidnapped," complained Abdullah. "We have gone down every street for blocks around, over and over. We have looked in every business parking lot. We have looked even in places people aren't supposed to park. The car is not anywhere."

"Could Hamza have found it first, and driven it away?" asked Taifa.

"No, he would not have taken the car," replied Abdullah. "He would have just taken the money. That's all he wants, same as us. If we found the car, we would just take the money. What would he, or we, do with the car? We don't need it, once we get the money. Neither does he."

"Where could the car be, then?" asked Taifa. "The thieves are dead, and can not drive it away. Oh, my, I had a terrible thought. What if someone stole the car? Someone who just wanted to steal a car, any car. Someone who did not know there was money hidden in it."

"Oh, Taifa," cried Abdullah in fear, "that would be awful! We might never find the car or the money ever. Or maybe we can. We were going to ask the police about the man Zahi told me about. Since his murder we have been afraid to talk to the American police forces. They might find out we are not really refugees but work for a Somali warlord. The Americans do not approve of Diric. However, the police can do things which we cannot. If we report the car stolen, maybe they will find it for us."

"Ah, Abdullah, that is a very good idea. I know their license number because Zahi would sometimes let me borrow his car. I had to know the license number so I could find it in a parking lot. Let the police search, using all their powers, and we just don't tell them why we want the car."

***

"It's not here," grumbled Hamza. "I know it must be here somewhere, but it isn't. Up and down every single street. We have looked in every driveway of every house. We have looked into every garage of every house. The car is not here."

"There are signs on some of these streets," noticed Bashiir, "that forbid parking at any time. What happens to cars that are parked there? Are the owners just fined? Are the cars confiscated and sold? What if the thieves parked in such a spot?"

"Yes, Bashiir, that is a very good question. I had not thought of that. What does happen to such cars? The police must do something about them, since it is illegal to park in those places. What? And how can we find out, without letting the police know who we are?"

***

"Is something the matter, Jack?" asked Marcy over breakfast at Katy's Diner on Monday morning. "You've been looking at the same page of that newspaper for twenty minutes, and you are not a slow reader. And when you take your eyes off the page, you stare out the window. Is this what I'm going to have to put up with at breakfast every morning?"

"Oh, I'm sorry, Marcy," apologized Jack, "and we've shared enough breakfasts over the years for you to realize this is not my normal morning routine. No, it's this ghastly murder case. It's been nagging at me all weekend long. The police have the bodies of two black people, minus their heads. I had two black people who wanted to hire me last week, the ones who doped me. I didn't want their job, and they were concerned about some unspecified enemies who wanted to kill them and steal their money.

"Despite all appearances, I do have a public-spirited side. That's one reason I helped arrest the French smuggler. I don't know if I can offer the police anything here. Two unidentifiable bodies, how can I offer to identify them? Even the police are stumped. The newspapers always say that; this time it's apparently true. Inspector Radcliffe must be going crazy with frustration."

"Well, then, you should help her," urged Marcy. "I like her, and she treated you politely during the kidnapping and art theft."

"Not Phyllis Radcliffe," corrected Jack, "her husband, Paul. He's the Homicide detective. Oh, my God! I've just spoken of them casually, using their first names and not their titles. I've never done that. Maybe I'm changing already. Anyway, you're right, I should help, if I can. And these may be two other people altogether.

"We have the measurements for the windows already. I will trust your judgment on the curtains and blinds. I should be through with the police by ten or eleven. I can join you then to discuss the new painting scheme we'll want in the house."

"Okay, that works for me; have fun being public-spirited."

***

"I'd like to speak to someone about the double murder," remarked Sorenson. "I might have some information about the victims."

"I know that voice," called Sam Mahoney, "and it always means long hours of work. How do you have information about this case? How do you *always* have information about so many of our cases? No, no, I won't complain. My wife likes the overtime pay. My chief likes the solved cases. I like the pats on the back. Come on back to Paul's office.

"Look who I found out in the lobby," he indicated as they entered Paul Radcliffe's office. "He says he has information about our victims. He probably went to school with them, and knows their names, address, phone number, and Social Security numbers."

"Mr. Sorenson, good to see you again," greeted Paul, coming out from behind his desk. "Phyllis tells me you have been much more civic minded lately. Is this more proof of that?"

"Yes, it is, actually," admitted Sorenson, shaking Paul's hand. "It's good to see you again, too, Inspector, and Sergeant."

"What, no Mr. Detective Inspector Radcliffe?" asked Paul.

"No, I'm trying to be less formal with people," confessed Sorenson, sitting down on the sagging couch. "I don't plan to call either of you by your first names, still, I can unbend a little. Sergeant Mahoney, have you switched Radcliffes? And where is Sergeant Feltz?"

"Oh, that's all connected," Mahoney told him. "Feltz got his leg broken in an accident last night, so Phyllis has loaned me to Paul. It should make you feel at home, having to put up with me again."

"Indeed, it does," allowed Sorenson with a smile. "Anyway, Sergeant Mahoney, you exaggerate a bit. I can only give you their names, address, phone number, and the license number of their car. *If,* that is, they are the people I met last week. And if they haven't swapped license plates, which is possible.

"I met a couple last week, a black man and woman, who wanted to hire me. They had seen the rather sensational article in *People* magazine, and wanted me to move a large sum of money to Africa. They wanted to move the money immediately. I told them I had to take care of some personal business first, and would call them the next day.

"Really, I wanted an opportunity to check them out as much as I could. I didn't like what I saw. Nothing criminal, necessarily, nothing quite right, either. I talked to Sergeant Mahoney to see if the money might be stolen and he couldn't find any really big thefts. The next day was Wednesday, and I couldn't get through to them on the phone, so I went to their hotel. They had checked out the night before.

"Do you know where they went?" asked Radcliffe. "Sam, have Gomez get us some coffee, he's on gopher duty this week. How do you like yours, Mr. Sorenson?"

"Cream, no sugar, thanks. I didn't know immediately where they went. They called me later in the day and I went to see them. I started telling them the problems involved in exporting a large sum of cash, especially into Africa. They were even more worried about corrupt officials than I was. While I was explaining the difficulties, the man put a damp cloth to my face and his wife bonked my cranium. Between their attentions, I passed out.

"When I came to, they were all polite and apologetic, and still wanted to hire me. I told them 'No' emphatically and absolutely. I'm not sure what they did while I was unconscious, although they did take my wallet out of my coat pocket, and put it back in the wrong pocket. Nothing was missing, and I don't know what that was about.

"That is all I have for you until I can see the bodies. The newspapers, naturally, did not have any pictures of the bodies. I'm not entirely certain that I really can identify them, but maybe I can. Can you take me to the morgue and let me look at them?"

"They're not pretty, you know" warned Radcliffe. "Headless and handless, and the amputations were done rather brutally."

"I know," answered Sorenson. "I read the account in the paper. However, seeing the bodies is the only way to know if these are the people I met."

"I'll take you," suggested Mahoney, getting out of his chair. "I haven't seen them yet, either, and I should, just to familiarize myself with all the evidence. Can you spare me now, Paul?"

"Of course. If Mr. Sorenson can put names to these bodies, we'll be much further along. We can't do much without names."

**

The Cook County Morgue, technically the Office of the Cook County Medical Examiner, is a large, squat building, with concrete walls and recessed windows that would look better in a gun emplacement. It is not supposed to be attractive. The people who work here don't care what the outside of the building looks like. The only other people who come here are those who are dead, or those who are trying to find their deceased friends or relatives.

Mahoney parked in the lot and they went inside. A clerk at a desk near the entrance pointed them to a door to the right. That door revealed another clerk at another desk.

"I'm Detective Sergeant Sam Mahoney. Berwyn Police Department, and this man is Mr. Jack Sorenson. We are here to view the bodies which were brought in last Friday from Berwyn. The headless couple."

"Oh, yes, let me look them up here," advised the clerk, checking his terminal. "John Doe June 7, and Jane Doe June 7. Unknown bodies are just John or Jane Doe, with the date of their arrival here. Rack 37 C and D. Come with me, please."

They went through a door to the left of the desk into a small anteroom, then through another door, thick and insulated, into the cold morgue storage room. Sorenson was surprised to see how very utilitarian it was. There was no wall of small doors each holding a chilled vault with a body, like in the movies, just open racks.

The room was full of industrial grade steel shelving, two long rows of shelves, fifty columns of shelves, five shelves high. Each shelf was a clean, stainless steel resting place for a body bag, though today about a third were empty. The clerk used a special type of forklift device to transfer the two bodies to rolling examination carts, and then wheeled the carts to the end of the morgue where Mahoney and Sorenson were waiting.

"I'm supposed to stay here and make sure you don't do anything weird with the bodies," remarked the clerk, "but I've seen these already, and once was enough for me. I'll be back at my desk. When you're through, please zip up the body bags."

"I see why he didn't want another look," commented Mahoney as he unzipped the first bag. "It looks like they had trouble hacking the head off. Four, five cuts before the one that worked. God, the place they cut these bodies up must look like a slaughterhouse. Only three tries for the woman, thinner neck, I guess. Not too much blood on the bodies, though. Which means they were dead before being hacked up. Anything in particular you want to see to identify them, Mr. Sorenson?"

"The woman had some sort of floral designs on her hands, but I don't think they were tattoos. They reached beyond her wrists, and looked almost painted on. To my untrained eye, they looked like Somalis I've seen on TV. And Somali women use henna to paint themselves – I looked that up afterward, trying to figure out who they were.

"Here, see this part, this is what I saw. The killers didn't cut far enough up her arms, and a tiny bit of the design still shows here. I'm sure this is the woman I met, and I presume this is the man I met. He didn't have any visible decorations on his body, so I can't say for certain. It's possible that the man got away, and that some other man was killed along with the woman. I think it's doubtful."

"So do I," agreed Mahoney. "Although, it is possible that the man you met thought his wife was cheating on him with this other man, and that he killed both of them."

"True, however, they both seemed to be worried about people who wanted to kill the two of them," said Sorenson. "Your suggestion is possible, and you should work on it as well, but I think these are both the people I met. Their enemies found them and killed them. Let's go back to Berwyn. Inspector Radcliffe is going to love my story today – all the juicy details he thinks I like to hide."

***

"Public spirit can ruin your day, Marcy," sighed Sorenson over his phone. "The two victims *are* the people I met last week, and I expect a long talk with Inspector Radcliffe. I have a lot to tell him, and he asks very good questions. I'll call you when I'm through here. I love you. Bye."

Sorenson put his phone away, and took a sip of his coffee. At least the police had good coffee, freshly brewed and not from a machine. He took a seat on one of the wooden chairs in Radcliffe's office, and leaned back enough to lift the front legs two inches off the floor.

"Last Wednesday I got a call from these people," began Sorenson. "They had seen the story in *People* magazine about me and the art theft. It mentions that I transfer money for anyone who pays me. They wanted to pay me to take some money to Africa for them.

"They began by saying that he was a Nigerian prince, and they needed the money to get him restored to his rightful place in Nigeria. I didn't believe that, of course, though I was too polite to say so. If they were really going to pay me a lot of money, I was willing to believe a lot of lies. I'm no ethnographer, but I've seen pictures of Nigerians in the news, and they didn't look like Nigerians. I've also seen pictures of Somalis in the news, and they did look sort of like Somalis. Their car has a Minnesota license plate, and Minnesota has a lot of Somali immigrants.

"They gave me their names as Zahi Smith, the man, and his wife, Bilan Smith. Yeah, I saw the irony of their using my own alias on me. They were staying at the Restful Motel in Oak Park, but they had moved out by the next day when I returned. I peeked in the window, and the room was empty.

"Their car is a recent Chevy Malibu, silver in color, with a dented rear quarter panel, and here's the plate number. They *may* have changed the license plates. The last time I saw them, I didn't see a car with Minnesota plates. Here is their phone number, as well. I have a friend who can check on license tags, and he looked up their plate. He says it's registered to a Mr. Zahi Smith, of Minneapolis. I didn't bother with the address; you can look it up for yourself.

"Your own alias, how ironic," murmured Mahoney.

"Yeah. He wanted me to move a million dollars to Africa. Yes, a million dollars. No. No, that's not right. That was the first number. Later *she* said five million. And still later they said several million, though they would have to count it to give me an accurate number. They pointed to two large suitcases in the room, and told me the money was in them. Both suitcases, they said. Each was big enough to hold maybe five million in hundred dollar bills. That's an estimate, based on handling Mr. Nolte's ransom money.

"I told them I had some personal things to take care of, so I couldn't start immediately. I really wanted to check them out, and to think about the job. I couldn't learn much about them, except to reinforce my opinion that they were Somalis and not Nigerians. I just didn't feel right about the job, either. Something fishy, something off. I trust my gut reactions a lot. Intuition has saved me from a lot of trouble over the years.

"On Wednesday when I saw them for the last time, they said they had counted it, and it was almost ten million. I really don't know. I never saw *any* money. And this is a guy claiming to be a Nigerian prince. I know that scam. Except he doesn't want *my* money, he wants me to take *his* money. So, maybe there is money here.

"My commission on ten million, I'd have made a cool million for myself. I don't like passing up that sort of money, but I've got to be alive and not in jail in order to enjoy it. And I wasn't sure I could meet those requirements."

Radcliffe swiveled in his chair, his head aimed at the ceiling, his eyes unfocused as he thought about what he'd been told. He faced Sorenson again and leaned toward him to ask his next question.

"Weren't you concerned about money laundering, or customs inspectors? Or are you just so sure of yourself that you thought you could avoid any problems there?"

"Oh, no, Inspector," Sorenson corrected him. "I told them that the U.S. lets you take as much money out of the country as you want, if you fill out a form explaining why you are moving so much money. If the request is approved, you're good to go. I told them they would have to fill out the form, and get it approved before I would do the job. They didn't have any objections to that. I told them they could do all that by themselves and save the extra million. They insisted I help them.

"I learned later, looking into the matter, that Nigeria lets you bring in as much as you want, also by filling out a form, and getting approval. I could see a problem there. I arrive with millions in cash, and find that the form is not going to get approved, and the money is going to be confiscated. That's part of why I declined the job."

"So, with this form approved, you would just waltz through customs?" asked Radcliffe. "Why, then, did they need you? Couldn't they have done it themselves? Am I missing something here?"

"Well, they were afraid of their enemies," explained Sorenson. "They didn't say who those enemies were, but they were convinced that they were after them to get the money. If I had the money, the enemies would not know this, and would keep watching this couple. They thought they would be safe as long as their enemies did not know where the money was. If they tried to bring the money with them, their enemies would find out, kill them, and take the money. I could bring it to Nigeria, or wherever, and once the money was safe, they would be safe. I'm not actually certain the destination was to be Nigeria, that's all they mentioned."

"Then, since they are now dead, the money is gone," Mahoney considered the facts, setting his coffee mug down on Radcliffe's desk. "And with that kind of money, and a weekend lead on us, the killers could be anywhere in the world by now."

"If you had taken this job when they offered it to you," asked Radcliffe, "would they have given you the money right away?"

"I think so," surmised Sorenson. "They were very impatient to get away quickly. The approval to export the money might have taken some time to get. For all the press I've had about moving money around the world, I really only work locally. I have no idea how long it might take to get that approval. Or how long it would take in Nigeria, either."

"Since it might take a long time, I suggested that I could help them move somewhere else in the U.S. to hide for the short term, or even permanently. They were adamant about going to Africa. If we had agreed last Tuesday, they probably would have given me the money then.

Sorenson let his chair settle back on all four legs and leaned toward Radcliffe. His arms rested on his legs as he looked intently at the policeman.

"They had only my phone number, not my address. I don't like giving my address to prospective clients. If I turn them down, they can't come back and pester me. So if the killers found them, they could honestly say they gave the money to someone who would take it to Africa. And that they don't know where I lived. They did know my real name, because of the magazine article, and maybe they could have fooled the killers about that. It doesn't matter, because that's not how it happened.

"Check with the Minneapolis police about them, and other Somalis they may have known. Look for their car, their luggage may still be in it. There may be some clues there about who they really are, what they were up to, where they were really going. All I know is they said they had a lot of money, and they were very afraid of some unknown enemies."

"There are Somalis from Minnesota who go off to fight with terrorist groups in the Middle East and Africa," remarked Radcliffe. "Could these people be connected with anyone like that? Did they say anything about politics or religion?"

"Not a word; they talked about enemies, with no indication of who they might be. If anything, they implied their enemies were Nigerians opposed to the prince coming back. If you aren't going to believe in the Nigerian prince part of the story, you can't believe in the rest, either."

"Well, thank you, Mr. Sorenson," complimented Radcliffe. "I appreciate your being frank with us. It's a nice change from our first meeting. The information you gave us should help us a lot."

**

"I talked to a man," commented Xidig, who was driving, "who told me they take the cars that are parked illegally to a place called the pound. He said it was near the police station, and it is kept locked up all the time. We can go there and look for the car. Even if the place is locked, we can find a way to get in. Here, this is the pound, Hamza."

"The sign says Metro Towing Service," objected Hamza.

"Yes, but this *other* sign says Police Impound Lot," indicated Xidig. "This is the right place. The gate is open. Can we just go in and take the money now?"

"No, there may be someone who will see us," warned Hamza. "If there is someone here, he will be with the police, or will call them. I think I see someone in that office. And we must not be seen carrying all that money. We will wait until after dark. The fence is not very tall, and we can easily get over it. Patience, Xidig. The money will be there tonight, and we will not have to confront the police."

Three hours later they climbed over the fence and began looking for the Chevy Malibu. No cars had Minnesota plates, but there was only one Malibu. It was silver with a big dent at the back end, and Bashiir noticed a map of Minnesota on the back seat.

"The license plate is wrong, but I think this is the car, Hamza. Let me open the trunk and see if the money is there. I have the keys we found in Zahi's pocket. This one is for a Chevrolet, but it doesn't work in the trunk lock. It fits the door, though. The back seat has only this map. I have no key that fits the trunk."

"Is there a switch to open the trunk?" asked Hamza.

"It's too dark to see in here, the overhead light is off," complained Bashiir.

"Don't turn on a light, someone may see it," cautioned Hamza. "We have a crowbar, use that."

Bashiir took the crowbar and pried the trunk open, and they looked at the big green suitcases lying inside.

"Ha, ha! You are right, Bashiir!" yelled Hamza. "Oh, how marvelous! Yahye will be very pleased with us. Here, take this suitcase… Wait, something is wrong. It is too light." He unzipped the cases. "It is empty! They are both empty! Oh, no! Bashiir, we must be cursed, the money keeps getting away from us! Now what will we tell Yahye?"

"Check the other bags, Hamza," suggested Bashiir. "They are too small to hold the money. Maybe there is a clue there to where they spent the night. Maybe the money is still at their hotel."

They found only clothes and toiletries. No room key. No hotel registration receipt. No millions of dollars. Frustrated, they threw it all back into the trunk and slammed the lid down.

Chapter Nine

Many Questions and a Few Answers

"Yes, sir, how may I help you?" asked Sergeant Lopez at the desk of the Berwyn Police Station.

"Yes, please, sir," replied Abdullah as politely and deferentially as he could. "My brother's car was stolen the other day. He does not speak very good English, so he wants me to ask you to look for it. It is a silver Chevrolet Malibu. The license number is 123 ABC. It is a Minnesota license plate. We have looked for it on the street, thinking he forgot where he left it. We cannot find it. Could you please find it for him?"

"All right, description, license. What year is it? 2010. Right. What's your brother's name? We will have to check the registration when we find the car to make sure it's the right one."

"His name is Zahi Smith," answered Abdullah. "We are from Somalia, and do not use last names so he called himself Smith. Is that allowed?"

"Oh, yeah, that's fine. Confusing if too many use the same name, but it's allowed. All right, I've got all I need. Give me a phone number, and we'll call you if we find it. We'll let the other towns near here know about the theft, too, still, it may take some time to find the car."

***

"Yes, sir, how may I help you?" asked Sergeant Lopez, still at his desk a short while later.

"Yeah, someone stole my license plates," complained the sunburned man in t-shirt and shorts. "I was parked at the MacDougal's on Roosevelt, near Harlem. That's the only place I've been lately where someone could have taken them. I only noticed it today, but it must have been last Tuesday, a week ago. I've been busy painting my house all week, so I didn't notice them gone."

"OK, what's the number?" asked Lopez.

"XY 4321, Illinois plate," the man informed him.

"Right, you should probably go to the DMV and report the loss. They'll probably have to give you a new set of plates. This is something that's hard for us to find. Sorry about that, pal."

***

"Hey, sarge, we've already got that number in the system," reported Patrolman Gomez. He was a rookie and was doing all the odd jobs in the station as a way to learn the ropes. He thought he already knew the ropes well enough from the academy, but he knew he couldn't argue with his bosses. "The stolen plates, we got that number on a car in the pound. It was brought in on Friday morning."

"Really? The guy just said his plates were taken, not his whole car. Are you sure?"

"Sarge, I can read the screen," mocked Gomez. "Illinois tag XY 4321, on a silver Chevy Malibu."

"Check the registration information on that plate. Make sure it matches the car. Someone may have stolen the plate to disguise another car."

"Oh, yeah, you're right, sarge," admitted Gomez. "That's the plate for a brown Subaru. What should we do?"

"You can go over to the pound and take the plates off that car and bring them here. I'll call the guy and tell him he got lucky. He won't have to go to the DMV after all. Hang on, before you leave, when you get the plates, be sure to get the VIN from the dashboard. We'll have to get some idea of who really belongs to that car."

***

"All right, sarge, I've got the plates for you," related Patrolman Gomez. "And the VIN. Which I know *you* do not want. You want *me* to look it up for you. Pleased to be of service, sarge."

"Thank you, Gomez. And yes, you look things up for me, because I might be busy dealing with the public. Not that anyone's here now. Still, someone might come in. And you are still a rookie, and need to learn how to look stuff up on the system."

"Yeah, sarge, right. I've been using the Internet as long as I've been alive, practically. Anyway, the practice is useful, since our system isn't the same as Google. Here's your info, sarge. The car belongs to a Mr. Zahi Smith, of Minneapolis, Minnesota."

"Zahi Smith?" asked Lopez, perplexed. "That's a weird name. Wait, that's the name of the guy who's brother came in to report a stolen car earlier. How does a stolen car end up with a stolen tag on it?

"Get Sergeant Vlach from forensics and go check out that car. He's got his own assistant, but you should pay attention to what he does. You won't be working with him any time soon, but all cops should know where *not* to put their own grubby fingerprints. See what's inside, passenger compartment, glove box, and especially the trunk. This is looking very peculiar."

***

"We're in luck, Gomez," instructed Sergeant Vlach, "they left the window open a little. I can slip this probe in and trip the door lock. I hate to have to force the door. The owner never likes that, and blames us for damaging his car. Here we go. Open the back door, Joe, and then get the trunk.

"Okay, Gomez, if you are looking at a suspicious car, use gloves if you can."

"Yes, sergeant." Gomez rolled his eyes. "They did mention this once or twice at the police academy."

"I don't know you yet, and want to make sure you know the proper procedures. If you don't have gloves, touch as little as possible inside the car. Even opening the glove box can leave your prints, and mess up someone else's. You can put your hand on the floor mat if you need to to look under the seat, but watch how you do it. Back seat, same thing. Nothing here except a map of Minnesota.

"Sarge, the trunk's already been broken into," called Patrolman Joe Chivas. "Looks like somebody used a crowbar on it."

"What a mess," grumbled Sergeant Vlach, looking into the trunk. "Opened suitcases, everything thrown together, this will take some time. Joe, get some pictures of what it looks like now, before we start moving things. Okay, Gomez, we've got a warrant, because the car was reported stolen. That means we can take anything out of it. If you stop a car and the owner lets you look into the trunk, you can't take anything. You can call for a warrant, but you can't touch a single thing, just look.

"Now that Joe's finished taking pictures, let's get to work here. I brought some big garbage bags along just in case we found something bulky, so let's put these small pieces into these bags. Give me a hand and we can slide a bag over each of these big cases, yeah, just barely. We'll take them back to the office to check these out. Last thing, Gomez. Close the car up nice and neatly."

***

"So did you learn anything useful from watching Vlach at work?" asked Sergeant Lopez.

"Yeah, he told me not to touch anything, ever," commented Gomez. "It wasn't very interesting, really. I had all that sort of thing in my training, you know. Still, it was a nice break from sitting in here, staring at my computer screen. Oh, hey, here's that name again, Zahi. Oh my God! Sarge, call Mahoney. That's his headless guy!"

***

"Zahi Smith's car has been in the impound lot since Friday, Paul," declared Mahoney, coming into Radcliffe's office. "Lopez checked and it was towed from the lot by Janura Park early Friday morning, but not *that* early. They must have parked there Thursday night, before being killed. Why should they park there? This case is getting even stranger, and it started out strange enough."

"Maybe the killers dumped the car there after the murder?"

Mahoney sat down to consider the suggestion.

"I don't think so, Paul. The car was intact when it was brought into the pound. The pound guys always check. Now, someone's broken into the trunk and rifled through their luggage. If the killers had the car, they would have done that before leaving the car. That makes me think the murdered couple left the car there themselves, and were killed before they could come back. That fits with the Medical Examiner's estimate of the time of death."

"From what Sorenson told us," mentioned Paul, "these are the people who came in early last week to ask you how to get in touch with him. Why are they back in this area again? Sorenson says they were in hotels in other towns around here, moving every night. They were afraid of being followed and killed, which was justified. So they weren't going to the park, or the swimming pool. Were they coming back here, to the station? Why? Did they decide, a little late, they needed police protection?"

"And, where's the money they said they had?" asked Mahoney. "Lopez says there was some small pieces of luggage full of clothes, and two big green suitcases like the ones Sorenson described as holding the money. Those were empty. If the killers had broken into the trunk, they would have taken the suitcases, and not just the contents. So, where's the money?"

Radcliffe got up and began pacing the floor, working on the puzzle. He turned and tossed a question at Mahoney.

"Did they hide the money somewhere before parking the car in that lot? If they did, why did they take it out of the suitcases first? If Sorenson is right, and they had ten million in cash, that's a hell of a lot of bills, even in bundles. Why take it out of two very handy containers? And Sorenson says he never saw any money. He told us they first claimed they had a million, then five million, and finally ten million. What if there wasn't any money, ever?"

"That's a horrible thought, Paul. Then we'd have a crime without any motive, except maybe just hate. Why would they have told Sorenson they had millions if they didn't? He would have checked before taking the job. He insists on being paid in advance, and would have expected to be paid a very large amount before taking this job. If there's no money to pay him with, what did they really want him to do?"

"Okay, Sam, there *is* money. There *was* money. Where? They weren't coming here to give us the money. That might have eliminated their risk, except they would have parked in our lot, and wheeled in the big suitcases."

"The city was finally re-paving our lot on Thursday," Mahoney reminded him.

"I forgot about that. Then we need to find where they last stayed. The room has undoubtedly been cleaned, and if they left anything, the manager must have it. Have Gomez call around to all the hotels in the area. He's not being kept busy enough as Lopez's assistant."

Mahoney called Gomez into Paul's office. He arrived with a fresh pot of coffee.

"Gomez, have you got a reply yet from Minnesota on that photo from their DMV? Did you get both names? Just Zahi? That's OK. One will do. I want you to call up every hotel, motel, and rooming house in the county. Start with anything close by first, then work your way out. Email them with the photo, and call to ask them to check their email. Ask them about tenants who might look like that and left unexpectedly or suddenly. If any think they fit our request, go over and get all they know. We need to know where these two people stayed the day before they were killed. Got it? Good"

"Have Lopez call that guy back," directed Paul, "the one who claimed to be Zahi's brother. Tell him we found the car and ask him to come pick it up. Once he's here, we can have a nice, long talk with him. He can tell us something about his brother, and who wanted him dead. And why.

"What about Sorenson? Phyllis liked the way he helped with the kidnapping and art theft. She once told me she could always squeeze more out of him, like a magic orange. You've dealt with him. *Can* we get more out of him?"

"He was very reluctant to cooperate last year when I first met him," Sam divulged. "He became more forthcoming when his friend was killed and he was in danger himself. In the kidnapping case, he was doing all he could to help his client. He had an interest in finding the crooks.

"He has no client here. The people who wanted to hire him are dead, and he says he didn't want their job anyway. I can't see how he's got any reason *not* to help us. I think he's told us everything. He figures if he tells us all he knows, we will go away and stop bothering him. That's what he really wants out of life."

"So we just wait for the brother?"

"We need more information, Paul, and he might give it to us. Until then, we're spinning our wheels."

***

"That was the police, Taifa," announced Abdullah as they sat in their motel room. "They said they have found Zahi's car. It is in their impound lot, and we can get it now."

"That is good news. Oh, what if they ask us about Zahi? The news program has a story about a man and woman found headless in an alley. We know that couple is Zahi and Bilan. How can we be claiming a car in the name of a dead man?

"The bodies can't be identified without their heads, Taifa. That's why Hamza cut them off. The police won't know who Zahi is or what happened to him. You did not come in with me to report the theft, so you can pretend to be Zahi. I told them Zahi did not speak very good English, so just smile and nod your head. Many Americans think that all foreigners are simple, stupid people. If they want some form signed, you can sign. Once we get the car, all of our problems are over. We will have the money. Yahye will not. And he will not know that we have it."

***

Sergeant Lopez recognized Abdullah when the Somali entered the station again. He wished he could see Radcliffe and Mahoney interrogate him and his friend, but the most fun he could have was to escort them to Paul's office. Abdullah was surprised to see a small office for a police inspector. *Surely such a high rank must deserve a bigger office, and a larger desk. This desk is hardly bigger than my coffee table at home, though taller.*

"This is Detective Inspector Radcliffe and Detective Sergeant Mahoney, gentlemen. Paul, Sam, this is Zahi Smith and his brother Abdullah, who reported the stolen car this morning."

Paul welcomed them. "Thanks, Lopez. Gentlemen, please have a seat, this may take a little while."

"Yes, sir, thank you, sir, but why should it take time?" wondered Abdullah, sitting on the edge of one of the wooden chairs. "We described the car, and you say you have it now. It is Zahi's car. His title papers are in the car. He will sign any release form you require. He does not speak much English, so I will translate for him. We wish to go back to our home in Minneapolis today if we can."

"We have a few simple questions to ask you," Paul told him. "When we filed your stolen car report, we checked with the Minneapolis police, just to get some basic information about Zahi. They said he is a good citizen, though they have heard some reports of someone who wanted to harm him for some unknown reason. I'd like to ask you if there is any truth to this report. Does Zahi have enemies?"

"Oh, no," objected Abdullah. "Zahi is a very modest man, well liked by everyone in our community."

Abdullah turned to Taifa and spoke in Somali, "Say something to me in Somali. Pretend you are telling me you have no enemies. They will not understand us." Taifa responded in Somali, shaking his head and looking innocent.

"He says everyone is his friend," argued Abdullah. "He minds his own business, and he is very helpful to anyone who needs help. Can we have the car now, please?"

"In just a minute," cautioned Paul. "We have to prove ownership before we can release the car. I could be in trouble for giving the car to someone pretending to be Zahi. So, can Zahi show me his driver's license?"

"Oh. Um, uh, he lost it last week," improvised Abdullah. "When he lost the car. He had been drinking and was careless. We are Muslim and we are forbidden to drink, but we are also human and we sometimes fail in our duty. I can vouch for him, I am his brother after all. Here is my license."

"Well, that's very good,' declared Sam. "However, we still have a problem. This is a picture of Zahi, from his driver's license, and it does *not* match this man. And we have reason to believe that the real Zahi is dead, killed last Thursday night."

Abdullah panicked. He had been so calm and cool, ready for any question the police might ask, just not for a question about a dead Zahi. *The police know about Zahi! They must know about everything. The money, stealing it from Yahye, Diric. We have to get away!*

He stood up abruptly, grabbed the edge of the desk, and dumped it into Paul's lap. A brief word in Somali, and Taifa followed him running out the door and through the open office. Men at desks were all around them, and they were all startled to see the two Somalis running past them.. Sam started after them while Paul righted the desk. Paul called the front desk to warn Lopez to stop the Somalis, but he was too late. They were gone.

Sam followed them out the front door, watching them get in a car and speed away from the curb.

"We passed the police impound lot on our way here, Taifa. If the car is there, we can just take it now. You can hotwire the car, can't you? They won't expect us to go there first, so we have a few minutes to get it. Here we are, you know what the car looks like. Go in and get it. Meet me at our hotel. I will pack up our bags, and we can leave this town."

Taifa ran into the pound, surprising the attendant in the office. Before the attendant could chase after the intruder, his phone rang. He groaned and picked up the phone.

"I ain't got time, I got a problem here," he shouted into the phone.

"If it's someone breaking in for a car, George, close the gate," ordered Lopez. "We have a couple of black guys trying to get a car out of the lot, and they don't want to answer questions about it. If this guy is black and trying to make off with a silver Chevy Malibu, that's our man. Don't let him get away with it."

George hung up the phone and ran into the gateway. He yanked one chain link gate away from the wall, then the other. He ran a strong chain between the two parts of the gate and secured the lock on it. Then he jumped back as a silver car came rushing at him. It bounced off the gate, and the driver tried to break through again, with the same result.

George, seeing the gate was holding, went back into his office and called Lopez. "I think this is your guy. He is seriously trying to take a silver Chevy Malibu out for a drive. I'd appreciate it if you'd send some guys around to pick him up before he destroys the gate. We're a *towing* company, you know, not cops, and I ain't armed."

Sergeant Doyle pulled his squad into the gateway to the lot a minute later and jumped out. He didn't need George pointing at the silver car pushing against the gate. He went into the office and out the door on the other side of the gate. Taifa looked forlornly at the policeman coming around the car, and put his hands on his head.

"Step out of the car, please," requested Doyle. "Lean against the car and spread your legs."

He patted Taifa down and handcuffed him. George opened the gate and Doyle led Taifa to his squad. He put him in the back seat and drove the two blocks back to the police station. He found no sign of the other black man they told him to arrest.

The Somali had resigned himself to being captured. He knew he had had little time to get the car out, and he had failed. He could see that Abdullah had gotten away, at least. All he needed to do now was to say as little as possible to the police about who they were, and where Abdullah was. That part would be easy if he kept quiet for half an hour. That was all the time Abdullah would need to get to their hotel, pack, and disappear. He had lots of experience.

***

Taifa sat in the bare interrogation room and waited for the torture to begin. The room was about ten feet long by eight feet wide, with a large table and four chairs. There was no clock, or anything else, on the walls. The floor was covered with scuffed, dirty, cheap tile, broken in places. The wooden chairs were not designed with comfort in mind. It was designed to make someone uncomfortable enough to talk rather than stay in the room any longer.

He had never been arrested in America before, and didn't know what to expect. *I know what al-Shabaab would do if they had captured me*, and he shuddered at the thought. *I know what Diric would do if he had captured one of the terrorists. Well, it wasn't much better, except they deserved it. How cruel would the Americans be? There were so many strange and marvelous devices all over America, surely they must have some especially horrid ways to torture a man.* He waited, and waited. Even the waiting seemed like torture to him.

They had spoken to him rather harshly when they first brought him back into the police station. On the other hand, they hadn't hit him, or pulled out any weapons or tools. They had made him empty his pockets, but they had not stolen anything. They even asked him to open his wallet and take out his driver's license. It didn't matter much if they knew his real name now. They had looked at the other things, and put them all in a big bag. A man came in and made a list of everything in the bag. He even counted the money in the wallet, and put it back. He gave a copy of his list to Taifa. Mahoney had watched all this, then left the room.

"That's your property list," mentioned Mahoney when he returned with Radcliffe. "If we let you go, that's a record of what you owned coming in here. You'll get it all back. *If* we let you go. Paul, I've got Saunders checking out the motel key."

Motel key? How could his key tell them anything? Was the hotel named on the key? Oh, no!

"Where is your friend, Abdullah?" the one called Mahoney had demanded. His manner was gruff, though he made no threats. "Where have you been staying? Is he going back there now? Come on, tell us what we want to know. We'll find out sooner or later, so make it easy on all of us and tell us now."

The man had continued that way for some time, but Taifa had refused to tell them which hotel they were in. However, he had forgotten he wasn't supposed to know any English, and had tried to talk his way out of custody. That hadn't worked at all and they had put him in this bare room all by himself. Now all he could do was wait for them to come back.

***

Sam entered Paul's office as he finished straightening up his desk.

"More good news, Paul. Saunders and Wozinski picked up Abdullah coming out of his motel room with a couple of bags."

"That didn't take long, Sam" remarked Radcliffe.

"Luck counts, Paul. Sometimes it's all we've got in our favor. Taifa didn't seem to realize the motel key told us where to look for his buddy. I put him in the other interrogation room. Who do you want to start with?"

"Taifa, he's been alone almost long enough now. He probably thinks Abdullah has escaped, and may be more willing to talk a little if he thinks the other guy is safe. We need to find out who they really are, and what their connection to Zahi and his wife is. Has Minneapolis gotten back to us yet?"

"Not yet. I asked for a full report on these guys. That may take a little time. I suppose they were trying to get the fabled money Sorenson mentioned."

"Sorenson wasn't sure it existed. If it did, it would be reasonable to expect to find it in Zahi's car. So I think you're right. But then, did these two guys kill Zahi? And if they did, why didn't they take the car and the money then?"

Mahoney sighed and shifted to a less uncomfortable spot on the hard chair. He thought a moment and answered Paul's question with his own questions.

"Lopez told us there was no money in the car, Paul. So did someone else take the money? Which leads to, did someone else kill Zahi and Bilan? Or did Zahi hide the money somewhere? In his hotel room? No, Sorenson said he had two big bags like we found. If he dumped the money out in his room, the hotel staff would have found a huge pile. The cleaning lady may have been tempted to keep it all, but that much money will attract attention, and someone would have talked about it. At the very least they would have reported it to the police.

"If someone had taken the money, that someone would have taken the bags as well. If Zahi needed two big bags to carry the money, it's too much to carry any other way conveniently.   Why not just leave the money in the bags, and take them?"

Paul scratched his head in confusion.

"So, these two guys didn't steal the money, Sam. And any other guys after Zahi didn't either. The money has disappeared. If they were full, those suitcases would have been fairly heavy. Zahi would have noticed if someone had emptied them and left them. That means that he must have emptied them himself. Did he have a place to hide the money that was big enough for the cash, but not the size or shape of the bags?"

"Money laundering," suggested Sam, half in jest. "You mentioned it to Sorenson, but think about a place to hide that much cash, in a different shape. A washer and dryer would do wonderfully. Too bad Zahi didn't have access to a laundry room. Let's go talk to Taifa and see what he is willing to tell us."

***

Paul was pressing his question again, and again. Pushing, figuratively, against a suspect often led to an inadvertent slip of the tongue. The interrogation room was stuffy, which bothered all of them, but he hoped it would annoy Taifa most.

"No, I didn't kill Zahi or Bilan. They were my friends. Abdullah and I had heard they had left Minneapolis, and we just, um, wanted to meet with them."

"Where were they staying?" asked Mahoney. "If you were going to meet them, you must have known which hotel they were in. Or were you chasing after them? We have information that someone was following them intending to kill them. Would that be you and Abdullah?"

"No, no, no! We wanted to help them. It was Hamza who wanted to kill them. Oh, no! I did not tell you that. I will not tell you anything more."

"Who is Hamza?" asked Paul. "Is he another Somali from Minneapolis? Where is he?"

Silence.

"I guess we're done with him for a while," mused Mahoney. "Let's try door number two."

Taifa wondered what door number two led to. *Americans have such strange expressions.*

***

In the other interrogation room Abdullah was pacing up and down, angry with himself for being caught. *Maybe Taifa got away with the car. He wasn't at the hotel by the time the police came, so he may have seen them and gone away. How did the police know where to find me? Has Allah abandoned me? Is this punishment for Zahi and Bilan's deaths?*

Radcliffe and Mahoney entered the room without saying anything. They took seats at the table and waited for Abdullah to sit. They looked at him steadily, which he seemed to find a little unnerving.

"Who was Zahi?" demanded Radcliffe.

"He was a friend of mine. From Minneapolis. That's all."

"Where is the money?" asked Mahoney.

"What money? I don't know anything about any money. Zahi was a poor man. We are all poor here."

"Who is Hamza?" asked Paul, who saw Abdullah start when he heard the name.

"I don't know anyone named Hamza," lied Abdullah awkwardly.

"Did you or Taifa kill Zahi and his wife?" asked Mahoney.

"No, they were my friends. We were all very close. I would never have harmed them."

"Did Hamza kill them?" asked Radcliffe, surprised that even a dark skinned man can go almost pale from fright.

"I do not know any Hamza. No. Do not ask me about such things. I did not kill Zahi."

"So, did Hamza kill Zahi and his wife and steal their money?" asked Mahoney.

"Who is this Hamza person? I do not know him."

"How much money was there?" demanded Paul. "Was it ten million dollars? Why did Zahi have it? What did he do with it? Where is it now? Why were you trying to get his car? Was it in the car? Does that money belong to you?"

"No, no, no. Please, I have done nothing wrong. I have killed no one. I have stolen no money. Please leave me alone!"

A man appeared at the door and called Mahoney out of the room.

"Sam, I just got a reply from Minneapolis about these guys, and that Hamza fellow," announced Tom Sweeney. "The cops up there have nothing serious on these two except they think they might be connected to some Somali warlord or other. Nothing definite. They're going to look deeper now that we're stirring things up.

"Hamza is another story. He's got a long rap sheet up there, mostly strong-arm and extortion. He's been mentioned in some nasty beatings, suspected in several robberies, and a murder or two, unfortunately, no evidence. Rumor has it he works for some Somali terrorist group. If so, he keeps it quiet. They think he's the muscle for a guy named Yahye, the big leader of the group. Here's Hamza's picture, and the two guys you've got in there."

"Thanks, Tom, that's a big help. Terrorists and warlords. Damn. Why can't they keep their stupid wars over there, where they belong?"

"I don't know anything about millions of dollars," Abdullah was saying as Mahoney re-entered the room. "If I ever had money like that I would buy a palace and live like a king."

"Who is Yahye [pronouncing it Yah-yee]?" asked Mahoney, and the blood drained from Abdullah's face again.

"Yahye [pronouncing it Yah-yay]? Who, who is Yahye? How should I know? I do not know him. I do not know where he is. I have never heard the name before. Who told you that name?"

"Okay, if you can correct our pronunciation, you do know Yahye, don't you?" asked Paul. "I have all day to talk to you. And you aren't going anywhere until you talk to me. I can charge you with first degree murder for the deaths of Zahi and Bilan. I can make a good case that you killed them to steal ten million dollars from them. The State of Illinois no longer executes people for murder, we will instead lock you up for the rest of your life. Now, all I ask of you is that you tell me things that I would like to know."

"No, I cannot tell you anything. You cannot scare me. You must have proof before you can convict me. I saw this on television. I am innocent."

"Let's go outside, Sam," suggested Paul, and they left the room.

***

"Yahye is a good name, Sam. It got a really nice reaction from Abdullah. Let's see what it does to Taifa." They went into the other interrogation room. Taifa was resting his head on the table, his hands covering his scalp as if to protect him from some impending disaster.

"Taifa, why did Yahye want to kill Zahi?" asked Mahoney.

"What! Who told you about Yahye? How could you know about him?"

"Abdullah is in another room down the hall," Paul revealed. "I think it's about time that you told us what we want to know. Do you want Abdullah to get all the credit for cooperating with us?"

"Abdullah would never talk to you. He is too strong. He is loyal to…."

"To his warlord?" asked Mahoney. "Is this warlord the enemy of Yahye's group? Who does the money belong to? We *can* find out the answers to these questions, you know. It will be better for you if we get the answers from you directly. Or would you rather go to prison for a very long time?"

"I will say no more. I don't know any warlord. There are no warlords in Somalia. I know nothing about any money. Leave me alone!"

"That's all right. We have enough from Abdullah anyway, Paul. Why waste time getting Taifa to repeat it. We'll have to let Abdullah go, but we can lock up Taifa at least."

"Wait, wait. You can't do that! I haven't done anything wrong. I didn't kill Zahi and Bilan. If you let me go, I'll tell you who did. Please don't send me to prison."

"That's better, Taifa," urged Paul. "Tell us the truth, and remember we will compare what you say with what Abdullah says. If you haven't broken the law, you won't go to prison. If you tell us everything we want to know, we'll even forget about you trying to steal Zahi's car. Now, who killed Zahi and Bilan? And why?"

"Hamza killed them both. I don't think he meant to, but he is cruel enough, maybe he did mean it. He hit Zahi with his fist *very* hard. He has big hands, and he is strong. Zahi was a small man. He fell to the ground and did not get up. Bashiir picked him up and told Hamza that Zahi was dead. He must have hit him too hard.

"Then he started to threaten Bilan with a knife, and she refused to tell him anything. He pointed to Zahi's body, and laughed at her. And she did something so brave. Even Abdullah thought she was very brave. She threw her head back and then forward and impaled her face on Hamza's knife. Shc killed herself rather than tell Hamza what he wanted to know. Oh, she was so brave!"

"My God!" cried Sam, shocked.

"What did Hamza want to know?" asked Paul.

"He wanted to know where the money was, of course. We all did. Didn't Abdullah tell you that?"

"Was it ten million dollars? Was it in big green suitcases in their car? Was that why you wanted their car?"

"Yes, yes, and now you've got it. I don't care. At least Yahye doesn't have it either. That's more important than if we got it for …. I keep talking too much. No more."

***

Abdullah was pacing back and forth in the other interrogation room, a worried look on his face. He wrung his hands together, ran them over his face, and pulled at his short hair.

"All right, Abdullah, what did you do after Bilan killed herself on Hamza's knife?" asked Paul.

"What! How could you know this? Are you sorcerers? What magic do you use to learn such things. You know everything already. I am doomed, cursed by Allah. He is punishing me. I will answer your questions then. Though if you already know, why do you ask? I don't care. Ask anyway. I will answer."

"What did you do after Bilan died?"

"Nothing. We could do nothing. We could not have saved them – you must believe me, please. I have only Taifa with me. He is a good fighter, but Hamza had Bashiir and Xidig with him. And they had guns, and we did not, only knives. I did not think they would kill them. Not before learning where the money was. And then, just like that, Zahi and Bilan were both dead. It happened so fast. There was nothing we could do then, of course. We went away quietly."

"How much money was there?" asked Mahoney.

"Almost ten million dollars, Bilan had said. She heard Yahye say how much, I forget just exactly how much. And Yahye was going to send it to to his masters in al-Shabaab. We had to stop him. It was Zahi's plan. Bilan cleaned Yahye's house, and she could get them in. She was our spy. They would take the money and give it to me. Instead, they took it and ran. So much money must have been too tempting for them."

"So, where is the money now?" asked Paul.

"I don't know. We could overhear what they said. If she said where the money was, we were going to try to get to it first. She said Zahi had hidden it, but she didn't know where. I think she did, but she said no more, and just killed herself."

"Oh, damn! I'm sorry, Abdullah. I should show more respect for the death of your friend. You've been very helpful finally. One more question. Do you know where Hamza is now?"

"No, I do not. I knew they were here, just not where. We happened to see their car on the road and followed it until they found Zahi and Bilan and kidnapped them."

"Thank you. Someone will come for you in a little while, so just rest yourself. Sam, let's check out the other room."

***

As Abdullah and Taifa were escorted to a holding cell, Mahoney and Radcliffe went back to Paul's office. Sam turned to Paul and said, "Ain't that a kick in the head. We finally find out what happened and we still don't know anything useful."

"Taifa confirmed everything Abdullah said, Sam. And it *is* a nice consistent story at last. I want you to ask the Riverside cops to do a luminol search of the park, just to confirm the murders took place there. I wish we had some idea of where Hamza is, and the money. You don't suppose Sorenson has it, and isn't saying anything about it, do you?"

Mahoney looked across Radcliffe's desk at the tired inspector and shook his head.

"No, I've gotten to the point where I trust Sorenson to be honest enough. Almost ten million is a vague number. He could easily keep two hundred grand, give us the rest of the money, and tell us that was all of it. We'd never know, and he could be a lot richer. I could see that, maybe, just not keeping the whole thing. If police work was easy, Paul, they wouldn't need us or pay us so much."

Chapter Ten

Night Work

Sorenson followed Marcy into her apartment at the end of a long day of talking to decorators and painters. He carried a bottle a wine light enough to not overwhelm their Chinese takeout.

"You gave in to me on every single thing we talked about today," complained Marcy as she set the table. "Not even a mock argument just for show. Have you gone soft, Jack? I like you being strong, the same way you want me to be strong. Why so accommodating?"

"You've seen my apartment, darling. It's plain. I've had it repainted over the years, and I choose the colors almost at random. I don't have a talent for decoration. I like art, I like music, I like books. I have no idea of what a room should look like, though. You *do* have an idea. So why should I try to impose my ignorance on your skill and taste?"

"It's an honest answer, I'll give you that. I thought it was because you were down after viewing the bodies yesterday. I'd have had to go to bed for the rest of the day if I had seen that. I guess you are still strong, after all."

"It didn't do my stomach any good. However, I don't have your artistic imagination. Locking myself away inside myself has also created a sort of defense against the world. Even truly unpleasant things can be shunted off to some back corner of the brain. The horrible part was not looking at their bodies, although that was bad enough. The worst thing was realizing someone hated them so badly the bodies had to be mutilated like that. I suspect that I'm talking about this more than you like. Let's change the subject. What furniture do we need for the house?"

"My mother told me when I was young that the very first, most important purchase every young couple getting married should make is a good bed."

"Young couple? Really? And don't we have beds already?"

"Mine is a double bed, a little small for both of us, as you've sometimes complained. And it's sagging. Yours is queen sized, old, and sagging, too. The bedroom is big, and I want a big bed, king sized, and very comfortable. Are you going to argue?"

"With logic like that, hardly. I've noticed my creaky bed myself. I have several chairs of varying ages and appearance, a decent enough couch, some small tables and desks. You have some nice pieces of furniture, and some bad ones, too. Favored relics, I suppose, of your starving artist days. I have my favorites among my collection, too, including a very comfortable reading chair. Maybe we can keep a few of these bits upstairs where only we will see them, and buy new furniture for the first floor."

"The house is so nice, it does need to have good looking furniture in the public areas. We'll have to sit down with the floor plan and little scraps of paper to represent chairs and things to see what we need. The living room and sun room is a big enough area, and there's the family room at the north end. Could we put your big bookcase in there, just to show people we know what books are?"

"That's a good idea. I like that bookcase, and don't want to get rid of it. I want to line the tandem room with shelves. I have a lot of books in storage, and you have a lot of books, too. I've always wanted a real library in my home. And now I can have it. My comfy reading chair, a comfy reading chair for you. Floor lamps to supplement the overhead lights. We'll also have to get some furniture for the guest bedrooms. Dining table? I haven't got a decent one. I like yours, but we need one for the breakfast area, and one for the dining room."

"We're going to make some furniture salesman's day by the time we're through, Jack. I like your suggestion for the library. It's not only a good idea, it shows you really care about this house."

"Of course I care about this house. How could you doubt that? This house will be ours, yours and mine. It will be us. A sturdy symbol of our marriage. Since deciding on marriage, I've gotten absolutely nutty about it. However, I *have* resisted the idea of having our marriage license engraved in brass on the front door."

"Silly! I *am* glad you feel that way. No, glad is too mild a word. Ecstatic? Is that too much? Touched to the bottom of my heart. I love you so much, and am so happy we will soon be married. I would say you have no idea how I feel, but I know you feel the same way. Isn't it a glorious feeling?"

"It is, dearest, it is. Back to furniture for a bit. Would you like to start looking, casually, tomorrow? I know a man who can give us a nice price, if we like his stock. I helped him out of a jam a few years ago, and he still thinks he owes me a favor. And there are a lot of other stores if we don't like his.

***

It was late evening, and most of the station house was quiet. The day shift had left, and it included many of the support staff. Most of the night shift was out on patrol. Detectives, however, weren't on the clock.

"More chicken, Paul?"

"No, thanks, Sam. I've had enough. I like their chicken but their fries are awful. We need to find another decent place for fast food."

"I should have taken Helen up on her offer to bring us a home cooked meal. Oh, well, this bucket can just go into the garbage. Here comes Sweeney with a smile. What's up, Tom? You're looking happy."

"Minneapolis sent us everything they have on Somali warlords, terrorists, gangs, and jaywalkers. Hamza is a seriously tough guy. Yahye is worse, although they can't prove anything. Witnesses keep disappearing. Their file lays out the whole structure of the two main groups. Yahye works for al-Shabaab, the terrorist group in Somalia. Abdullah works for Diric, a minor Somali warlord. Diric's also on the government's list of bad guys, further down.

"There have been rumors in Minneapolis that Yahye was collecting money for al-Shabaab. Mostly by extortion and robbery. Abdullah has his own gang there, not so nasty. They do seem to get into fights with the al-

Shabaab bunch, but no one talks about it. Oh, and why I'm so happy. I'm going home now. See you in the morning."

"Goodnight, Tom. Well, Paul, let's at least pretend to look this stuff over tonight. We have pictures of all of these guys now. I'll have copies made and we can send Saunders out tomorrow to check all the hotels and motels in the area. I'm hoping he did well on the sergeant's exam and some practice won't hurt him."

"You keep worrying about Saunders passing that sergeant's exam. Is he your secret brother or something?"

"No, I've just noticed over the last couple of years that he has a good nose for police work. You may remember old Fred Prchal, I think he was still here when you started. His daughter Joan is a sergeant now. He gave me a lot of support and guidance when I was where Saunders is now. It wasn't required, but it helped me, and I want to give Saunders the same little boost. He's going to make detective some day, and I want to have him helping me when I make Inspector."

"Inspector? Yeah, I can see that, Sam. You've got the brains for it and the tenacity. Two big cases in two years to your credit. Now maybe a hand in a third. I'll be glad to see it happen. Meanwhile, however, we've got a case that doesn't want to be solved. Where are the killers? Do you think they're still in the area? Are you thinking they won't leave without the money? Or have they already found it?"

"If I lost a buck in Milwaukee, I wouldn't waste any time looking for it. Or even ten bucks. However, if I lost ten million bucks, I'd be turning over rocks looking for it for a *very* long time. And these guys belong to a terrorist organization. Imagine what the next guy up the chain of command is going to do when you tell him you don't have the money. They're still here. We just need to figure out how to find them."

"They wanted to find Zahi, Sam, and they did. He's dead so they have no one to ask about the money. Abdullah doesn't think Hamza knows he's here. All either party wants now is to get the money. And no one knows where to find it. Where *could* he have hidden it? He's a stranger here. He doesn't know of any good hiding places. Although he might find one by accident. Sorenson only met him briefly two or three times. What was he doing when he wasn't talking to Sorenson? Was he actively looking for a hiding place?"

"Why hide it when he wanted Sorenson to help him get it out of the country? And why empty the suitcases? They were an easy way to move the money. If he dug a hole to hide the money, it would make sense to dig a hole big enough for the bags, and just drop them in. Oh, God. I just had an awful thought, Paul.

"What if he put the money into a coffin? It might hold the contents of the suitcases, even if it's the wrong shape. And then had the money buried in a grave somewhere? Maybe he thought he could come back for it when the heat was off him. Dig up the coffin at night, and put the money back into the suitcases. Which is why he still had them."

"Oh God! No! I don't want to think about that." He sighed. "Tomorrow morning, get Sweeney to check all the cemeteries in the county for burials since early last week. Sorenson says he saw the suitcases as late as last Wednesday, and he also says he never saw any money. So they could have done a switch like that anytime after they got to Berwyn. God, this will be awful. I don't want to have to get exhumation orders on dozens of burials."

***

The cell was not very large, but it wasn't cramped for the two men. Two bunk beds, a sink, and a toilet. No chairs. No table. No window. Gray walls. They sat on the bottom bunk and talked in Somali.

"They said you had talked," claimed Abdullah. "Who else could have told them about the money?"

"They said *you* had talked," countered Taifa. "They are very sneaky. And who told them about Yahye? I didn't. You say you didn't. How did they know?"

"They are sorcerers, I think, and can learn things from spirits. They seemed to be less angry with us after we told them about Hamza and

Yahye. Maybe they will let us go soon. We can't do anything while we are in this jail. They won't even let me call Ali to ask him for help. All we can do is wait. We must pray for Allah to help us. They can't stop us calling on him for help."

"At least they have not accused us of killing Zahi and Bilan, Abdullah. Americans take murder more seriously than we do in Somalia. Trying to steal the car from that lot is not so great a crime. They will let us go. Then we can try again to find the money."

"I have an idea, Taifa. What if Zahi did here what we wanted him to do in Minneapolis? What if he put it into a luggage storage place at a train station? When we get out, we must look for such a place. Zahi was daring to steal from Yahye and from us, but he was never very clever. Bilan was, but I think, from what he said when he called me, that this was all Zahi's doing. And he would have remembered our orders to him back home. A checked luggage office in the train station."

"The policeman said they have the green suitcases, and not the money. Zahi must have put the money somewhere else. How can we go to the luggage office, with no claim ticket, no description of the bags, not even knowing which station to search?"

"We must try anyway, Taifa. Once we are out of jail, we can start looking. It may take time, but the money is here, someplace. We will find it. We *must* find it."

***

"Yahye is very unhappy," grumbled Hamza. "You all know what that means. We must find that money very soon, or he will send someone to kill all of us. Yes, even me. The money was not in the car, only the suitcases. The woman said Zahi had hidden the money. Where? Where could he have hidden it? He didn't know this city any better than we do. And he took the money out of the suitcases. Why?"

"We were looking for the big green suitcases," answered Bashiir. "Zahi knew that. What if he bought some other color suitcases and put the money into them. He then keeps the green ones to mislead us."

"Very good, Bashiir," argued Hamza, "where are the other suitcases, then? You all saw the suitcases, in Yahye's house, and in the car. The money they held would be a big pile and hard to hide without being inside some container. That is why Yahye used the suitcases. Zahi stole the money, and he would have much trouble hiding it without a container. So your idea is good, Bashiir. Nevertheless, I repeat, where is that container?"

"Where could he have hidden the money, in whatever sort of container he had? We must look at all the places he stayed. Did he leave some bags behind, to be picked up later? Did he meet someone and persuade that person to take the bags? He was a very friendly man and persuasive in his speech. Where else could he have hidden the money?"

"Maybe a storage locker," suggested Xidig, "there was one in Minneapolis not far from our house. Many big lockers, anonymous, everything inside hidden from view. Even a small one is bigger than he would need for two big suitcases, not that it would matter. He could lock the money away and it would be safe. Much better than trusting the money to some stranger."

"That is possible," agreed Hamza. "That is a very good idea. Only where is this locker? And where is the key to open it?"

"Oh, no, Hamza," confessed Bashiir. "When we broke into the car, I had Zahi's keys. I threw them away in disgust when we didn't find the money. I didn't think we would need them again."

"Did you leave them in the car?" asked Hamza.

"No, I just threw them away from me. I was frustrated and angry. I threw them far down the lot. They may still be there. We can go look again tonight."

"We will need a light to find them," observed Xidig, "and the light will attract attention."

"Maybe use a very dim light," suggested Bashiir.

"We need a tool to help us," declared Hamza. "I saw a man using a long stick to find metal things on the ground. There was a big magnet on the end of it, and he just waved it around the ground, finding metal items. He said he got it at a big hardware store. We can find such a store here, and get one. Then, with just a dim light, we can still find the keys."

**

Xidig let the others out by the fence, and pulled around a corner to park their car out of the way. By the time he returned, they were over the fence. He joined them and held the small flashlight. It wasn't as dim as he would have liked, but it's small beam wasn't too noticeable.

"I threw the keys off in that direction," indicated Bashiir. "I threw them hard because I was angry. I think they landed somewhere near that van."

As they walked down the lot a half moon was rising and helped them a little. Near the van they switched on the small light and looked at the ground. The light wasn't very helpful, however the magnetic stick worked quite well. Most of the things it found were bolts and washers, however.

Hamza knelt down and waved the stick under the van. Nothing. They tried under the next car, and the next. Nothing. Xidig took the stick and walked over the whole area, slowly moving it back and forth. Nothing.

Bashiir took out a stronger flashlight and carefully turned it on so the beam only went under the cars. Nothing. Then, as he moved it, something glinted. He went closer and saw something under a tire.

"Xidig, bring that stick here," Bashiir called. "I may have found it."

The others hurried over to him. He turned on the light again, pointed close to the ground by the tire, keeping the light from being seen from a distance. There was a shiny key showing beneath the tire. There seemed to be more keys, and the tire was resting on top of them all.

"These must be the keys," decided Bashiir. "They are in the right area. This car must have been moved here after we were here last night. Can we push the car and move it?"

With a little effort, the three men managed to roll the car forward a foot. Bashiir bent down and picked up the keys.

"Yes, these are the same keys," he exclaimed jubilantly. "I recognize them. Now all we need to do is to find the locker they will unlock."

"How many storage places are in this town?" asked Xidig as they went back over the fence and walked to their car.

"This town is very near Chicago," lamented Hamza. "That is a much bigger city than Minneapolis, and Minneapolis has a great many storage lockers. So Chicago must have even more. Still, Zahi would have taken one near his hotel. We can start with ones near his last hotel. We can start in the morning."

Chapter Eleven

Not Here, Not There Either

"His name is Zahi, and he looked like me, but smaller and with just a little bit of beard on the end of his chin. He would have rented the locker last week."

The man looked at Hamza with a bored expression. "I told you already. I don't have *any* empty lockers. I haven't had any empty lockers for months. Your friend may have wanted to rent a locker from me last week, but I didn't have one to rent to him. Got that? I can't say it any plainer, buddy."

Hamza walked back to his car. He was depressed, unhappy, angry, afraid. *Yahye is going to kill us all if we can't find the money. And find it soon. So many storage places, and none had lockers to rent. We've been to ten so far today, and there are more on the list the man at the hotel gave us. Maybe Xidig has had better luck with his list.*

"Call Xidig and tell him to meet us for lunch where we ate yesterday," Hamza told Bashiir. "I am hungry and frustrated and so angry I want to kill someone. And I have no one to kill. Yahye does. He will kill *us*. Where is that money? How could that little fool Zahi hide it so well?"

Xidig was already there when Hamza and Bashiir arrived. They ate in glum silence. Xidig's search had been as fruitless as Hamza's. Hamza finished his meal and looked out the window, watching the traffic go down the road. A bunch of cars all close together, then one, then two, then none. Then another bunch.

He sighed, such a lot of failure today. This whole week. *What can I do if I can't find the money? Yahye will kill me. There is no question about that. I would not follow him if he did not kill me for failing the cause. But I don't want to die. Not for this. Can I run away? Did running away help Zahi? Maybe I can run harder and more carefully than he did.*

"Maybe we should just call these storage places," suggested Xidig. "It will save time, and we have phone numbers for all of them. If no one answers, it's the same as finding no one there when we go in person. It will take us days to visit all these places on our lists. We have only two cars, but we have three phones."

"That is a good idea, Xidig," agreed Hamza. "We will go back to our motel room and call from there. It is quiet there, and we will not be disturbed. And there is tea in the vending machine."

"It is not near where Zahi and Bilan stayed," objected Bashiir.

"That does not matter," countered Hamza. "The telephone reaches everywhere. We could call Cawil, Yahye's master in Somalia. We could tell him we have failed utterly, and ask him to kill us. I do not want to do that. But I think we can call these storage places."

***

"Buck up, Jack," comforted Marcy, "it's not like writing personal notes on Christmas cards. Wedding invitations are easy. We pick a design, give them the date of the wedding, and a list of our friends with their addresses. The printer handles all the rest. We don't even have to lick the stamps."

"It's not the work that I object to, Marcy. It's the embarrassment of having to admit how few real friends I have. George Peterson should have been my best man, but he's dead now. Fred Orzinski is a good replacement. I've known him almost as long, and we've been almost as close. A half dozen men I know from a variety of bars, mostly civilized. A few other men I've met at the opera with you, mostly men I'm not very close to.

"I have lots of clients, and I'm friendly with some of them. But not to the point where they know who I really am. Some I don't want to get close to, for fear of their doing something careless and getting caught. I can be sociable with the gamblers, but I still won't consider inviting them to my wedding.

"Oh, except, of course, Herman Nolte. The only client I have that I really like. How odd. I am opening up to the world, Marcy, and it is surprising to me how it happens. Pleasant, even. I used to talk to some of my clients, just shooting the breeze. Nothing major.

"Herm used to …. Look, I'm calling him, not by his name, but by his nickname! Wow! I *have* changed. Herm used to chat with me like that when I brought him his winnings. Making a successful bet pleased him almost as much as making a good stock deal. He got talkative, and I enjoyed the talk, too. And over the years, we talked more about our lives. Not that I told him anything serious about mine, but I was closer to him in those days than to any of my other clients.

"I got even closer with the kidnapping, and the ransom, and all that. We talked more seriously about things then. He's the only client I have who knows my real name, or was until the press found out about me. He's on the list, definitely. And I know you like his wife Gladys."

"I painted their portrait, and I tend to like people I've painted. It's easier to paint a good likeness if I feel some affinity towards my subject. No, I should turn that around. It's harder to paint a good likeness if I feel some animosity towards my subject. Anyway, I do like them both, and I'm glad you want them to attend.

"I hesitate to suggest this, Jack. But what about the Radcliffes, or Sergeant Mahoney? I know they're cops and not part of your regular social circle, but you have gotten along with them pretty well in the last year or so. You don't seem to mind helping them out when you can. And it can't all be a sense of civic duty."

"Oh. I hadn't thought about them. We had a very rocky beginning to our relationship, but it has smoothed out rather nicely. Yes, put them on the list. They may not come, anyway. Here are some more names for you. My mechanic, my favorite local grocer, the guys I play pinochle with. They all have wives. Melissa's family, of course, even if they're hosting the party.

"Your parents, my parents. They'll all be overjoyed to attend. I know they were ecstatic when we told them we're getting married, but they'll be in absolute heaven to see that it's true. And Miriam and Jim, her husband. I used to work for her before Melissa took over, and she always treated me well. She gave me a break once when she could have tossed me to the wolves."

"I do like your choices of friends, Jack. You like people who are a lot like you. Not secretive, but loyal, trustworthy, dependable. Herm cared enough about Gladys he would give away every dime he had for her safety. She said she still felt like a newlywed after a dozen years of marriage. You've told me what Miriam did for you, and that *was* an act of courtesy she didn't have to offer.

"With my friends, we are now up to about sixty people. And the numbers for each of us are pretty close, so don't think you're such a recluse. I'll get this to the printer this afternoon. Will you take care of telling Melissa how many are going to come? The menu is set, but I know you want to surprise me with something at the dinner. So go ahead and make your arrangements with her."

"You are just as bad as my mother. Dad was always trying to surprise her with a special gift or dinner, and she always knew in advance. He never figured out how she knew. He used to think I was telling her, but even after I left home, she would always know. I'll still try to surprise you."

***

Three phones made checking the lists easier, but no more successful. By evening, they had called all the remaining places, and none of them had rented a locker to a black man or woman in more than two weeks. Hamza was frustrated again. *I want to do something, preferably something violent. I like action, and violence. It solves so many of my problems. Well, not with Zahi, but I hadn't intended to hit him so hard.*

Hamza left the room and went to the motel's lobby to get some more bottled tea. It was not as good as home-brewed tea, but it was acceptable and available. The vending machine was in an alcove to one side of the lobby. He could see the desk clerk greet some people who just came in. Two policemen. They showed something to the clerk. It looked like a picture of someone, then another picture, and another. The clerk looked at the pictures and seemed to be thinking. Then he said something to the policemen and pointed to the corridor leading to Hamza's room.

Police! Why are they here? They can't know I killed Zahi. They have the bodies, but they can't know I did it. No time to worry about why they are here, I must get away.

He rushed back to his room and threw the door open wildly.

"We must leave immediately! There are policemen here, looking for us! Get your bags, and we must run, now!"

They ran down the corridor, away from the lobby. As he went out the door into the parking lot, Hamza looked back to see the two policemen at the open door to his room. *It wasn't just my imagination or fear. They are here looking for me! What do I do now?*

As they got into their cars, Hamza shouted to Xidig, "Follow us!" He came out of the parking lot so rashly he almost hit a car in the street. Xidig had to swerve violently to avoid the same car, now stopped, its driver staring angrily at the reckless drivers all around him. Other drivers, brought to sudden stops by the first car in their way, honked their annoyance.

Behind him Hamza could see the policemen running to their squad. He turned down a side street to get out of their sight. Maybe he could twist his way through these streets and lose the police. After a mile of driving fast and a great many turns, he pulled over to the curb. There was no one behind him except Xidig.

"How did the police know where to find us?" asked Xidig.

"I don't know," complained Hamza. "I don't know how they knew about us, either. They can't possibly know we killed Zahi and Bilan. The news is still saying they don't know who was killed. Why are they looking for us? We must find another place to stay, and quickly. It is almost night."

"If the police are looking for us at the motel, they will check all the motels, won't they?" asked Bashiir. "Where can we go if all the hotels and motels are closed off to us?"

"There," indicated Xidig, pointing to the backyard of a house nearby. "There is a tent in that yard. We can get a tent and camp someplace. The police will not expect us to be camping in the woods. We have lived in tents in Somalia. It's not that bad."

"Ah, that is a very good idea," agreed Hamza. "I have been arrested by the police in Minneapolis, and know how they do their jobs. It is as you say, Bashiir, they will check all the hotels and motels in town. Then they will look at the next town, and the next. They become fixed on one idea, that we must be in a motel. It will not be possible for them to think of us in a tent. But we should not just camp in the woods. That place we killed Zahi had a sign forbidding overnight camping. We must find a proper, lawful place. And we must do what Zahi did to hide his car. We must steal some license plates from local cars. Let us do that first."

An hour later, with stolen plates on their cars, they were talking to a gas station attendant.

"There's a nice place west of here called Camp Bullfrog Lake. I've camped there a few times, and you don't need a tent, they'll rent you one. It's not expensive, either. Just go down here to Archer Avenue and turn left. Go west a few miles and you'll see the sign. It says Maple Lake, but the Bullfrog Lake campground is there, too. Have a good time!"

The campground did have tents to rent, and a place to put one. They had to go out again for food and blankets, but the night was warm and the tent was dry. It would have to do as their new home. *At least the police won't look for us here. And neither will Yahye,* thought Hamza as he dropped off to sleep.

***

Mahoney walked into Radcliffe's office looking upset. He plopped down on one of the hard chairs without caring for how hard it hit his rump.

"Saunders just called in to say he almost caught those Somalis, Paul," groused Mahoney. "He was checking out a motel down in Bridgeview, and the clerk said he thought he recognized the photo. He pointed to the corridor, and there was one of the guys. He turned and ran, got his buddies, and they went out the back way before Saunders could get them. Saunders blames himself for being slow, but it did take him a moment to realize he had his man right in front of him."

"Bridgeview? That's getting pretty far south. Wozinski says they were in Cicero last week, before the murders. If they keep hopping around it's going to be hard to find them. All they have to do is go back to someplace we've already crossed off our list."

"I told Saunders and Wozinski to leave copies of the pictures everywhere they went. If they show up anywhere, we'll hear about it. But if they're looking for the money, the way we figure it, they can sleep anywhere in the county, or even beyond. What's an hour coming back to Berwyn to search? Especially as they know now that we're after them. I'm going to give these pictures to all the street and patrol cops, just to make sure every pair of eyes we have is looking for them. They can sleep somewhere else, but they have to look for the money here."

"True enough, Sam. But we have the same problem they do, we're all looking for the money, and none of us has any idea where it might be. Keep Saunders checking the hotels and motels. Have Wozinski start looking at storage lockers. Zahi might have rented one to hide the money. We have time. Since no one knows where it's at, the money isn't going anywhere. When Saunders is done with the motels, have him check with rental offices. Did Zahi rent a cheap apartment or office to stash the money. Where was he living before he was killed? We need to find that place."

"I'll put Wozinski on the rental offices. If the money's in a storage locker, it's still there. It takes a couple of months for the owner of the lockers to sell off the contents for non-payment. But if Zahi rented an apartment instead of a motel, he may have left the money there, or at least some clue to where it is. And the landlord of an apartment may be more impatient about his rent. If he goes looking for his money and finds a fortune, we may never see it."

"That's all to the good, Sam. I'm going to get us some extra, unsuspecting, help. The State's Attorney agrees we can let Abdullah and Taifa go. We've got their written statement about the murder, and their addresses in Minneapolis. I would prefer they go home, but I think they'll stay and keep looking for the money, like all the rest of us. So I'm going to have Gomez tailing them. If they head north, he's back to work for Lopez, but if they stay here he'll be there if they find the loot. Ah, here they are now."

Patrolman Gomez opened the door to Paul's office and ushered in Abdullah and Taifa. They were in their own clothes again, and appeared uncertain about what would happen to them now.

"Sit down, gentlemen," offered Radcliffe. "We told you that your cooperation would get you released, and it has. The prosecutor has decided not to charge you for trying to take Zahi's car. You are now officially free to leave Berwyn and Illinois. You should go back to your homes in Minneapolis. When we catch Hamza we will ask you to come back here to testify against him at his trial.

"I realize that America is very different from Somalia. I wouldn't know how to live in Somalia. I imagine you must have trouble adjusting to life here. The police in Minneapolis say you've committed some crimes, but not really serious ones. We Americans prefer that people don't commit crimes. We can forgive those who try to change their ways. That's what I would like you to do. Try to leave those feuds from Somalia behind you. You're not there now and can live peacefully here. Think about what happened to Zahi and Bilan and try to lead more law-abiding lives. Goodbye and good luck."

                                   ***

"Gladys suggested we have dinner with them ages ago," Marcy reminded Sorenson. "Way back in the Stone Age, practically. Two and a half weeks ago, before we went to Paris and you became famous. Eons ago. I know you've been busy with dead non-clients, and we've both been busy with house buying and being madly in love. But they did invite us. And now they're expecting us tonight. I told you yesterday. And the day before. And on Sunday."

"I remember now, dear. The discovery that my two non-clients had been murdered pretty much drove a lot of things out of my mind. I'm sorry about that. We will go and dine with the Noltes. I recall now that they think I have saved the world, or at least their world. I do hate having to remind them how little I actually did. But their praise is enjoyable, and I usually don't get *any*."

"Good, because I want to deliver their portrait. It is finally dry enough to give to them for framing. I know they will like it, because I love it. And the artist is always the ultimate expert on her work."

"Not any shortage of modesty there, huh? But you showed it to me before we left for Paris, when it was still fresh. And even I think you outdid yourself. You must like them a lot. Your portraits of people you really like are always much better than your other portraits. Like that one you did of Melissa for Tony. Sargent couldn't have done any better."

"Oh, it's nice of you to say that, dear. But it's pure flattery. I only wish I could paint like him. But thank you for saying it. Now, hurry and get dressed. I have the painting in my car and if you don't get moving, we'll be late for dinner."

Chapter Twelve

Yahye

Two weeks passed and nothing had changed. Hamza and his henchmen were still camping and looking for the money. Abdullah and Taifa were still lurking around Berwyn, also looking for the money. The police were still looking for the money. Only Sorenson and his friends didn't have any interest in the money.

"How are you holding up, Angela?" asked her father, Tony.

"Oh, I'm fine, Tony. It was sweet of you to insist that I work here at the pizzeria for a couple of weeks, but it wasn't necessary. Not really. I was shocked at finding those bodies, and it *is* a nasty memory. But I didn't spend a lot of time looking at them, either. Professor Small took our law school class to the morgue once to show us what we might have to work with, if we worked on murder cases. This was worse, but I'm tough. I'm not a kid anymore. Tony Jr. and I can deal with unpleasant things. You and Melissa made sure of that."

"That's good. It's a terrible thing to happen to someone. I feel awful thinking about those poor people being hacked up like that. So cruel, so evil. I'm just glad it doesn't concern us. It's wrong to think about how the bad publicity might hurt the hotel, but it's also a human failing. We always think of our own problems. Still, I asked Father Joe to say a Mass for those people. Even if they were Muslim, it won't hurt them, and it's the least we can do."

"Melissa says that Gertie is going to quit because of the murders."

"Gertie?"

"Yeah, Gertrude Palgrave. She calls herself Sexy Susie for the guests. She's into spiritualism and seances and all that. She's afraid their spirits are going to haunt the hotel."

"Sexy Susie was named Gertie? I think that's one reason Melissa doesn't want me running the hotel, I'd have trouble keeping track of who is who."

"Oh, I forgot to tell you. That cop, Radcliffe, stopped by a few days after the murders to show Melissa and me a picture of the murdered guy, before he died. He wanted to know if we had ever seen him around the hotel, or in the area. We hadn't, of course. But I was thinking about it again today, and his face struck me as familiar from somewhere.

"Then I remembered something I had seen before the murders. I saw him, or someone just like him, coming out of a building near the tracks. He got into a car and drove off. But a couple of years ago, when we all had the flu, you asked Jack Sorenson to take me to the hospital to see the doctor. Jack did, but he stopped on the way to pick up something from that building. He called it, mysteriously, as he always does, his 'secret lair.'"

"Did you tell Radcliffe?"

"No, why should I? I didn't remember this until just today. This guy wasn't near the hotel, and he was alive. It was a couple of days before he was killed. And I'm not entirely sure it was the same guy."

"You're studying to be a lawyer; you should know enough to tell the police even the most trivial details. If your school isn't teaching you that, your grandfather will give you some extra lessons when he comes in for Jack's wedding."

"All right, Tony. You're just like Melissa. You always know the correct thing to do, and why. I'll talk to the cops tomorrow."

***

The campground was quiet at night. There were some other people camping, but they stayed by their own tents for the most part. A few had gathered around a campfire a hundred yards away, but they were not talking loudly. The moon was rising, casting a pale light over the tents. It would have been beautiful to Hamza, but he was preoccupied. They had been here for two weeks already, and had still not found the money, or any clue to where it might be.

Hamza stared at the campfire without seeing it. *I can't believe how badly things are going for us. I need a new idea of where to look for the money, and I can't think of one. I know what Yahye will do to me, to all of us, if we can't find the money. And soon. I have no ideas. I am a failure. I am not used to failure. Al-Shabaab does not accept failure.*

Across from him Xidig and Bashiir looked just as glum. *We have spent two weeks looking at every storage locker place, every place one could leave luggage, every place to rent a room. We haven't found a single trace of Zahi and Bilan visiting any such a place. And we have found plenty of proof that the police were often there ahead of us. What are they looking for? The money, maybe. But do they know about the money? How could they?*

His phone rang. "Hamza here," he answered. "Yes, all right, thank you for telling me that. What else? Abdullah? No, I haven't seen him here. Isn't he in Minneapolis? I wonder if he *is* here, or was here. Thank you. Goodbye."

"Who was that?" asked Xidig.

"That was Mahmoud, calling from home. He says Yahye is healthy again and they are coming down here tomorrow. I will have to tell him where we are. He will kill us if we don't have the money, but how can we hide from him? But Mahmoud also said that Abdullah is no longer in Minneapolis. He thinks he may have come here looking for Zahi and Bilan. Could *he* have found the money? Could they have given him the money before we killed them?"

"No, Hamza," decided Bashiir, "if they had given Abdullah the money, they would have all left Berwyn. We would not have found the thieves. So if Abdullah is here, he is looking for the money, too. But where is he? The men at the lockers told us the police were looking for a locker Zahi might have rented, but not about any other Somalis. He didn't get the money from Zahi, and he isn't looking where we are looking. So where is he?"

"Could something have happened to him?" asked Xidig. "An accident, or maybe he got arrested by the police. They were looking to arrest us, maybe they arrested Abdullah too."

"Ah, that is an idea," allowed Hamza. "I will call the police in the morning. We cannot risk going to their building, but I can talk to them safely on the phone. I will say he is my friend and he has disappeared. I will ask if they know where he is. If he has been arrested, they will tell me. There are other aspects of this that I must think about, too. Maybe this will help us with Yahye. Let me think this over."

***

"This is Detective Sergeant Michael Feltz. I'm not available right now, so please leave a message at the tone."

"Oh, um, this is Angela Maguire. I'm calling about that double murder at our hotel. I think I saw the murdered man coming out of a building at the corner of Oak Park and Stanley, the northeast corner. It was a few days before he was killed, so maybe it doesn't mean anything. But I thought you should know. Call me if you need more information. You have my number."

***

Hamza's call was transferred to Detective Sergeant Mahoney.

"My friend Adbullah, he's a Somali and has no last name. He's from Minneapolis, and he was here in Berwyn and now I can't find him. Has anything happened to him? I'm worried about my friend."

"Oh, yes, that Mr. Abdullah. I'm afraid your friend was arrested a few weeks ago for trying to steal a car from the impound lot," Mahoney made up a convincing half lie on the spot. "He's sitting in jail here. You could visit him, if you want. The information I have here says that no bail has been set for him. I think that's because he's a foreigner and from out of state. I'm sorry I can't be of more help to you."

Your friend Abdullah. Right. Abdullah would have told his friends he was still here, and free. If you don't know that, you aren't his friend. Probably one of his enemies. So why should I tell you anything useful. Come in and visit. You can't talk to Abdullah, but Paul and I would like to chat. Oh, yes.

"Abdullah is in jail," Hamza told his men, "for trying to steal a car from the impound lot. That has to be Zahi's car. The car is still in the lot, but the suitcases are empty. Xidig, Yahye should be here by early afternoon. Let me know when he gets here. I have to think some more about this. I may have a way out for all of us. A way that will please Yahye."

Bashiir and Xidig walked away and let Hamza make his plans. He was never happy to be disturbed when he was plotting something. And he was almost as harsh as Yahye when he was unhappy. Best to leave him alone. Bashiir looked over their food supplies, thought about having to feed Yahye and Mahmoud tonight, and went out for more food.

Yahye arrived at one in the afternoon, and looked ready to kill everyone in the tent. He was tall and broad, with a thick black beard broken by a slash across his left cheek. With his beard combed the gash stood out so much it distracted from the other scar across his forehead. He had a two edged knife in a sheath at his side, and his hand was never far from the hilt. He got out of the car and gave a dismissive glance at the campsite. Yahye walked up to Hamza without looking at the others and spat at the ground between Hamza's feet.

Mahmoud, Yahye's driver, had an impassive face. He was still weak from an old leg wound so he was not a serious threat of doing them harm. But Xidig knew that Mahmoud was even more dedicated to Yahye than Hamza was, and would never turn against their boss. He also knew Mahmoud would be given the task of killing them, and that he enjoyed making death slow and painful.

Hamza welcomed Yahye as cheerily as he could manage. He gave him some freshly brewed tea and some fresh fruit. Yahye accepted the food and drink, but not in a friendly manner.

"I know you are upset with us, Yahye," admitted Hamza, "but I think I have some good news for you. Just today I learned that Abdullah is in an American jail near here. I have been thinking about this all day, and I think I finally know where the money is hidden. It will not be easy, but with some effort I think we can get it for ourselves."

"Really? After all this time, just when I arrive to kill you for your failure, you suddenly discover something you couldn't find earlier. How very convenient for you! Tell me, Hamza, where is this newly discovered hiding place? And why could you not have found it sooner? Answer me, and quickly. My knife is calling for blood."

"I hadn't known Abdullah was here," objected Hamza, swallowing with difficulty. "But when I learned that, it made me think differently about where the money must be. Zahi did not have the money. We thought he had hidden it somewhere, and we have been searching for it without any success. But if Abdullah was here, it seemed likely that he would have taken the money from Zahi. But then they would both have left.

"So Zahi did not give the money to Abdullah, and still had it himself. And Abdullah was arrested for trying to steal Zahi's car from the police lot. So the money was in the car. When the police arrested him, they found the money. When we found the car in the lot, the suitcases were there, but empty. So the police took the money and have it in their building. They took the money out of the suitcases and put them back in the car in the lot.

"Xidig says he watches an American police program on TV, and the police put things into a locked room called an evidence locker. We can break into the police station and the evidence locker, and then the money will be ours again. Very simple."

Yahye stared at his henchman as if he were a raving lunatic.

"Very simple. Just break into an American police station and help ourselves to what we want. Do you not suppose the police will try to stop us? How many policemen do they have? In Minneapolis there are hundreds of police. Do you think you and these few men can fight hundreds of policemen? What are you thinking, Hamza? Is your fear of dying driving you insane?"

"No! No! But with you and Mahmoud, we have five brave men. We can send back to Minneapolis and get more men, and more weapons. And explosives. We can set off a bomb and kill many of the police with that. And if we attack in the middle of the night, a great many of the police will be home, asleep."

"Hmmmm. Perhaps this might work. Let us talk about this some more. Is this tent all you have for shelter? It is not big enough for all of us. Can you get me another for Mahmoud and me?"

"Bashiir, ask the man in the office for another tent, and this other campsite next to ours. If one is available, ask for a cabin. One cabin will hold all of us and will give us more privacy. Now that Yahye is here, we will be making plans which the infidels must not hear."

"That is good, Hamza," agreed Yahye. "We must be very careful around these strangers. Walk with me down to that lake. Are there boats we can use there?"

"Not really boats. Little things they call kayaks, like a small canoe."

"Good, we can row them out into the lake, right? Rent us a pair, and we will row into the middle of the lake, and no one will hear what we talk about."

A few minutes later they were paddling away from the dock. "Ten dollars? Was that the right price?" asked Yahye. "It seems too small. I do not care, it saves us some of our money. Pull further out. Here, this is good.

"Speaking of our money, are you certain the police have it? We must not be rash or careless about this. If we attack the police building we will be declaring war on them. America is not like Somalia, we cannot just fade into the rural areas and disappear. The police will come after us in large numbers. And they will call up all the other layers of police in this country. You know as well as I do how many types of police they have here – city, county, state, FBI, drug police, immigration police – we can't possibly fight all of them.

"So we must be very certain the money is in that building. Did you see the police take the money into the building? Or are you just imagining this because you need to please me? You have always been a loyal supporter, Hamza, but a weak loyalty is no virtue. I would hate to have to kill you, and your men, but I cannot allow failure from anyone. So, tell me, honestly, do you really know the money is there?"

"No, I do not. I am sorry, Yahye, but I do not know this absolutely. But it must be there! Zahi did not put it into any storage locker. He did not leave it at any motel. The suitcases were still in his car, but empty. The police must have unloaded the money to count it, then stacked it in their evidence locker. Then they put the bags back in the car. It must have happened like this."

"Fool! Why would the police put the suitcases back in the car? Those bags were evidence, also. They would have had to take the money out of the bags to count it, yes. And they may have stacked the money by itself. But they would have kept the suitcases too. They never let evidence out of their sight. And you said Zahi's personal belongings were in the car still. That proves the police did not move the money. If they had, they would have moved Zahi's bags as well. For a while there, I thought you might have been right.

"Abdullah is here, you say? If the police arrested him for trying to steal Zahi's car, then he doesn't have the money either. So the money is here somewhere. Could he have buried it somewhere?"

"No, because he would have buried it in the suitcases and the police have them. Bashiir thought maybe Zahi put the money into different suitcases, because we were looking for the green ones. Even if he did, we don't know what those look like. Or where they are. It just goes around and around, Yahye. Every idea we get keeps running into dead ends."

"Oh, Hamza, you just missed it! Didn't you hear what you said? If Zahi bought new suitcases he could have buried the money in them, and left my suitcases in his car. That is how the money has disappeared. The police do not have it. Abdullah does not have it. We do not have it. Zahi does not have it, but he did have it, and buried it so we can't find it.

"Now, where could he have buried it? It must be in a place where he could dig a large hole without attracting any attention. If he dug at night, he would have needed a light."

"Yes, it was the dark of the moon that week."

"So if he uses a light, he attracts someone's attention. And where can he dig? He has no house here. He can't dig in a motel parking lot. Even nice motels with small lawns won't be big enough for him to dig a hole large enough. You said you killed him in a forest. Could he have buried the money in that forest?"

"It is possible. Or in some other forest. There are many forests around Berwyn, some of them quite large. It would be very hard to choose the right forest, and find the right spot. It's been three weeks since he would have buried the money. The ground would have settled by now. How could we find the place now?

"Oh, wait, Yahye! I forgot! There was no shovel in Zahi's car. Not in the trunk. Not in the back seat. How could he dig a hole without a shovel? And he would have kept the shovel, so he could dig the money up later."

"Ai! Hamza, you are right. It is as you said, every new idea just shrinks up to nothing. How can this little man who helps his wife with woman's work outwit us?"

"Bashiir had another idea, Yahye. He thought that Zahi might have given the new suitcases to some other person to keep for him. Bashiir said Zahi was a friendly, outgoing person. He could make friends easily, so maybe he persuaded some American to take the suitcases."

"That still doesn't help us, Hamza. Who is this imaginary American? And where do we find him? Row us back to the dock, Hamza. My illness still affects me a little. It was a long drive here. I am tired and want to sleep. We will talk more later."

***

"What are you reading, Xidig?" asked Hamza. "I did not know you liked these American magazines."

"I don't, they are so shallow. Nothing about the Prophet, peace be upon him. Only about people who are famous for a day or two, and then disappear into forgetfulness. But I am bored and it keeps me from thinking about my bride. We have been looking for the money for so long, and it has been such a waste of time. At least in Minneapolis I could have been squeezing some more money from some storekeeper."

"Where did you get that magazine? I do not remember you buying it when we went for food yesterday."

"I found it when we broke into Zahi's car. It was in his luggage in the trunk. I took it with me, and I've been reading it when I get bored. I've read the whole thing several times over."

"That is not the cover of a magazine. What magazine is it?"

"Oh, it's, um, *People* magazine," disclosed Xidig, flipping the pages over. "Zahi left it folded open to this one story, and it is so creased it always opens to this page now."

"Why was Zahi interested in that story? If he flattened the page that way, he must have thought there was something important there. What is it about?"

"It is about some American who helped capture some art thieves in France. It says he pretended to help the thieves move the stolen art and money to France, and they were arrested. The story is a month old, but I have nothing else to read. Do you mind?"

"He moves money to a foreign country? Are you sure that's what the story says?"

"Yes, right here. It says, 'He told the thieves he could move the stolen painting and a million dollars in cash to Paris for them.' He must know the same tricks that we use to get our money to Somalia."

"How long have you been reading this story over and over?"

"Ever since we broke into Zahi's car. Two weeks, three weeks. Why? I haven't been neglecting my searching for the money. I only read it when I have nothing else to do."

"Come with me and bring that magazine. Yahye must be told about this."

"Please, don't tell him. I don't deserve to be punished for reading an American magazine. I promise I will only read the Qur'an from now on."

"Don't worry, you will not be punished. You may even have earned Yahye's praise. And you know how little he praises anyone."

***

The cabin which Bashiir had rented had four bunk beds, and a private room with two single beds. There was no proper table, or chairs, although the porch had a pair of benches. Inside, there were some small tables, barely taller than the beds, which could be moved together to make a large, low table. Having no chairs was not a problem, since they were used to sitting cross-legged on the floor to eat in Somalia, and the low table was just the right height for that. They had to cook on an open fire outside, but they had to do that with the tent, also. The cabin was more comfortable than the tent, and even had air-conditioning. As the summer heated up, they were finding that a very nice luxury.

Yahye had claimed the small side room with two beds as his private room. Hamza would have offered it to him anyway, and Yahye knew that. But he wanted to remind them he was their leader by insisting on taking the room for himself. He had been napping for two hours when Hamza and Xidig awakened him.

"What is it? Why do you disturb me? It had better be something very important!"

"Oh, Yahye, the pieces are starting to fall into a pattern," reported Hamza. "When we talked earlier, I told you that Bashiir suggested that maybe Zahi had made some friend and given the money to him to hold until Zahi came back for it. We had no idea who that person might be, or even if he existed.

"And now I found Xidig reading this American magazine story about a man who moves money around for people. He can take money to foreign places for anyone. Just like we will send this money to Cawil when we finally find it. And he lives here in Berwyn. The magazine came from Zahi's car and he must have read this and thought this man could help him. Maybe to get the money out of the country, or at least to hide it."

"Hamza, this is wonderful!" exclaimed Yahye. "At last we have a clue to where the money is. I think you are right – Zahi must have seen this man as a way to hide the money. Let me put this together as a whole picture. Zahi has our green suitcases full of money. He wants to avoid being seen with them, so he buys some suitcases in a different color, and transfers the money.

"But he still does not want to be found with the money. It is difficult to move around all the time. He wants to hide it until he feels he is safe. So he finds this man, and asks him to hide the money for him. Now the money is safe, and Zahi thinks he is safe, too. Yes, this is a good plan. If you had not killed him, Zahi could have continued denying he knew where the money was. He could have lied about its location, and hoped to escape when we went looking for it. Yes, this is good. Who is this man?"

"It says his name is Jack Sorenson, and here is his picture. It only says he lives in Berwyn, but it does not give an address for him. Zahi must have come here to meet him. Perhaps we can find him in a telephone book."

"No, Hamza, you cannot find me or yourself in the telephone book. We have cell phones, and those are not listed in the book. Would you like the police to know where you live? If it gave us his phone number, we could call him, but it doesn't. However, I have used services on the internet for finding people; remember that man who tried to cheat me last year? He hid his address, but I found him anyway.

"Use your phone to search for him. We know his name, and he lives in Berwyn. These search sites want to be paid for their information, so use that stolen credit card you have. No one will trace this search to us then." Half an hour later, Hamza threw his phone down in disgust. "Four Jack Sorensons in the Chicago area, none in Berwyn, and none who appear to be the right age. How old is this photo of him?"

"The magazine said he uses an alias sometimes," Xidig reminded them. "What if Jack Sorenson is the alias, and not his real name? What if he has more than one alias?"

"Oh, Xidig, must you make our work so much harder?" Hamza groaned in misery. "He must be known by that name to someone, somewhere."

"He has an apartment," Yahye pointed out, "and therefore he has a landlord. When I first came to Minneapolis, I rented an apartment. My landlord knew who I was, though not what I was doing. Still, he never talked to the police about me. Maybe this man has a discreet landlord who knows his name, but who doesn't talk about him."

"This is possible," agreed Hamza. "Yes, it makes sense. But how do we find the landlord?"

"We are looking for one man in a large city," explained Yahye. "One man, one apartment, in a city with many apartments. However, there are always more apartments than landlords. Some of the larger apartment buildings in Minneapolis had maybe a hundred or more apartments, but only one landlord. One landlord might also own several properties. We can talk to the landlords, and find this Sorenson."

"How do we get them to tell us where he is?" asked Bashiir.

"We tell them we want to pay him some money," suggested Yahye. "Say we talked to him about buying his car, but we've lost his address. The landlord will be happy to help us and his tenant. Use your phones to make a list of landlords in Berwyn. Start with the ten with the most properties. We can go out in the morning and call on each until we find the man."

***

Mahoney was now working for both Inspectors Radcliffe. Paul's case was not quite cold, but definitely cooling down. Phyllis had some work in hand that needed an occasional sergeant's help. This morning he walked into Paul's office with some new information.

"Gomez is still following Abdullah and Taifa around," Mahoney told Paul. "They've been going to all the same places we've already checked. I was going to take him off the job, but I got a call this morning from someone who said he was a friend of Abdullah and was looking for him. I think it's one of the killers. He must have just learned Abdullah was here.

"I fed him a story about Abdullah still being in jail, and told him he was welcome to stop by for a visit. If the killers are looking for Abdullah I'm going to keep the tail on him, for his protection. It may be a way to find the killers, even if we don't find the money."

"That's interesting, Sam. Why would they suddenly think Abdullah is here? These guys are in rival gangs. How closely do they watch each other? How much of Yahye's gang is here? Who's left up there to notice Abdullah is gone? I wish we had some idea of what the hell is going on."

Chapter Thirteen

Unwelcome Visitors

"Most of the day gone before we found his landlord," grumbled Yahye, "and he gave us four different addresses for one man. Bah! He did at least say this was the most expensive. It should be where he lives. This is a large building, but the number over this door is the right one. We have his apartment number."

Hamza opened the outer door and they entered the small lobby with the mailboxes for the tenants. The inner door had a glass panel and was locked. Through the glass they could see the staircase going up to the first floor.

"All right, get your guns ready, but keep them out of sight," ordered Yahye. "Up the stairs quickly. Be quiet and we will overpower him when he opens the door."

***

"I'm still not comfortable with Sorenson," complained Radcliffe. "Phyllis likes him. You like him. He's the most charming, ingratiating fellow imaginable. Maybe that's my problem with him: He's too likeable. I think about the things he does to earn a buck, and I worry about his basic honesty. You say he's fairly honest. Fine, I can't expect everyone to be a saint, and 'fairly honest' works for me most of the time.

"But there's something nagging at me, anyway, Sam. If he intended to keep the money from the start, why talk to us about it at all? We wouldn't have known about it, or his connection to Zahi and Bilan. I understand that objection. If he didn't want anything to do with the money, he wouldn't have it now, and he would tell us every detail. You think he has told us all he knows. But here is where I keep getting stuck: He does barely legal favors for people; he moves large sums of money around nonchalantly; he's secretive about his clients. What else isn't he telling us?"

"You want to talk to him again, don't you?" interpreted Mahoney. "I understand your concerns about his honesty. He does draw a fine line between what the law allows and what *he* thinks is allowable. But I think he's on our side of that line in this case. I'll call him and ask him to come in for a chat. I don't think he has anything more to tell us, but I'm willing to watch you question him. I learn useful techniques from your interrogations."

Mahoney went to his desk and pulled out his phone. *Three in the afternoon already. Call Sorenson and get a cup of coffee. The day is rushing past too fast. No, it's been almost three weeks since the murders and we've got damn little to show for our work. Time is speeding by and crawling along, both. Ugh.*

"Sergeant Mahoney, how nice to hear from you again," said Sorenson. "How's that murder case going? I haven't seen anything about it in the news lately. Oh, that's what this call is about? Well, I've already told you everything I know about it. Inspector Radcliffe thinks otherwise? Is he still upset because I kept him out late a year ago so his house could be robbed? Or does he just not trust me on principle?"

"It doesn't matter. When a policeman wants to talk to me, I'm always available. It saves a lot of time and trouble that way. I can't guarantee I will satisfy him, but I will be happy to cooperate. Especially as I have no fish to fry in this matter. I'm busy packing right now because I'm moving soon, and I want to finish a couple of boxes. I'll be there in about half an hour."

Sorenson hung up his phone and heard a knocking on his door. As he unlatched the door, it was forced open by several men with guns. He was grabbed and pushed back into the room.

"Yes, this is the man in the picture," noted Yahye. "Good work, Hamza. You were right about that magazine. Now, tell us, dog of an infidel, where is the money that Zahi gave you? If you do not tell me at once, I will give my men some new lessons in how to torture a man into talking. Where is the money?"

"Money? I have no idea where it is. I don't even know for certain that there *is* any money. Zahi claimed to have some money, but I never saw it. And he never gave it to me."

"Ah, yes, Bashiir, a wooden kitchen chair, that is perfect. Xidig, cut those cords from the blinds. Tie him to it, tightly. Even the bindings should be painful. Let us start with the simple techniques. Hamza, you are big and strong. Would you please punch this man several times in his stomach, just to soften him up?"

"Ten is enough for now, Yahye. If I hit him too much at a time, he will get numb. A pause makes the next blow even worse."

"Ah, you have learned well. Now, scum of an unbeliever, where is the money?"

"I don't know where the money is. I haven't seen the money. Zahi only showed me two big suitcases and said the money was in them. Look around. You won't find them here. I never had them or the money."

"Of course we won't find the suitcases here. The police have them, and they are empty. The police don't even care about the empty bags. Why should they? I don't want the luggage, I want the money. Where is it? Xidig, Bashiir, search this entire apartment. Look anywhere the money could be hidden. Look in those boxes. Hamza, what are you waiting for? Hit him some more."

Yahye walked around the apartment, watching his men and looking at Sorenson's possessions. He did not seem impressed with what he saw. He watched his men searching for the money, dumping out the boxes onto the floor. He glanced at the titles of the books spread across the room. He watched Hamza beating Sorenson, appreciating his technique. *He's very good, I'm glad I gave him the task.*

Sorenson reflected on the beating, too. *He's skilled, very professional. Better than some mob thugs I once knew. He hits hard enough to cause pain, but not hard enough to make me pass out. No broken bones, yet, but my midsection is getting increasingly tender. It's manageable so far. I just hope they hold off on breaking bones for a while. Or the really nasty stuff with hot wires and sharp knives. I wish they would just believe me, but they can't. They're too certain that I must have the money to believe that I don't. Damn!*

"Enough, Hamza! All right, Mr. Sorenson, friend of my enemy, accomplice to the man who stole from me, a man who has no Koran, not even an infidel Bible, a man who believes in nothing! Tell me where the money is. Tell me now! Tell me now before I have Hamza get cruel."

"The money isn't here. I believe you now when you say Zahi had the money, because you obviously believe that. But he never showed it to me. He never gave it to me. I. Do. Not. Know. Where. The. Money. Is. Wouldn't I tell you if I knew?"

"No, you want that money for yourself! I know you Americans. You will do anything for money. You will take this beating and hope that I will leave so you can keep the money. I will not leave here without the money. I will not kill you, I will only make you wish you were dead. If you tell me now I will spare your life. If you don't tell me soon, I will make you pray for death. And I will not give it to you. Why should I be kind and put you out of your misery when you refuse to help me? Now tell me, where is the money?"

"You don't know all Americans. You don't know me. I will do a lot of things for money, but not risk my life foolishly. It would be foolish, wouldn't it, to believe your phony promise of kindness. You will kill me whether I tell you where the money is or not. You may prolong my death, but you will kill me in the end. I can't keep the money if I'm dead, so why shouldn't I tell you right away, so you *will* kill me quickly and end the beating. It doesn't matter. I still don't know where the money is."

"Hamza, do you have your knives with you?"

"Yes, Yahye. I always have them with me. Here, let me spread them out for our little victim. So nice, so sharp. But I will save the knives for later. First, I want to burn him. Beating a man softens him up a little, but not enough. Some men can stand it. Some will make themselves stand it to show how tough they are. It is the scent of the meal, but not a real taste of it.

"Burning turns a man to jelly. It is very hard to tolerate the electric jabs, the smell of your own flesh roasting. Most men tell everything they know when they are burned properly. If they don't, *then* there is the knife. The knife always delivers. A man thinks I will cut him deeply and dangerously. But I make little cuts, here and there, always in painful places. Places a man does not want cut. He will talk before the day is over.

"Xidig, unplug that long extension cord and give it to me. Watch and learn, youngster. Cut off the head, like killing a snake. Then split the cord between the two wires just like this, see? Now I strip the covering from the wires for about two inches. Plug it in again and I will show this infidel what a nice toy I have just made."

"Bashiir, rip off his shirt," ordered Yahye. "Now, Hamza, show us your specialty. I have not seen you do it in months, and I so enjoy it."

***

"Saunders, check out this address," directed Mahoney. "It's the apartment where a Mr. Jack Sorenson lives. You've passed the Sergeants Exam and get your stripes next month. Consider this a little prelude for you. He said he was coming in to see us, and he's not here yet. I want you to go and give him a personal invitation to come here. If he declines, call for a warrant. If he's not there, well, just call me."

***

Saunders parked his squad almost legally in a bus stop and went into the apartment building. *How odd,* he thought, *for him to live in such an ordinary looking place. That case a year ago involved lots of money. Okay, maybe he didn't handle it, but he had a lot to do with the kidnapping this year. And now he's supposed to have millions? He sure hides it well.*

Saunders was about to knock on the door when he heard sounds inside the room. Someone screamed, apparently in pain, a man with a harsh foreign accent was demanding something. Another scream. Saunders stepped back from the door, and called in on his radio.

"Dispatch, I need immediate backup at South Oak Park and West Twenty-first Place. Possible assault in progress. Tell Mahoney his man may be in trouble. It sounds like several suspects. I will wait for backup unless it gets worse. Out."

He leaned against the door, listening for hints of what was going on inside. *More talking, quieter now. The rough voice again, demanding information about something. Another voice, Sorenson? It might be his voice, but it's strained. Can't tell what he's saying, he's too quiet. Oh, God! Not another scream!*

If they're torturing Sorenson, I've got to go in. How many of them are there? Does it matter? I promised to protect the public. Unconditional. Not only if it was safe for me. Oh, well, they'll give Wanda a nice medal and a pension.

He tried the doorknob and it turned. He pushed the door wide open and charged in, badge in his left hand, gun in his right. He shouted, "Police! Freeze!" Five men surrounded Sorenson, who was tied to a chair, his head hanging limply down. One of the men was prodding Sorenson's bare belly with a long wire.   One was watching with sadistic glee, and shouting "Where's the money?" at Sorenson. The others stood looking on, with expressions of grim satisfaction on their faces.

They turned to look at Saunders coming in. They looked in surprise, then in amusement to see only one cop coming in. Then in panic to hear in the distance, and getting closer, the sound of sirens, a lot of sirens. Hamza tossed the sparking live wire at Saunders, distracting him. Yahye snarled, cried out something in Somali, and led his men into the rear of the apartment. Saunders yelled "Freeze" again and shot at their backs. One man staggered a bit but kept on running. The back door Yahye expected to find was easily unlocked and they fled down the wooden fire escape, knocking over a trash can on the back porch.

Saunders ran after them and from the porch could see the Somalis running down the street to three cars parked by the building. He raced down the stairs, almost tripping over the trash can, and got to his squad just in time to see the three cars speeding away down West Twenty-first Place. He called the dispatcher again with his update, and went back inside.

Saunders walked back up to Sorenson's apartment, feeling depressed. *So close to catching them! Should I have waited for backup? No. Sorenson looks alive but I couldn't be sure from outside. And the sirens might have made them run off anyway. I did the right thing, no matter what the brass might say. Catch the crooks. But save the taxpaying public. Can't always do both.*

Sorenson's chest was covered in sweat, his belly with large bruises and small burn marks. His face showed pain and anger, and he was struggling to free himself from his bindings. Saunders knelt behind him and used his pocket knife to cut the cords and free him.

"How are you feeling, Mr. Sorenson? I'm sorry I didn't get here any sooner. Did that hurt? I'm sorry, this cord is tough and my knife is dull. Mahoney sent me to bring you in for a talk and I heard them torturing you. Do you need medical care? Was that guy using a live wire on you? He looked like he knew what he was doing, and enjoyed it."

"What the hell!" roared Mahoney as he came in. "Are you all right, Sorenson? God, you look awful. Have you called for an ambulance, Saunders?"

"Right behind you, Mahoney," declared the first EMT.

"Hiya, Jake," Mahoney casually greeted the man. "I've got to talk to this nice man, so I'd appreciate it if he lives a while longer. Do your usual magic on him, please."

"Sit back down, sir, please," requested Jake. "I need to check you out before you go for a walk. What do we have here? Ah, nasty bruises, burn marks. Let me check for broken bones. Tell me if I'm too rough. No, no, sore, but not broken. I'm afraid we can't do much for your bruises but a little pain gel. It'll help the burn marks, too. There's only a couple of them. Do you want to go to the hospital?"

"No, thank you very much," gasped Sorenson with an effort. "The man beating me knew how to hurt without physically damaging me too much. If I'm too sore tomorrow, I'll stop by then."

"Tough guy, huh?" mocked Jake.

"You said you can't help with bruises. I know the hospital can't either.
All they can do there is check for internal ruptures and I would feel them
now myself. I've been beaten before and know what damage feels like.
Rub on the pain gel, because it *will* help. And accept my thanks for doing
all you can."

"I shouldn't have asked, but I was trying to be polite," replied the EMT.
"You *are* going to the hospital, now, whether you want to go or not. Not
because I like to be thorough in my work, although I do. Not because I
might get fired for letting you decide this, although I might be. Because
you may think you feel OK enough, but you can't see inside your body.
We'll take some X-rays and then *we*'ll decide if you go home tonight. Got
that?"

Sorenson stood up to prove to the EMT just how fine he was, and his legs
buckled under him. Jake and Mahoney grabbed him and kept him from
hitting the floor.

"I told you, you can't decide how well you are right now," Jake insisted.
"Mac, help me get him on the stretcher. The stairs are a straight run down,
so carrying him down should be easy enough. Sam, you can come to the
hospital with us and talk to him there if you want. It'll be a while before
someone looks at the X-rays and decides on keeping him overnight."

"Can't you give me a break?" begged Sorenson. "I'm getting married
Sunday. Everything's set, preacher, hall, dinner, guests coming in from
out of town."

"I *am* sorry, Mr. Sorenson," commiserated Jake, "but you don't want to
collapse in the middle of the ceremony, do you? You'll probably go home
tonight, unless there *is* internal damage. But we *do* have to check on that.
Grab the other end of this stretcher, Mac, and let's get him into the
wagon."

"Wait!" Sorenson shouted. "Where's my phone? I need to call Marcy.
She'll have a fit over this, and I won't blame her. Mahoney, do you see it

somewhere? They came in just after your call, and I dropped it. Yes, that's it. Thank you."

"Move him now, Mac, before he asks for a beer," grumbled Jake.

***

Sorenson punched the autodial button for Marcy's number once he was strapped into the ambulance. Her phone rang three times before he heard her cheery voice saying, "Marcy Delancy."

"Hello Marcy. I have another confession for you, some bad news, and a request."

"Jack! What's happened? You sound awful. Are you involved in something you haven't warned me about? I told you I wouldn't overrule your job decisions but I would like to know what you're doing. And what kind of 'bad news'? You're not calling from the hospital, are you?"

"No, well, not yet. I'm in an ambulance on my way there. I got beat up pretty well by some thugs this afternoon. That's the confession and I'll tell you all about it later. The EMTs insist on taking some pictures of my insides to make sure I'm fine. My stomach got punched a lot, but not enough to cause internal damage, I think.

"That's the confession. The *bad* news is that I was almost all packed up and the thugs unpacked everything for me. The apartment is a mess and I'm too sore to bend over and clean it up, even if they let me go tonight. Which leads to the *request* : could you please call Melissa and ask her to send Anthony and some of his friends over to redo the boxing. I've left the door unlocked.

"You can come see me in the ER, but Sergeant Mahoney will be monopolizing me, I'm afraid. He wants to know why people are beating me up, almost as much as I do. I really don't want to scare you. Just more adventures and scary ones, too. And now more assisting the police in their investigations, as the English say."

***

Marcy entered the screened off cubicle in the ER right behind Inspector Radcliffe. Sergeant Mahoney was sitting on a chair, making notes in a small book, and looked up as they came in.

"Good evening, Paul," remarked Mahoney, "and you too, Ms Delancy. Sergeant Sam Mahoney. We met earlier this year at the party for capturing the kidnapping art thieves. Sorenson is still in the lab, posing for X-rays. He should be back soon. The doctor, Dr. Crippen, is over there, reviewing his notes on Sorenson."

"How is he, Sergeant?" asked Marcy apprehensively. "He told me he was fine, sort of. But he doesn't like me to worry about him, so he sometimes plays the tough guy."

"He's got a very nice, very colorful, collection of bruises all over his belly. He told me they were just trying to soften him up for the serious torture, with electric wires. He shrugs that off, but electric shocks can do serious damage."

"When you called, you said he told you it was a bunch of Somalis," Paul Radcliffe began. "Does he know if they were any we're interested in? Although it would be hard to believe there are two groups of Somali thugs running around Berwyn."

"Oh, I sincerely hope not," moaned Sorenson as a nurse wheeled him into the cubicle. "This one was more than enough for me, thank you very much. Mahoney, thank that nice EMT for insisting on bringing me here. My stomach hurts way more than I had expected it to. That guy didn't hurt anything but the muscles. And they are *so* sore right now!"

"Jack, tell me the truth," urged Marcy, "how are you? Is there anything broken or damaged? We *are* getting married Sunday, even if it has to be here in ER. I'd prefer you were healthy enough for a honeymoon."

"I hurt, love, but I think it's just pain from a hard beating. The X-rays will be here in a minute and will tell us for certain."

"You can't fool me, Jack. 'Just a little pain.' Ha! Your face is contorted with pain like someone was nailing your head to the floor."

"No, I can't fool you. Yes, it's been a long time since I've been beaten like this, and I've forgotten how bad it feels. As soon as they let me out, I'll let you take complete charge of me, I promise."

"So, you caught part of my question as you came in," mentioned Radcliffe. "Did you recognize any of these men?"

"No, but the only two Somalis I ever met were Zahi and Bilan. They mentioned enemies, but never gave them names. The goons who attacked me, on the other hand, couldn't *stop* calling each other by name. The thug who beat me was named Hamza, the man in charge was named Yahye. Two other guys who helped were called Bashiir and Xidig. The names mean nothing to me, but I remembered them just in case I survived long enough to talk to you again."

"Thank you for that." Radcliffe's face glowed with pleasure when he heard names that matched the ones Abdullah had given him. "Hamza is the one who killed Zahi. You're lucky to have survived him. One of Zahi's friends says that Hamza killed Zahi without intending to by hitting him too hard."

"So, why were they after me? I get that they were after Zahi's mysterious ten million bucks. They told me so, but I don't know where that is any more than you do."

"I owe you an apology, Mr. Sorenson," said Radcliffe. "I've never been comfortable with you. I always thought you were just a little too slick, despite Sam's protestations that you're honest enough. I'm sorry you had go through the third degree, but I trust you now. Did they give any indication of where they expected to find the money?"

"They thought *I* had it, that Zahi had given it to me. I told them I had never seen any money, only the two green suitcases that supposedly held it. They told *me* that you guys had the suitcases, empty. They really believed that Zahi had given it to me, and that I had hidden it for him. They searched my apartment, opened all the cupboards, emptied all the boxes I had just packed for moving out, sliced up my old sofa. Thorough, but fruitless. And how the hell did they ever find out about me?"

"Everything about this case is a pure mystery," observed Mahoney. "Why should this be any different? I have no idea how they could know about you. Maybe one of them saw you visiting Zahi, but they should have found you much sooner in that case. When he first came to see me, Zahi said he saw a story about you in *People* and wanted to hire you to move money for him."

"When they came in, Yahye declared I was the man in the picture. Maybe he saw the same story, but why would he connect that story to Zahi? Zahi told me the killers had found him and Bilan, but that was before my last visit. They weren't killed until the next night. So the killers knew Zahi and Bilan were here for at least one day, maybe more, before killing them. Why? Why not grab them and the money as soon as they could? And what did they do with the money?"

"That's our problem too," admitted Radcliffe. "I had thought they had given it to you. As a preparation for a trip to Africa, or just for safekeeping. I don't think that any longer. It's a shame, because it would have made this part of the case so much easier.

"You don't have the money. They didn't have it with them when they died. It wasn't in their car. It wasn't left in any of their motel rooms. We have the suitcases it was held in. You've told us about the green suitcases, and so have their friends from Minneapolis. What could they have done with that much cash?

"Sam made the horrible suggestion they had hidden it in a coffin and had it buried. We've checked all the burials in the county for the week before the murders, and all are legitimate local deaths. There's not a storage locker available within fifty miles of Chicago, and hasn't been for months. We've checked the left luggage rooms at the train and bus depots. Nothing. Could they have said something, anything, which might have given you an idea of what they would do with the money?"

"Only that they wanted me to take it out of the country for them. Even the last day I saw them, when they doped me, that was their plan. I have to admit, I didn't understand their doping me. Zahi was very apologetic about it afterward, but why do it at all? They didn't take anything from me. They took my wallet out and put it back in the wrong pocket, but nothing was missing from it.

"I'm sorry, Inspector, but I don't have a clue as to what happened to the money. They had that Wednesday evening and all day Thursday to hide it. Maybe they found some place that was such a great hiding spot that no one can suspect it. Have you tried looking in the storm sewers? Maybe they put the money in plastic garbage bags and stuffed them into a sewer."

"Oh. My. God. What an idea!" exclaimed Radcliffe. "That would account for the empty suitcases. They would need them again when they came back for the money. And properly bagged, the money wouldn't get soaked in the sewer. The weight should keep it from getting washed down the sewer, I guess. This is going to take a lot of men a lot of time to check out. How did you think of this, Mr. Sorenson?"

"In my misspent youth, I had occasion to use the sewers to avoid pursuit by hostile individuals. I can't recommend them as a way to travel, but they are very private. No one thinks about them that way. I used them once to hide some, um, 'investment' money for a friend. I've also seen a story from Omaha about a gun that was used in a killing being found years later in the sewer. But I really don't care about where the money is. What I want you to do is find these killers before they find me again."

The doctor came into the cubicle and interrupted their conversation. He had some X-ray pictures in his hand that he had been examining. And a few sheets of paper in his other hand.

"Mr. Sorenson, I've checked your X-rays, and there is no internal damage. I've written a prescription for some pain pills. Take them for at least three days, and follow these instructions. The EMT said you tried to tough it out. Don't. Pain is a sign of trouble. There may not be any real damage, but the pain tells me, and you, that something is hurt. Hurt means damaged. Be a good little boy and take your medicine. I don't have any lollipops, but as an alternative treat, you can go home."

"Thank you, Dr. Crippen," Sorenson murmured meekly. "The pain is not getting better with time. I guess I'm not as young and resilient as I used to be. I'll take the pills, I promise, and take it easy. Thank you for your time, and care, and for allowing me to leave. I don't really like lollipops, anyway.

"Inspector Radcliffe, I'm getting tired, and I'm out of ideas. May I go home now?"

"Oh, certainly, Mr. Sorenson. Thank you for your help, and for this idea. And we'll do what we can to find the killers. That's a promise."

***

"What were the police doing there?" yelled Yahye back in their cabin. "How could they have known we would be there? *We* did not know we would be there. How could *they* know?"

"This man who moves money," suggested Bashiir, "may be wanted for moving money illegally. I was looking at Xidig's magazine, and it says he may or may not be honest. Maybe we were just unlucky to be there when they came to arrest him for something else."

"But so many policemen!" shouted Hamza. "They would not have used so many to arrest one man. If they knew we were there, they would have sent that many men. But how could they have known we would be there?"

"There was just the one at first," remembered Xidig. "The others were still approaching when he came into the room. It doesn't matter; we got away. And they did not follow us here. Later tonight, I will go out and find another set of license plates for Yahye's car. If they do not see any sign that we are from Minnesota, they will be less likely to look our way. But we still do not know where he hid the money."

"Yes, and if the police arrested him for anything they will search his apartment," decided Yahye. "We searched, but maybe we missed the hiding place. The police will have more time, and other ways to make him talk. If the money is there, they will take it. And that will be very bad for us."

"Maybe not, Yahye," objected Hamza. "If the police find ten million dollars they will brag about it. You've seen the police showing off how many guns they took from that gang leader's house in Minneapolis. Imagine what they will do with millions of dollars. We just have to watch the news reports. If the police do not have the money, we keep looking. If they do have it, we steal it from them."

"Break into the evidence locker," Yahye sighed at what he still regarded a stupid idea. "I still think that is a very difficult and dangerous thing to try to do. We may have no choice, but I will *not* do it without proper preparation. We must get more men from Minneapolis, and more weapons and explosives. And we'll be pursued by all the American police, the FBI, the Army, everything! It will be hard to get away. We must have a fool-proof plan."

***

"I should take you home and put you to bed," said Marcy. "But it's been a long day for me, too, and I'm hungry. I haven't any food left at home. The fridge is empty, except for the remains of a gallon of milk and some yogurt. I'll have to go out, but I don't want to leave you alone like this."

"I'm sore, very sore. But you can leave me alone for half an hour while you get something. Hell, order in some food. Actually, I'm starting to get hungry, too. I'm not sure if I can handle food, but maybe some soup."

"Melissa suggested we come by tonight to try the bisque she wants to serve at the wedding. Do you think you can handle that? And the drive to her place?"

"You have to drive me somewhere, and Zoltan's bisque experiments are always worth trying. Let's give it a try."

Twenty minutes later they walked into Melissa's restaurant. She greeted them personally and brought them to the private room.

"What's the matter, Jack?" asked Melissa. "You look like you've been sentenced to death, and they aren't going to wait for dawn. Marcy called and said something bad happened to you. What was it? Are the details really that scary?"

"He's told me, along with the police," said Marcy. "He has to tell me, it's part of our bargain for life."

"I know I do, dearest one. That's part of why I'm so down. This is scary for both of us, I think. I never wanted you to be affected by my life choices. What I want may not matter any more. Let me tell you what happened, as near as I can figure it out, Melissa.

"Zahi's killers are still in town, now with some more of their friends, and have somehow decided that I must have the money. I have no idea how they could think that, or how they associated me with Zahi. The gang beat me and asked me where the money was. I kept telling them I didn't know. They kept beating me. When they started on the nasty stuff with an electric wire, I started screaming. A very nice policeman came bursting in, in the best Hollywood manner, to the sound of sirens on the way. He was coming to see me anyway, and his timing was both fortuitous and welcome.

"Everyone wants to know where the money is. I wouldn't want to have it. It killed Zahi and Bilan. It may yet kill me, because the murderers think I have it. They want it and will do anything to get it. And that leads to you, dear one.

"Right now they probably don't know about you. But come Sunday and our wedding, they will find you when they find me. I do not want to put you at risk. Especially because I made a mistake. I can't give you up, and won't, no matter what army comes after us. But it depresses me no end to think that I have put you in danger. Unintentionally, but still in danger."

"You know I don't scare easily, Jack. I've had hard times once, and can take my lumps. Well, maybe not physical ones, but the psychological kind. I trust you to protect me, even from wild killers. I don't know *how* you will, but I trust you to do so. I know you will not leave me vulnerable. I know any danger I am in is a danger to you even more. Yes, they will try to hurt me to make you talk. I understand what hostages are for. But I won't be afraid. And I don't want you to worry about me. The police know about these men now and will find them. But you do need to start watching your back more."

"No. Oddly enough, this time they attacked from the front. First time that's ever happened. Oh, my, Marcy. I just joked about what happened today. Maybe I'm getting over it already. I hope so. It's been such an awful afternoon."

"We get married on Sunday, and I want you fresh and eager. I don't want some drudge mumbling 'I guess so' when the JP asks if you want to marry me. Everything is set, we have nothing to do before the ceremony. We have our tickets for Paris, our hotel reservations, even a table reserved at the best restaurant in Paris. Stop worrying, that's an order from your loving wife-to-be. Take tomorrow off and relax."

"If that's the kind of order you're going to give me, I will surely enjoy being married. But I can't take off tomorrow. July starts on Monday, when we will be in Paris. And I have rich men who want me to pay their mistresses and their mistresses' landlords. And they want to pay me for doing this. It takes half a day, and I've already set it up to get them to make their payments tomorrow instead of Monday. I promise to relax when I've delivered the last envelope. It's easy work, it will pay for the honeymoon, and if I don't do it, they'll stop using me, and then what will I do for a living?"

"Yes, you are coming out of your gloom. That's the wise-cracking man I want to marry. Yes, you may go deliver money for rich men. Just be sure to bring home enough to pay for our honeymoon."

"Jack, I've known you since forever," observed Melissa. "I've known every scrape you've ever been in, with the law, with the mob, with small time crooks. This is the worst, isn't it? I'm glad you told me as well as Marcy, because we can help too. Tony Jr. took care of your apartment. He and his buddies packed everything up and moved it to our garage. Not the furniture, just the boxes. That problem is covered.

"The real problem for you is to stay safe until Sunday. You haven't said so, but it's obvious. Tony Jr. offered a solution for that, too. He has a small apartment he uses for entertaining his girlfriends. He can't bring them here, obviously, and he doesn't want to offend his father and me by bringing them to the house. He left a key and says it is clean and ready for you and Marcy. No one will know you are there, and you can stay the whole weekend."

"Ah, Melissa, you are such a good friend," acknowledged Sorenson. "And so is Anthony. Thank him for us when he comes home tonight."

**

Hamza looked at his phone, then stuck it back in his pocket. *Two in the morning and all these infidels will be safely asleep and unable to see or hear anything,* he thought. He looked around the street carefully. There was Sorenson's apartment building, dark all over. No lights showing anywhere. No one was in sight. No pedestrians, no cars, especially no policemen lurking in dark corners. He knew how to search for a police stake-out, and there wasn't one.

He went to the rear stairs to the apartment, and crept up to the back door. It was locked, but he had expected that. His jimmy forced the lock open and he listened at the door. Silence. No one moved inside. He pushed the door open and went in. Room by room he went through the apartment. He looked for his knives and didn't find them. *Damn police took them, I suppose.* There was no one in the apartment. He went to the back door again and flashed a small light. Soon Yahye and the others were coming into the apartment.

"The boxes that were here are gone now," noticed Yahye. "If they have removed them, they may have removed the money as well. No, you emptied them, didn't you? Still, we must search this apartment very thoroughly. Either the police have found and taken the money away, or it is still here. Before we raid the police station, we must be certain the money is not here. Tap the floor, tap the walls, look for hiding places. Do not overlook any possible hole. We have the rest of the night if we are quiet, so start looking."

His men ripped open the mattress on Sorenson's bed, emptied the freezer in his fridge, and pulled the bookshelves down from the walls. There was nothing hidden. There were no other obvious hiding places. Hamza stopped Bashiir when he raised a crowbar to smash a wall.

"No, Bashiir, it's not in that wall. Can't you see that the paint is old and dirty? If he made a hole in the wall and covered it over, the paint would look fresh. Yahye, we've looked everywhere. I've even checked for loose floorboards. The money isn't here."

"It's getting close to dawn. Let's go back to the camp before his neighbors begin to awaken," ordered Yahye.

Chapter Fourteen

The Wedding

Mahoney was back working full time for Paul Radcliffe, Sorenson's torture having refocused their attention on the still invisible terrorists.

"Gomez just called in, Paul." Mahoney walked into Radcliffe's office to report the next morning. "Abdullah and Taifa left about nine, taking the interstate north. He followed for a while to make sure, but when they got on I-90 going toward Rockford, he figured they were leaving for good. He'll be back in an hour, he says. I'll get the details then. I wonder if Abdullah just gave up, or if he thought the killers are after him."

"Abdullah knew they were here. He saw them, even if they didn't see him. He's spent two weeks poking into every empty gopher hole we've looked into, with the same result. That's got to be frustrating. I was kind of hoping he might lead us to the money. I was even willing to use him as bait for the killers. I'm glad he's taken himself out of danger, though. I told him when we freed them to go home and be good. I guess he finally decided to to that."

***

"Mr. John Smith to see Mr. Costello," Sorenson told the receptionist. He usually saw Mr. Costello on the first of the month, the busiest day in the man's schedule. That meant a wait for his client to find time for him. The end of the month found Sorenson ushered right into Mr. Costello's office at once.

"Here's the envelope for Jill," offered Mr. Costello. "And one for her landlord, and yours. I've added a little extra to yours, a sort of wedding present. You never talk about your personal life, but you said you're going on a honeymoon next Monday. I can make the connection between honeymoon and wedding, no trouble at all.

"I've dealt with you for a long time now. Two mistresses, and other things. You've always been dependable and discreet, and I appreciate that. You've never raised your rate or asked for a tip. Hell, even my wine merchant asks for a tip. Anyway, don't refuse the gift. It's a wedding present, not a tip. I hope you have a long and happy marriage. Happier than mine, at any rate."

"Thank you. If I don't ask for a raise or a tip, it's because I'm afraid you might realize you're already overpaying me. There are a lot of men with mistresses who handle the money themselves, you know."

"Yeah, and they don't have jealous wives hiring detectives to trail them everyplace they go. Mine has given up on the divorce lawyers, but I still don't want to make her mad. I cheat on her, but I still do love her. And complain about her. Crazy, but that's life. See you next month."

***

Sorenson entered Anthony's tiny love nest with a merrier expression on his face than he had left with. His stomach was still sore, sensitive enough that his belt hurt. But he had had a profitable morning.

"I have finished my monthly errands, darling, *and* obeyed your command. Every one of my errant husbands felt overjoyed at our marriage and gave us wedding presents. Never have so many false lovers made two honest lovers so happy. You wanted enough to pay for our honeymoon, and I have more than succeeded. We can stay in Paris for a month."

"That's wonderful, Jack, but we need to be back in two weeks anyway to close on the house. Living well with you is only part of the deal. We must live well in the perfect house. I finished, finally, getting all my paints and painting supplies packed. The movers can pack everything else any way they like, but I need to know that my oils and acrylics aren't tossed in all jumbled together. It's just noon, and we're both done for the day. Wonderful!"

"'Oh, how sharper than a serpent's tooth it is to have a thankless child!'" quoted Jack facetiously. "Have you forgotten our parents are coming in this afternoon?"

"Oh my God! I did. When are they arriving? Jack, this is horrible! I haven't given any thought at all to our parents. Oh, dear, they'll be sitting there in the airport all alone, not knowing anyone, wondering where we are."

"Easy, love, take it easy. We have half an hour before we need to leave for O'Hare. And they won't be lost and friendless. Since they're all coming from Phoenix, I bought them seats together on the same flight. They've also known each other for almost as long as we've known each other. Hardly friendless."

"It's just that I've been so busy with planning our wedding, and our house, and worrying about you, I've completely forgotten them. Where are we going to put them up? Neither one of us has a spare room, much less two. And we can't impose on Anthony's generosity, not that his pied-a-terre is big enough anyway."

"Your father wanted to stay at the Holiday Inn. Mine wanted Motel 6. I talked to them earlier this week about where they were going to stay. I'm not throwing us a cheap wedding, especially where our parents are concerned. They're getting the Palmer House. It may not be the best hotel in Chicago, but it *is* very good, and *I* like it. It has a nice old-fashioned feel while being an up-to-date modern hotel. I have a limo coming for us in a few minutes. It will take us to the airport, pick up our parents and their luggage, and bring us to the hotel.

"We can spend the rest of the day with them and get a room for ourselves for tonight and tomorrow night. Anthony was kind to give us his little flat, but it *is* rather too little and the Palmer House will be just as safe. We can come back to Berwyn tomorrow so they can see the house, even if we can't get in yet. And you can pack for Paris while we're here. How does that sound?"

"Melissa once told me you calculate everything you do. I don't know if I'd call this calculating, but I'm glad you take such pains over your plans. I had wanted more time to pack up stuff here for the move, but that can actually wait until we get back. Time with my parents, and yours, is more important."

***

The Somalis were gathered in their cabin to discuss how to find the money. There was more than enough room in the cabin for them, much better than the cramped tent. They had better privacy now, too, and air-conditioning as well.

"Hamza, your idea could be disastrous for us," declared Yahye. "But you have convinced me that the police must have the money in their evidence locker. I cannot think of any place else it might be. We know that Zahi did something with the money. We know that Abdullah does not have it. We searched this infidel's apartment and he does not have it. Zahi did not put it into some storage locker or any other place to leave luggage. The police must have it.

"I do not like this, but a fact is a fact, and you have proven it to be so. We must plan this attack with the greatest care. One little error and we may all be dead or in prison. American soldiers are very tough warriors. We have seen them in videos, how they are fit and aggressive and are never stopped. But American policemen are not like their soldiers. We have seen many fat, slow, lazy police. They can barely drag themselves out of their squads. Even Americans laugh at them for eating donuts all day. They are not as tough as we are.

"But there *are* many of them. If we attack, even at night when most are away from the station, they will call for help. We must get the money before any help can arrive. We must try to overwhelm them at the beginning. Maybe we can keep them from calling for help. Hamza, this was your suggestion. Have you actually given it any thought?"

"Yes. A week ago I first thought the police might have the money. I had no reason to think it then, but it was a possibility. I went to look at the building, at night, very late when no one was about. I walked all around the building and have given it much thought since you arrived. I think I know how to attack it with the least effort and danger to us."

"Then you must show me. Take me there late tonight and tell me all about this place and your plan. The rest of you will come with us, so I don't have to repeat what Hamza tells me. We will all attack, and we must all know the plan, especially as the rest of our men will only be told when they get here. Mahmoud, I want you to drive to Minneapolis early in the morning, but I also want you to hear the plan. So get some rest now while you can. We will wake you in time to see this building."

***

It was midnight, with a waning crescent moon mostly obscured by clouds. No one paid any attention to the men looking at the police station.

"You see, it is almost all two stories tall," explained Hamza. "This east end seems to be offices, like the police stations in Minneapolis. The west end with the tall walls looks like that exercise place near us. The Americans call it a gym. I don't know why they would have a gym in a police station, so maybe it is where the cells are. At any rate, you can see there are windows only at the top of the walls. It is secure because of the walls, but I think it is too big for just the evidence locker.

"In the back of the building here are more windows, which means more offices. But there is one area here which has no windows and is not too large. This must be where they store the valuable evidence, where no one can easily break in. I would be afraid to blow a hole in the wall right here, because we might accidentally destroy the money. But there are doors, one here and one on the other side of the building, which should let us get into that area without having to go through the whole police station.

"These doors have glass panels in them, so we can get in without having to use explosives. That will give us some element of surprise. A few moments at least before anyone knows we are there. There are few cars in the parking lot this late at night, so there can't be many policemen to stop us. The front door of the station is always open so the local people can come in and ask for police help.

"Some of us can go in the front way and kill the man at the desk. Then they can find the radio man and kill him. The rest of us go in through the back doors and find the evidence locker. We may need to blow open the door to that room, but such rooms in the TV shows always have a desk near the door, Xidig says. So we find the room, break into it, take the money out, and get away. If any police try to stop us, we kill them."

"Well planned, Hamza," approved Yahye. "We will need more men for this and more weapons. And explosives. We will also need some more big suitcases to put the money in. We will get three, no, four suitcases. It will be easier to load them up if we have extra space in them. Mahmoud, in the morning I want you to go to Minneapolis and get the rest of our men. Bring all of our weapons and ammunition. And steal explosives from that quarry we talked about. You know the plan, and this is the time to do it.

"This is Friday. You can be in Minneapolis by mid-afternoon Saturday if you leave early enough. Get the men and equipment together quickly. You should be able to steal the explosives tomorrow night, and then bring the men and gear here on Sunday. I will let the men rest while I explain the plan to them. We can then attack late on Monday night, when the moon will be totally dark.

"Bashiir, I want you to get the suitcases. You bought the ones that were stolen, so you know how big these new ones must be. Get four of them, we won't have time to pack carefully while we are robbing the police station. Later we can repack them."

***

Melissa's hotel lobby had never looked lovelier. There had been many political gatherings and celebrations in the past, but political banners and bunting couldn't match the stands of flowers which filled every nook and corner today. Sorenson wore his best tuxedo and his patent shoes shone with special glare. Marcy looked angelic in a creamy gown that trailed across the floor. She had a chaplet of small white roses.

A red velvet rope blocked access to the stairs to the upper floors. The lounge on the second floor, overlooking the lobby was discreetly hidden by a gauze curtain which allowed the residents of the hotel to watch the wedding without intruding on it.

The justice of the peace took his place in a front corner of the lobby, facing the crowd which spilled into the bar and the restaurant. A man and a woman, both smiling broadly, stood before him, listening intently to his words about the sacred nature of marriage and the responsibilities of each to the other. He ended in the traditional manner.

"Do you John 'Jack' Sorenson take this woman, Marcy Patricia Delancy, for your lawfully wedded wife … "

"I do, absolutely."

"Do you Marcy Patricia Delancy take this man, John 'Jack' Sorenson, for your lawfully wedded husband … "

"Oh, I most certainly do."

"Then by the authority invested in me by the State of Illinois, I hereby pronounce you man and wife. You may, well, yes, carry on."

***

"Miriam, and James, how are you?" Jack asked Melissa's parents at the reception. "It's been too long since we talked properly. Last night doesn't count; it was all about my recent adventures. I want to hear what you two have been doing lately. Still going to the Diamondbacks games?"

"Are you kidding? It's been hot as hell this month. What I want to know is what took you so long to get married?" asked James McBride. "You were mooncalfing around Marcy back when Miriam owned the hotel."

"That's what I wanted to know, too," interjected Harald Sorenson. "Was is so hard to say 'Marry me'?"

"Don't blame Jack, either of you," apologized Marcy. "Blame me. He used to ask me all the time. For a while he would ask on the anniversary of the first time we met, every year. I kept telling him 'Not until I become a successful artist.' He finally convinced me I was one, and he was still waiting. Marrying him now is my penance for not doing it earlier. Oh, no, that doesn't sound right! It's his long delayed reward. Is that better, Jack?"

"That certainly sounds better, but you've never spent more than a few weeks in my company. Wait until after the first couple of months before you cancel that 'penance' remark. I will, however, do my best to keep our life from being penitential, and that's a promise."

"Never mind your father, Jack." comforted Dorothy Sorenson. "You know how he likes to blow off steam about nothing at all. He's been on cloud nine ever since you told us you and Marcy were getting married. Me too. He's been bragging to anyone who'll listen about how his boy has made it big in the big city and is now marrying the most beautiful woman in all of Chicagoland. Don't try to deny it, Harald. You have."

"I'm happy Jack stayed with you, Marcy," remarked Ellen Delancy. "Lots of men would have gone off looking for someone more willing to marry. It's a good sign when a man is persistent in love. And a woman, too. You've never really dumped him. You just said 'later' over and over."

"Ah, they've been as good as married for years, long as I've known 'em," commented a glum looking man who had just walked up. "I'm Lefty Spicoli, a friend of Jack's from way back. Him and me went to high school together once upon a time."

***

"Jack, Marcy, this is so wonderful!" congratulated Angie Orzinski. "Fred's upset, he bet me you two would never get hitched. I hope you have as good a marriage as Fred and I have had. Who's moving in with whom?"

"We're buying a house," revealed Marcy. "We both have too much stuff and we want to have space to entertain."

"Yes, I've turned a new leaf, and won't be the recluse you used to know," admitted Jack.

***

"Congratulations, Mr. Sorenson," offered Paul Radcliffe. "Is that too formal, Phyllis?"

"Yes, it is, dear, he's not a suspect in anything, even if we only see him at the station."

"Well, it's hard to call him by his first name when he never uses ours. Still, congratulations Jack and Marcy. I wish you the very best for the future."

"Thank you both, Phyllis and Paul," replied Sorenson with a wink.

**

"Helen, this is Mr. Jack Sorenson, the man who has provided you with that new washer and dryer," announced Sam Mahoney to his wife.

"I thought you paid for them," replied Helen.

"I did, with the overtime money he forced me to take working on that kidnapping and art theft case. Congratulations, Jack and Marcy, good luck, best wishes to both of you."

**

"Ladies and gentlemen, Zoltan, our chef, tells me that dinner is ready. Will you please enter the restaurant and find your places?"

"I trust you have not let my standards slip, Melissa," remarked Miriam.

"Mother! How could you even *think* such a thing? You trained me so well that I can't help but keep them, and I've trained Angela just as well. I could have let her run this affair, and you'd have been just as pleased."

"How could I doubt you? And I know Angela is as good as you. I'm glad that the business will be in good hands for years to come."

**

"… in conclusion, I propose a toast to the bride and groom, Marcy and Jack … "

"My God! I've never had such a wonderful meal!"

"He helped ransom my wife from her kidnappers, got them arrested, got the money back, and refused most of the reward I offered him."

"He's about to give me the biggest commission for selling a house I've had in years."

"Yeah, a year ago I warned him someone was after him, just before they tried to run him down out front here."

"He's done favors for us, just little kindnesses, you know, all the time. Fred's tickled to death about being his best man. Never expected it, but he's so happy for Jack."

"I've been friends with Marcy since she came back from her first visit to Paris, studying art. We roomed together for a while. She introduced me to Jack way back then, and never took my advice to marry him. Until now. I'm so happy for her, and him too."

"Ladies and gentlemen, our friends, our families. Jack has yielded to me the task of saying 'Thank you'. He said he's married now and can't ever again expect to have the last word, so he wants to get used to it right away. But we do thank you for coming, and for your long years of waiting patiently for this wondrous day. *I* put it off all this time, and now I wish I hadn't. I wish we could have gotten married twenty years ago when we first met, thirty years ago, even in grade school. Well, I'm happy, which is what you've all been wishing for us. And Jack's happy. Thank you all, from the bottoms of our hearts. You are the best people we could have ever known. And now we have to leave, or we'll miss our flight to Paris. We're going on a honeymoon!"

***

Jaali was one of Abdullah's followers, another of his spies. Bilan had worked in Yahye's own house, picking up what news she could on the one day she cleaned. Jaali worked at Yahye's favorite coffee house, a small, intimate place with no privacy for talking. Yahye and his men spoke Somali freely in front of Jaali because they hardly noticed him. His grandparents had moved to Somalia from Kenya, so he had learned Somali as a child but he looked like a Kenyan. To Yahye, he looked like any other black American who wasn't Somali. He dressed like an American, he must be one. And Yahye knew that Americans didn't know a word of Somali.

"Mahmoud came back and talked to the others of Yahye's men," reported Jaali to Abdullah. "They ignored me as usual and I pretended not to hear anything, also as usual. He is gathering all of Yahye's men and they are going to some place near Chicago called Berwyn. He thinks the money Zahi and Bilan stole from him is there, in the police station."

"No, it is not in the police station," Abdullah corrected him. "I was there and the police thought I had the money. They do not have it. They do not know where it is any more than the rest of us do. I believe that Allah had placed a curse on that money, and the curse killed Zahi and Bilan. And now Allah has taken the money to Paradise and given it to them as a reward for taking it from Yahye."

"Why would Allah kill them with the cursed money and then reward them?" asked Taifa.

"You should not question the ways of Allah," demanded Abdullah. "He does what He does. He knows things we don't know, can't know."

"Well, wherever the money really is, Yahye thinks it is in the police station," repeated Jaali. "Mahmoud took some of his men last night and stole some explosives. Today they are going south, and tomorrow night they will attack the police station. That is all I could learn."

"You did very well, Jaali," Abdullah praised him. "Take this money, it is all I have left. Don't worry about me, my brother Ali will give me more later."

Abdullah went out for a walk in the warm summer evening air. *I thought I was through with Yahye and his evil plots. Surely the police in Berwyn would find him and lock him up. They haven't. And now he wants to attack them. He always thinks he is tougher than anyone else. Even with all of his men, how can he think he can overcome all the police in*

Berwyn? They will call for help. There are a great many police near Chicago.

I should warn them, shouldn't I? But what are they to me? They are not my kin, not of my tribe, not Somali at all. But they did us a favor and let us out of jail without any charges. That police inspector spoke to me the same way my grandfather used to. Be good and stay out of trouble. If I had done that Zahi and Bilan might still be alive.

The imam said the same thing to me yesterday. I am so tired of all this fighting. I fought in Somalia and had to flee. I fight here and my friends die horrible deaths. I must go somewhere else, and take Taifa and Ali with me. I could not bear to have them die like Zahi and Bilan. They are the only family I have left now. And I must do something too. I must take a stand for good as the imam told me. He said Allah rewards those who do what is right. It is right to warn the Berwyn police. I will do it. I should call the inspector. No, it is very late already. He may be asleep. Anyway I have only his office phone number, and he won't be there now. I will send him an email message.

Back in his room, Abdullah started his laptop, waiting for the desktop to come up. It was an old computer, not very fast, but he had bought it for very little and had taken a class in using it. He used it mostly to send messages to Diric, but he was through with that now. Tonight he would send a message to Berwyn.

"Subject: Attack on Berwyn Police Station

Dear Inspector Radcliffe, I am Abdullah, the Somali from Minneapolis. You treated me very well when you did not have to, and you told me to be good and obey the laws from now on. You sounded like my grandfather. My imam also told me to do good. So I have decided that I must do good to you. I have heard that Yahye has sent for all of his men here and all their guns and explosives. They intend to attack your police station late on Monday night. Yahye thinks the money is there. I don't know where it is, but it is not there. You know this as well. But Yahye does not know this. I have a spy, I had a spy, I am

not doing Diric's work any more. I am leaving
Minneapolis and going somewhere safer for me and my
brothers. I will tell you where I go when I get there. Oh,
my spy, he overheard all this and told me. He also said
that Yahye is staying at a place with bullfrogs. I think that
is the word he used, it is unknown to me. Does it mean
anything to you? I hope this lets you defend yourselves
well and capture that beast Yahye. Goodbye. Your friend
Abdullah."

Chapter Fifteen

Making Plans

Mike Feltz let his wife steer his wheelchair into his cubicle. He grinned, somewhat sheepishly, at his friends who welcomed him back to work. He looked around at his surroundings, making sure he could get around without his wife when she went back home, and that anything he might need was within easy reach. He kissed her, thanked her, and watched her head off.

"Welcome back, Mike," Paul Radcliffe greeted his partner. "I see a sturdy cast on your leg, and a wheelchair, and I make this deduction. You are here because you're going crazy at home. And maybe driving Anita crazy too."

"Both. I was getting snappy and she didn't deserve that. If you've never broken a leg, you don't know how much you depend on your wife for *everything*. I can't go out in a squad, or chase down clues the way I should, but maybe I can help think. Another brain cell or two can't hurt, can it?"

"Here you go, Mike, put your brain cells to work on this pile," offered Mahoney, dropping a large stack of papers on Mike's desk. "That's the headless Somali case and any help you can give will be much appreciated. I'll make a deal with you. You think up a new question, and I'll chase down the answer."

"All right guys, it's nice to be back here. Let me check my voicemail and email first, I probably have a list a mile long. I'll read what looks important in this stack and come talk to you about where this case is going, Paul."

***

Paul went back to his office and looked at his own email inbox. *A message from the city about overtime, spam that had slipped past the department's filters, a reminder from the Chief about the staff meeting this afternoon, a message about ...*

Paul ran through the station to the Chief's office, interrupting a meeting between the Chief and an Assistant State's Attorney.

"Excuse my breaking in this way, Chief," Paul exclaimed hurriedly. "I just got an emailed warning that the station is going to be attacked tonight."

"Attacked?" shouted the Chief and the prosecutor at the same time.

"Remember that Somali we had a couple of weeks ago, Abdullah? He went home, eventually, and now he says he's heard about this plot. He thinks we were nice to him for not keeping him locked up and he wants to return the favor. He says the terrorist gang's boss Yahye is calling all his boys down here. He thinks that money is stored *here* somewhere and wants to break in and grab it. Abdullah says Yahye is staying 'at a place with bullfrogs' but he doesn't know what that means. I don't either."

"Is this for real?" asked the prosecutor.

"I think so," answered Paul.

"Then I better get back to my office and start alerting everybody with a badge in the state. Oh, boy! What a way to start the week!"

"I actually needed to finish that conversation, Paul," complained Chief Wenzel. "Well, if we're still here tomorrow, I'll ask him to come back. You believe this email. How much detail does he give?"

"An attack sometime tonight, probably with explosives. He doesn't say when exactly, or how many men Yahye has with him now. Not much to go on, I'm afraid. We should prepare as best we can."

"I don't really want to see the station house blown up. The city may not want to pay for a new one. What's this about 'bullfrogs'? How does anyone stay with bullfrogs? Is he hiding in a swamp?"

"When Chicago was first settled, there were some swamps, but they got drained. There may still be some small marshy areas around Chicagoland, but not any serious swamps that I know of. He's a foreigner and maybe he misheard the word. His English is pretty good, but still it's possible."

"Camp Bullfrog Lake," announced Mike wheeling himself in awkwardly. "I went to your office to tell you about my voicemail, and saw an email on your screen. It's a county forest preserve campground. I camped out there a couple of years ago. It's southwest of here. South of Burr Ridge, just south of the Des Plaines River and the ship canal."

"How would a bunch of Somali immigrants currently living in Minneapolis ever hear of such a place?" asked Paul.

"They do advertise a lot, especially with people who might be asked about a campground. Sam told me you've been hunting for these guys in all the motels. Maybe they decided to camp instead."

"I'll call the State's Attorney and fill her office in on this," added Chief Wenzel. "If they can put together a large enough task force, we can fight them at the camp instead of in town. Paul, send one of the more careful men with pictures of these guys we know about. Have him check out the campground as inconspicuously as he can."

Paul went back to his office and sent for Saunders. Sam Mahoney looked up curiously, not having heard any of the furor yet.

"Sergeant Saunders, let me congratulate you on passing the exam, getting your stripes, and even saving our Mr. Sorenson," Paul praised him. "I now have something dangerous for you. You know the people. You've seen their pictures and you've met them in person. We have a report that those Somali thugs may be hiding at a campground called Camp Bullfrog Lake. Mike can show you where it is.

"Go home and get into civvies. You're not a detective, but we're short of detectives with legs and this calls for discretion and disguise. Look around the place and try to spot any of that gang. Even one will be enough to confirm that's their hideout. Try not to be seen by them. When you rescued Sorenson you were in uniform. Maybe they won't recognize you out of uniform, but don't take any unnecessary chances."

"Yes, sir. Um, can I ask for help, sir? I just got these stripes today. I know a cop is expected to handle whatever comes his way on his own if he can. And just spying on these guys won't be hard or really dangerous. But if you want to know where their hideout is, it's got to be because you want to raid it. That means more men than we have here. It means the Sheriff's Police and probably the State Police. You want someone to work with them. I'm too new to do that. I don't feel confident saying 'no' or 'maybe' to a whole bunch of guys who outrank me."

"Let me go with him, Paul," suggested Mahoney. "The rest of the investigation is going to be on hold while we go after Yahye and his gang. You've got Mike back now to handle easy stuff here. And you know I don't mind telling brass hats where to go."

"All right, Sam. Despite your last remark, you also know how to coordinate with other agencies. You've got an unmarked car with a radio so keep us up to date. Both of you, use your cell phones to get pictures if you can. It would be useful to making plans if we know where these guys have their tents. If they're definitely not there call in for our next guess."

***

Bill Saunders looked at his closet. *I need something civilian that says "very much un-cop" boldly and obviously. Ordinary casual looks too straight arrow. Shorts are fine for the lower body. Maybe a rock t-shirt? Do Somali thugs know about rock music? What about that White Sox World Series Championship t-shirt? They don't know baseball either, probably. But I've worn that shirt so much the design is mostly rubbed off. And painting the bedroom in it last year didn't make it look any better. Ooh, neither does the rip. Perfect. Most casual thing I have. Sunglasses top it all off.*

"Ha, ha, ha!" laughed Mahoney when he saw Saunders. "Paul said get disguised and you sure did! That's great, Bill. We can't be seen together now, but we should be separate anyway. Less suspicious. If they think I'm a cop, they will *never* suspect you.

"I've been thinking about our approach to this. I will go into the office and ask where our targets are camped. The guy in charge may not know their real names, but I'll show their pictures. You come in five minutes later, and he tells both of us. I leave first and go back to the car. You head out to scout their area.

"Be careful walking about. Some of them have seen you, remember. They may not have got a good look while they were running out the back door at Sorenson's place, but some people have a good eye for faces. When you find their tents, find a secluded spot to take some pictures. See if you can get pictures of them too. We need to know how many of them are here now."

"Got it. Wish I had a dog. Walking a dog around the place would be great cover. I'll manage. Do you have any idea of the layout of this place?"

"No. Feltz has been there and he says the lake is about three hundred yards across, more or less. All the tenting areas are along the lake, with cabins farther back from the shore. He says we can get a map of the place at the office, which is the first building we'll come to from the highway."

***

The campground office was in the largest building at the site. Soda and snack machines guarded the front door. Inside were racks filled with information about tourist attractions nearby, a few chairs, and a counter. A smiling man stood behind the counter thinking about where he wanted to go for lunch. It was almost noon and he was getting hungry.

"I'm Detective Sergeant Sam Mahoney from the Berwyn Police Department, and I'd like to ask you about some of the people who are camping here."

"Berwyn? This is Willow Springs. Ain't you a bit far from home?"

"Yeah, I am. But this is important. I can get a local cop to come here and ask my questions if that makes you any happier. But it won't make *me* any happier, and I'll be sure to point out to him any deficiencies in your sanitary conditions, garbage handling, overcrowding, or whatever I can find. Or maybe you'll just cooperate because it's a nice day for cooperating."

"Geez, take it easy, man. I don't need any hassle. What do you want to know? I'll be right with you, sir, when I finish with this gentleman," he said to Saunders who had just walked in.

"He's with me, actually. We want to know about some black men camping here. They have probably been here a few weeks. They are Somalis, from Minnesota."

"There aren't any cars here with Minnesota plates, unless they're at the south end. I don't check on the cars normally. If someone pays the fees, I don't care where they're from. There *are* some black guys in the big cabins in the center. They had a tent here at this end of the campground for a couple of weeks but the end of last week another couple of guys showed up and they took a cabin. Then Saturday they took the other big cabin.

"I couldn't tell you if they're Somalis or not. What do they look like? These guys are just black guys. A couple of them have an odd accent, but that's all. They've stayed close to their cabins and haven't caused any trouble."

"Do they look like any of these pictures? Especially this one or this one?" Mahoney showed him his mug shots of the Somalis, emphasizing Hamza and Yahye.

"Yeah, this guy was here first. This other guy is the one who just arrived just a few days ago. I think I've seen a couple of these other fellows too. They don't come up to the office very often. They go out sometimes, and I guess they buy groceries when they do. But they leave our vending machines alone."

"Have you got a map of the campground? Two or three would be best."

"Yeah, here take what you need. Say, what's going on? You're cops. Are these guys wanted for something?"

"Should we tell him, Sam?" asked Saunders.

"We have to tell him sooner or later. These are serious criminals, part of a terrorist gang from Africa. They intend to attack the Berwyn Police Station tonight, which is why we are here now. My Chief is working with everyone else in Illinois law enforcement to put together a task force to take them down. We want to fight them here, with few civilians around, rather than in the middle of a city.

"At some point, when the cavalry is gathered together ready to come riding in, we will send a few men through the campground and evacuate the innocent campers. Bill, you know where to go looking. Get started now. I need to talk to this man some more. Excuse me, sir, I haven't asked your name. I'm sorry."

"Uh, I'm Bob Olson. We haven't got a lot of people staying here right now. It's been a cool, wet spring and the weather has only just lately turned nice. No one wants to go camping in the rain. These guys you're interested in, they've been here since the middle of June. Our rules say you can only stay six nights, but with the weather so bad I wasn't going to turn away paying customers. Park District or not, I want this place to pay its own way. I'm a taxpayer, too.

"We were busy over this weekend, but most of those people have left. I've got, uh, five tent sites rented out, all facing the lake. The only cabins in use are the ones you're interested in. Good thing you're here today. Fourth of July on Thursday is going to bring out a lot of campers, especially as it's going to be hot all week."

"That's good. Thank you, Mr. Olson. My partner is going to check on the cabins and try to get some pictures of them, and maybe the people. What are these cabins like inside? How much room, windows, stuff like that?"

"Here's a floor plan. One window in the small bedroom, and one on each side of the room with the bunk beds. The plan gives you some idea of the size and space inside. Not too bad for a bunch of kids, but for eight or ten adults it's a bit crowded. There's air-conditioning, and the windows have screens to keep out the mosquitoes."

"All right, I'm going back out to the entrance to link up with whoever is coming to do the raid. We will wait until they're ready before warning your other guests. One thing, though. Don't rent out any boats this morning. I don't want to have to try to get people in off the lake."

"Sure thing, Sergeant. Do you think there'll be a lot of shooting? I mean, I'll be out of here with everyone else, and there isn't a lot of stuff here to get shot up, really. But I'm kinda worried anyway."

"I wish I could give you a better answer, but I don't know. These are part of a Somali jihadist group, and are used to warfare back there in Somalia. They commit serious crimes here, too. They have guns and we've been told they have explosives as well. A lot will depend on how much surprise we can get on them."

"Oh, here, take a couple of these maps too then. They show all the trails through the woods around here. You can wander a fair distance in all directions through the forest. Maybe some of your men can use these trails. Here's one that goes right behind those cabins. Our map shows it, here, see."

"Thank you very much, Mr. Olson. Who do you report to? I'll put in a good word for you with your boss for your help."

***

The showers and restrooms for the campground were conveniently located in the middle of the grounds. Saunders found it was also convenient for taking pictures of the two large cabins the Somalis were in. He could stand at the corner and poke his phone around the edge. He saw one or two going in and out, taking a smoke break. He hadn't seen any "No Smoking" signs as they came into the grounds, but the park district probably didn't allow smoking in the cabins. He moved to some other spots and soon had a good selection of pictures of the cabins from almost every angle.

The door opened again and men started leaving the cabin. One went to the other cabin and said something. That cabin emptied also. They *were* empty, someone locked them up. The road through the campground made a big loop, and the men walked to the south end of the loop. There were no tents anywhere near that area. They were out in the open, alone, and no one could eavesdrop on them.

Clever, thought Saunders. *All very public and still very private. I'd love to be able to hear what they're saying, but there's no way I can get any closer. Take some pictures, and then go find Mahoney.*

***

Yahye waited for all the men to cluster about him. He didn't want to shout his orders. There may not be many people camping here, but any of them might talk to the police if they heard his plans.

"Mahmoud has told you what we are going to do. I have seen this police station. It is built of brick, but the doors are plate glass. They will not stop us. Gather around and look at this map. I drew it to show where we must go in. This area here is where we believe the money is stored, in the evidence locker. This room will be locked. It may have a chain link wall or bars to keep people out, but we can blow a hole in those.

"Hamza will go in through this door on the opposite side of the building. I could not very well ask the police for a guided tour of their building, so I have to guess about these things. Hamza's door may lead to a corridor across the back of the building to the evidence locker.

"I will go in through this door, on the same side as the evidence locker. This door may also lead to a corridor going to the evidence locker. We will each have six men with us, which should be more than enough to overpower any policemen who might be there late at night.

"Bashiir, you will take five men and go in the front door. There is a man at the desk in the lobby. Send in one man first as if to ask that man a question. When he is distracted, the rest should rush in and kill him. Find the radio room and kill anyone there. If they can't call for help, we have a better chance of success.

"Xidig, you are in charge of the suitcases. You and Mahmoud will stay by the cars. When we tell you which door to come through to get the money, bring the bags right away. We must pack the money into the cases as fast as possible. We don't know what sort of alarms they might have. We can't be certain that no one will stumble in upon us as we are at work. So we must not waste time.

"You all know each other. Do not hesitate to kill anyone else you see. Do not worry about the noise. This building is not close to many houses and late at night the people will be sleeping. We will attack at two in the morning. I want you all to go to sleep at eight tonight, so you will be fully rested for the attack. Are there any questions?"

"Who will take the money?"

"Hamza, note that man's name. He is too stupid to be part of our band," Yahye's voice dripped venom, menacingly. "I will take the money, of course. It will go into my car, with Mahmoud driving. No one else will ride with me. We have five cars and two vans and every driver will take his vehicle back, the riders can arrange themselves as they like. Now, are we done?"

His tone of voice meant, "We are done and don't think otherwise if you value your life." The meeting was over.

***

Saunders watched them all go back to the two cabins. A few stayed outside to smoke and chat, the rest went indoors. He walked back to the office and learned that Mahoney had taken his car back down the entrance drive. He walked a few hundred yards and found him talking to a State Trooper. Looking back over his shoulder he saw that trees blocked all view of the campground from here.

"Sergeant Bill Saunders, this is Captain Raul Olivera of the State Police," Mahoney introduced them. "Did you see anything interesting? How many are there, do you know?"

"There are twenty-three of them, in these two cabins," he told them, pointing to the spot on the map. "Despite the heat, they are mostly staying inside."

"Yeah, they have air-conditioning in the cabins," reported Mahoney.

"Once in a while someone comes out for a smoke break, but he goes back in. Right now, there's half a dozen outside smoking and talking. They do not seem interested in the rest of the campground. It's mostly empty and they probably feel that makes it safer for them.

"A little after I got into position, they all came out and went to the far end of the place, where they could see anyone who tried to listen in on them. The boss guy, this one, Yahye, talked to them for a while. He showed them a piece of paper, and pointed at it from time to time. Maybe a map of our police station.

"When he was done someone asked him something and it made him mad. I couldn't hear what he told that guy, but the man actually cringed. Yahye stalked back to his cabin. I couldn't see any weapons, but there are cars parked right by the cabins. Here's the photos I shot, Sam. Who do I send them to?"

"This inter-agency work is always complicated where it should be simple," commented Olivera. "You have your office's email on your phone already. Send copies there, and they'll distribute to the rest of us. Keep the originals on your phone, so we can study them here.

"I've got my boys back up the road a bit including a small SWAT team, and we've got a SWAT team coming in from Fifth District, that's the biggest one outside Chicago. When the local departments heard of an attack planned on Berwyn's station house, they all wanted in on the job. We can't use that many men, and some haven't had any training for something like this. Chicago is sending its SWAT team as well. Three trained SWAT teams and a lot of regular cops should be enough."

"Twenty-three of them is going to be a serious challenge," observed Mahoney. "If we can catch them off guard, we might be able to trap them inside the cabins. Tear gas should force them out gasping for air, and make it easier to arrest them. Is the air-conditioning going to have any effect on the tear gas?"

"It might help disperse it, but it's a windy day and we'll have to break the windows to get the gas inside. Open windows on a windy day will let the gas blow out. We can still dump enough gas in to give them problems.

"The State Police SWAT team isn't all that big, and they cover the whole state. We've got half a dozen men available today, but the other teams are bigger. I want them to work out a joint plan they think will work and give me their opinions. You can offer your suggestion, Sergeant Mahoney, but it's still their decision. Well, in the end, it's my decision as captain. But I usually take a SWAT commander's advice."

Olivera's phone rang and he stepped aside to talk. He hung up and told Mahoney and Saunders "Fifth District SWAT team just showed up. I want to bring all three team leaders here to check out the area. I've got the aerial photo from Google Maps, the camp's maps, your pictures. We can sneak through these trees to get a closer view too. Then they can go make their plans. I'll be back in a bit."

"What are we going to be doing in all this, Sam?" asked Saunders. "I've only got my service revolver with me, and I forgot to get any extra ammo when I changed clothes. I'm willing to go in with the rest, but I feel a bit unprepared."

"I've got my revolver too, and a shotgun and bullet proof vest in my trunk. But I'm not thinking about doing anything but providing backup. That's what I did during the shoot-out in Chicago with the art thieves. We have trained men to make the raid, and we should *not* pretend we are their equals. It's a little embarrassing for a cop to say he isn't up to any challenge, but sometimes it's true.

"You haven't been on the force all that long. We haven't had anyone killed in the line of duty for a few years. But I remember the ones who died. We all do. And I remember their widows. The last thing I ever want to have to do again is tell one more woman that her husband died a hero. We'll do what they ask us to do, and hope *they* take most of the risk. What was it the cop said in *The Untouchables*? Our first duty is to go home alive at the end of our shift."

Olivera returned and three other men in body armor got out of his car. Olivera made the introductions.

"Sergeant Bill Saunders and Detective Sergeant Sam Mahoney, Berwyn Police. Lieutenant Max Schwarz, Fifth District SWAT. Lieutenant Tomaso Garcia, State Police SWAT. Lieutenant Rich Morales, Chicago SWAT."

"Hiya, Rich, nice to see you again," Mahoney greeted him.

"Got another shoot-out for us, huh?" asked Morales with a grin. "I thought Berwyn was such a quiet town, too."

"We're going to have to walk back along this drive a bit," explained Olivera. "The trees give us good cover here, but the office blocks our view of the cabins the terrorists are in. From the bend up ahead, we should be able to see the cabins and the rest of the campground.

"Here, you can see it's all pretty flat and open. Those two big cabins are the ones we want. You can see everything from here with your binoculars. This map shows a trail passing right behind these cabins, and there are other trails in the area. There are a lot of recreational spots in these woods, all connected by these trails. Tell them your suggestion, Mahoney."

"Well, it's just an idea, but if we can sneak up on them unexpectedly, we can trap them inside the cabins. Toss in some tear gas and they won't be in any condition to fight back."

"Not a bad idea," agreed Garcia. "Uh, oh, there's someone coming out."

"Yeah, they sometimes come out to smoke, then go back in," explained Saunders.

"All right, let's go back and make some plans. Can we ask you two Berwyn cops to take care of evacuating the civilians? We won't be making our move for at least half an hour, probably, but it's best to start them moving early in case they balk. Try to send them out one at a time, too. We'll direct them to a safe spot to wait."

***

"Nobody's going to steal your belongings," declared Saunders as patiently as he could. Four of the campers had been startled when they were asked to leave, but they hadn't argued. The fifth camper and his girl friend were reluctant to go anywhere.

"Your stuff will be here, safe and sound. The whole area will be crawling with cops in a little bit. We just want you to leave because there may be a lot of shooting, and we don't want you getting hurt."

"Just leave us alone, why doncha? We aren't anywhere near those cabins. We'll be okay. Just go away and let us be."

Saunders sniffed the air and commented, "No one will go after your stash, either. We aren't interested in what you're smoking. All we want to do is keep you safe. We want to take these men down without a big gun battle, but if one breaks out, we won't be able to protect you. And canvas won't stop bullets. Leave your stuff here and it will still be here when you come back. Everything. Or would you rather get busted now? Your choice. I don't care as long as I get you out of danger."

The couple got into their car and left, looking back to make sure Saunders wasn't digging through their gear. He watched them go and looked around. *Everyone was cleared out and the men in the cabins had apparently not noticed anything happening. Good. Now to join Sam covering the exit.*

***

"All right, everyone's here finally," directed Captain Olivera. "Get all your men together and we'll brief them on the plan. Listen up, men, this is a different sort of police raid. We're not soldiers, we're policemen. Our job, here as elsewhere, is to serve arrest warrants on suspects. We have warrants on some of these men, so this is a proper, legal raid, but it will not be a normal raid.

"They are Somalis, which means they are black. We all know how the news media can blow things out of proportion when black men get killed by the police. Don't kill them all recklessly. Don't risk your own lives by trying *not* to kill them. Wound them, capture them, kill them if you have to, but be able to justify it.

"These men are not ordinary criminals. They aren't gang bangers or drug dealers who will surrender so their lawyers can get them off. These men are members of a Somali terrorist organization.   These are men who think of themselves as soldiers, warriors for Allah. They are fanatic and will very likely not want to surrender. Not without a serious fight anyway.

"Sergeant Saunders, come here. This young man, despite his appearance, is actually a cop, and has just won this year's 'best undercover disguise' contest. He is a Berwyn cop, and has been keeping an eye on the terrorists' cabins. Sergeant, I would like to ask you to continue keeping an eye on them. Are you willing to go back to your hiding place and let us know when all of these men are indoors? And to take video with your phone? I want video evidence that *we* did not start any fighting."

"Yes, sir, I can do that. I've got good cover there, so I should be safe."

"Thank you. All the rest of you have body cams. I want them turned on now. Garcia, you've got the smallest team, so you go through the woods and come out right behind the cabins right here. Schwarz, you go with Garcia on the same trail, but you go longer and come out farther south on this trail. Use these trees as cover and get as close as you can to the cabins. The near one has two windows facing that side, so be careful.

"Morales, you have the biggest and most experienced team. You get to knock on the front door. I want you waiting in this area here, just outside the camp. Schwarz, you will call Saunders when you get in position. Garcia will be set by then too. Saunders will let us know when they're all inside. As soon as he gives the word, Morales, you race down the road to the cabins. Get out, take up defensive positions, and tell them to come out with their hands up. Just like the movies.

"And just like all the action movies, I don't expect them to come out meekly. We'll keep demanding they come out but we'll do nothing aggressive. When they shoot, and I think they will, I want Garcia and Schwarz to toss the tear gas in through the windows and block the back doors. These windows will be closed with the air-conditioning on, and they all have screens. You may have to slash the screens before smashing the windows and tossing in the gas. Be careful.

"They are jihadists, terrorists. They fought in Somalia. They will fight here. Expect them to fight back, even with the tear gas. I don't think they'll have gas masks, but they may try to tough it out. Don't give them any targets. Is everyone clear about his job? Then let's do this."

Chapter Sixteen

The Battle of Bullfrog Lake

Saunders made his way back into the campground carefully. He used the trees along the entrance road to cover his approach to the office. He had seen the front of the cabins, and knew they each had a skinny slit window next to the door. He considered his route and decided to go from the far side of the office to the lake, then along the shore until he was opposite the bathhouse. That would then provide cover for the last stretch, up to his lookout spot on the bathhouse corner.

One man had been outside smoking as Saunders maneuvered himself into position, but he had ignored Saunders completely. After a few minutes he went back inside. Saunders got out his phone and made sure he had a good view of both cabins. He could see both front doors easily, and had an angled view of the south windows in both cabins. *Not perfect, but it will have to do.*

Fifteen minutes later he saw a man in body armor sneaking around the edge of the woods behind the cabins. *Okay, that must be one of Garcia's men. I won't be able to see Schwarz's men from here, but they're supposed to call when they're in position. Here's the call now.*

"Saunders? Schwarz here, we're set."

"Good, everyone is inside right now. I'll call Morales and we'll get this thing rolling."

"Lieutenant Morales, everyone is in place, and the suspects are all indoors. It's all yours, sir."

***

Mahoney watched the SWAT trucks, civilian APCs really, speed quietly down the road. He was with the other officers from Berwyn, guarding the road out of the camp. A small wall at the entrance created a choke point that was easy to guard. Other police departments were fanning out through the woods, behind the SWAT teams to block any exit that way. *Great,* thought Mahoney, *all these suburban cops wandering in the woods. I hope they do some good. Hell, I hope they don't get lost.*

Morales had no worry about getting lost. The road went past the office and curved around toward the target cabins. He told his drivers to park on both sides of the cabins, leaving an opening for Saunders to film through. His men jumped out of their vehicles and took up positions behind their vehicles and the others parked there. He picked up his bullhorn and shouted "This is the police. We have warrants for the arrest of Yahye, Hamza, Bashiir, and Xidig. Please come out at once with your hands in the air."

***

"WHAT! Police? Why are they here?" shouted Yahye angrily. "How did they find us here? Who told them we were here? Did any of you betray me? Tell me now and I will kill you mercifully!"

"No one talked, Yahye," claimed Xidig, trying to control his leader's temper. "We would all be arrested. Who would want that? Does it matter how they found us? If someone betrayed us we can wait to find out who did it later. Now we must think of a plan to get away from here. Look, they are all around our cars. How can we escape without them?"

"We could go out the back door," suggested Bashiir. "We can go through the forest, there is a trail right behind us. We will have to steal other cars, but we can get away."

"That is not good, but it is safer than fighting our way to our cars," agreed Yahye. "Check the back door, Bashiir. Make sure it is safe. Xidig, call Hamza in the other cabin and tell him what we are going to do. The rest of you, get your weapons ready."

Bashiir opened the back door and saw three men in body armor half concealed in the trees. One man was pointing a rifle at the door. Bashiir pulled out his pistol and shot twice at the man. Then he slammed the door and locked it.

"They are waiting for us out back too," he told Yahye. "We are trapped in here!"

"You are surrounded. Come out with your hands up." The bullhorn boomed its warning again.

"Do not panic, fool," yelled Yahye. "You have been in battles before, back home, and against the police in Minneapolis. You have always survived, as have all of us. I do not like being enclosed like this, but the walls give us shelter. They cannot see us, so they cannot shoot at us. We can shoot at them from the windows. They are in the open and that makes them easy targets."

Hamza was listening to Xidig talking about going out the back when he heard the gunfire from the other cabin. The renewed call to surrender made him decide to break out the front way. He could see a dozen police there, but he didn't know how many might be in the woods. And could they find their way out of the woods in any event?

Hamza opened the front door and fired at a man hiding behind the nearest police truck. His first shot missed, but his second may have hit the man. A dozen bullets were fired back at him and he shut the door.

***

"All right, they are shooting at us, time for us to fire back," ordered Olivera on his radio. "Let's get that tear gas into those cabins now. Keep under cover, and take your time to make aimed shots. Remember, we want live prisoners, but don't be too obsessive about that. Wounded counts as alive."

SWAT team members were already in place, crouched below the windows on both sides of the cabins. At the order, they stood up, one slashed the screen and broke the glass, the other tossed in two tear gas canisters. Finished, they pulled back to a safer position to watch the buildings.

Smoke poured out of the windows, but more was visible inside. Three windows to a cabin, and each window had been hit with two gas canisters.

The buildings were full of tear gas, and the windows weren't broken enough to let it all out.

Lieutenant Schwarz had arranged his men in a line across the back of the most southerly cabin. With no window at the rear, he knew they couldn't see his men and positioned them in trees on both sides and two even right at the back door. The door opened suddenly and a man ran out. One of the two cops tripped him and he fell. Someone inside saw what had happened, fired two shots, then pulled the door closed again. A faint click indicated the door was now locked.

The man on the ground was trying to get up, but the man who had tripped him had also jumped onto his back. A brief scuffle and the man's gun was knocked away. The second cop produced handcuffs and bound their prisoner. They brought him to Schwarz, while two others took their place.

***

"Hamza, they are behind us as well as in front," revealed Yahye on his phone.

"I know. Cabdi tried to run away out the back and he was captured. What are we to do, Yahye? Some of my men cleaned and loaded their rifles earlier and put them back in the cars for tonight. We all have pistols, and seven still have rifles. We have ammunition but how can we break out?"

"I have the explosives. I will keep some for the evidence locker tonight, but I can make two bombs with the rest. Get your men ready. When I have made the bombs, Xidig will call you again and we will all rush out the back doors. Before these policemen can shoot at us, Bashiir and I will throw our bombs at them. We can then run into the woods. You have been here longer, Hamza. Which direction should we go when we get into the forest?"

"One day when we couldn't find the money and I was frustrated, I went walking in the forest. After a short while I came out of the woods and there was a road with traffic on it. If we go west, we should find that road. It was less than a mile, I think. Maybe half a mile, even."

"All right, we will do that. Tell your men. Give me five minutes to prepare the bombs. Don't go out until Xidig calls you."

"Filsan, take that Uzi and get in the doorway. Lie on the floor and when I open the door, spray all those cops out there. Let me tie this rope to the door handle. There, fire away."

Filsan fired off two full clips of ammunition before Hamza pulled the door closed again. The police were forced to duck even lower than they had been. They had fired into the open doorway while they could, before the flood of bullets forced them into hiding, but they didn't have any easy targets.

Hamza didn't care about that. *I can lose a man if I have to, as long as the police are distracted. They will now think we are trying to soften them up to go out the front way. Our cars are there, they must suspect we want to get our cars. So they won't be looking quite so hard out the back.*

***

"What the hell! Where did they get a Tommy gun?" roared Olivera, crouched next to Morales.

"It's just an Uzi," Morales consoled the trooper. "I recognize the sound, very distinctive."

"Just an Uzi! Ha! Just as dead if it hits you! I think we've waited long enough, Lieutenant. Crash one of these tanks of yours into the front of that cabin. Do the same to the other, just for good measure."

Over his radio he ordered "All you men, get ready to rush inside once the doors are breached! You men at the rear, be ready to keep them locked inside."

Schwarz sent some more of his men to the back door of the south cabin and set others to watch the side windows on both. Garcia brought his men up to the blind back door of the north cabin. He brought a four foot length of branch he had found on the ground, intending to use it to block the door.   Just as he was about to wedge it in place, the door sprang open and two men rushed out.

Yahye and Bashiir were surprised to find the police on the doorstep. Bashiir had seen them hiding in the woods, not waiting for them so close by. Yahye threw his bomb to the south, where he could see other policemen surrounding Hamza's cabin.

Bashiir merely dropped his bomb as he and Yahye ran. He thought they would get away from the blast and that it would kill all the police at the door. But he forgot that the rest of his friends were coming out behind him. The bomb went off as Yahye and Bashiir reached the trees. It was powerful, but not as powerful as Yahye had imagined. Three policemen fell to the ground, and four terrorists who had just rushed out and were right on top of the bomb.

The other bomb landed near some of Schwarz's men, but Yahye's toss was wild. The bomb only wounded some and diverted their attention from Hamza's exit. But Schwarz had more men than Garcia and most of them were away from the blast. They began firing at the terrorists fleeing past them. The terrorists were shooting back and the scene quickly became a shambles. The terrorists had thirty yards to go to get to the tree line, with no cover. Five fell before they could make it.

The SWAT trucks broke the front of the cabins into kindling and pulled back to let the police on foot get inside. The cabins were quickly turning into scenes of utter chaos. Tear gas still swirled in the air, not that the police minded, since they had gas masks. Somalis were crowded into the bunk rooms trying to get out the back doors and firing shots wildly at the police in front and behind them. The police had no trouble with targeting. The ones coming in the front saw only terrorists squeezing out the back doors. The ones in back saw only panicky Somalis pushing out the back doors. A few managed to force their way through the police lines and escape into the woods.

Five minutes of intense shooting and confusion had finally ended. Olivera walked into the north cabin and looked about. Three men were on the floor, dead or wounded, four more just outside the back door. Two men who seemed unharmed were being handcuffed. He went out the back, stepping gingerly over the wounded men in the doorway. Three policemen were down, too. Medics were already treating them, and taking one off on a stretcher with speed.

The south cabin was pretty much the same. Five men shot outside, two of whom were being covered over. Two more dead inside, and another pair of prisoners. He went back outside and the SWAT team commanders came up.

"I've got three men wounded by that bomb, one pretty badly," reported Garcia.

"I've got two wounded, but not badly," advised Schwarz. "They were farther from the bomb blast."

"I only had two men wounded out front," noted Morales. "One man hit in the arm early by a rifle, and another hit by a ricochet from that Uzi."

"What about the Somalis?" asked Olivera. "How many can we account for? Did any get away?"

The sound of gunshots from the woods seemed to provide an answer to that question. Olivera punched a number into his phone.

"Pete, send a couple of the local backup squads south down Archer. We seem to have some suspects who got into the woods. I can hear gunfire and maybe they're being handled. But I don't want to take a chance on any of these guys getting away. Archer runs straight along here, so anyone crossing is going to be easy to spot."

A long, loud staccato burst of gunfire made them look at the woods again.

"That's the Uzi again," observed Morales. "So he got out. Let me check out the body count for the rest."

"Garcia, you don't need to stay with us," directed Olivera. "You had the smallest crew and took the worst damage. Go take care of your men, and thank them for me, please.

"Lieutenant Schwarz, have your men help get the wounded Somalis out of the cabins. They can't be treated there."

***

Mahoney found Saunders still sitting at the corner of the bathhouse.

"How are you doing, Bill?" he asked. "Was it bad up here? I couldn't see anything from where I was, but it sounded awful."

"Yeah, it got really hairy for a while. Some guy opened up on us with a full auto gun of some sort and then they set off a couple of bombs. And then Olivera turned the SWAT boys loose on them. Oh, man, I don't ever want those guys mad at me! I'm okay. A bit scared, to tell you the truth. I was safe here, but I've never seen a shoot out, except in the movies, and those aren't real. This was. Scary, but I am okay. Really."

"Well, send your video to headquarters now. The news media will want to know all about this, and we need to show who shot first. Damn, they're still shooting out there someplace in the trees! Nothing for us to worry about now. The Chief wants us back as soon as Olivera is through with us, so let's go find him and ask for permission to go home. We started this party but someone else gets to clean up."

***

"Captain, out of twenty-three terrorists, we count four killed, ten wounded, five captured but not wounded," said Lieutenant Schwarz. That leaves four unaccounted for. We've been matching them to the pictures you gave us, and it looks like Yahye, Hamza, Bashiir and one other got away. We didn't have pictures on all these guys. We may be able to get the other's name by interrogating the survivors."

***

"La Grange isn't all that close to here, Captain, but they offered a big detachment and we put them in the woods behind here," commented Lieutenant Morales. "They were doing all that shooting earlier. They called in to say they have one dead, two wounded in custody, and the guy with the Uzi got away. They had three of their own wounded. They should be coming in soon."

"Thanks for the report, Lieutenant. So there's only one left on the loose. One with a sub-machine gun, but if he's alone someone should be able to pick him up. Oh, hello, Mahoney. We've got some pretty good news for you. Only one guy got away, so I think your station house will be safe tonight."

"That's wonderful, Captain. Do we know which one got away?"

"No. We know that Yahye, Hamza, and Bashiir got away earlier with another man. All I know just now is that the one with the Uzi got away, but one of the others is dead and the other two are in custody."

"Whose custody are all these men going into?" asked Mahoney. "I don't really care because the county will try them no matter who holds them. But I might want to question some of them. Hamza and Bashiir are wanted for a killing I'm working on. And Yahye tried to torture a man in Berwyn."

"So many departments helped with this, and so few have the capacity to hold all the prisoners that we're just going to send them all to the County Jail. That all right with you?"

"Oh, sure, just curious. I knew you didn't go through all of this as part of a catch and release program. Lieutenant Morales, Bill says you did a great job with your rams. I'm sorry I missed it. I'll be sure to watch the videos."

"Do that, they should be pretty exciting. Nice to work with you again."

"Captain, do you need Saunders and me for anything else?" asked Mahoney. "We haven't been doing all that much anyway. Well, *he* was, but not me. If we're through, we'd like to get home."

"Yeah, take your men and go. The State Police forensic team will be here soon to process the cabins. The ambulances are loading up. We really have nothing for you to do. Take care. And thanks for your help, Sergeant Saunders. You did well today."

**

Filsan got to the edge of the woods after wandering lost for an hour. *Where am I? How am I going to get back to Minneapolis? I've got my Uzi but with very little ammunition. I need a car. I can find my way north with a car. I have a dangerous gun. Even if it is almost empty it will scare someone into giving me his car. Which way should I go, east or west? Chicago is east of here, I think, and it is full of police. So I should go west, away from the police.*

Peering out from the edge of the forest, he saw a couple of squads sitting on the side of the road, apparently keeping watch for anyone escaping from the fight. That settled his plans. *Stay inside the tree line and go west, away from those policemen.*

After a while he felt safe enough to walk on the shoulder of the road. He walked down the road for a long while, carrying his Uzi at his side, away from the road. Nothing but woods on this side of the road, so no one could see it. Cars went past him in both directions, but they went by fast. The drivers showed no interest in stopping for him. He kept on walking, hoping to find a car that was stopped somewhere. Another half hour of walking brought him to a building set back a bit from the road, behind a wall bearing the sign St. James Catholic Church.

Catholic Church? Where's the steeple? Churches have steeples like mosques have minarets. But there is a parking lot. Maybe there is a car I can steal.

There was, and he didn't even have to show his gun. He had stolen cars in Minneapolis and this one was easy to break into and start. He left the parking lot and turned west again. Up ahead he saw a busy road going north. North was where Minneapolis was, and he turned quickly. He turned too quickly, missing the red light. Worse, he missed, figuratively and literally, the ambulance speeding through the intersection. Worst of all, he missed seeing the squad following the ambulance.

The policeman in the squad decided the ambulance was doing fine, but that rude drivers should be given nice fat tickets. He flipped on his lights and siren and went after the small car. It sped up, so did he. The small car turned off down a ramp and turned right. The cop smiled. He knew this area and it seemed the other driver did not. There was a way out, but a stranger would get caught before he could find the exit. He kept on the small car's tail and called for backup.

He chased the small car into a truck repair lot and trapped it. The driver got out with an Uzi in his hands, and pointed it at the squad. The cop ducked beneath his dash and made a more urgent call for backup. He peeked over the dash to see the man he had chased so casually coming toward him. The gun was still pointing at him.

I can't out-shoot that thing. If he gets closer, I'm dead. I haven't even got room to turn around and run. One chance. Shoot first and hope for the best. Dear God, please bless this bullet.

He drew his pistol, sat up, took a second to aim, and fired through the open window. Whether it was really blessed, or because the range was so short, the bullet hit the gunman between the eyes. He had been raising his sub-machine gun to fire it and just fell in a heap. The cop uttered a prayer of thanks, got his shaking under control, and stepped out of his squad. He kicked the Uzi away from the man on the ground. He knew the man was dead, but procedure said to kick the gun away. Two backup squads showed up, sirens blaring.

"What's the fuss, Bert? You made it sound like you were facing Dillinger or Capone. And here you are just standing around calm as can be."

"Yeah, look at that, Willy," Bert said, pointing to the gun. "He was coming for me with that. I didn't want to find out if he was serious. He looked serious. That was good enough for me."

"Wow! Is that an Uzi! I've never seen one in person before. Where did he get that?" asked Willy. "Damn good shot, too, Bert. Right between the eyes. That is some shooting! Good for you!"

The radioed report about a sub-machine gun brought more local police and two State Police squads. The State Police officers photographed the entire area, concentrating on the dead Somali and his weapon.

"This guy was involved in a big shoot-out in the woods east of here," declared Captain Olivera. "We will let you take the body and process the scene. But we're taking the Uzi. The Feds will want it and I'll turn it over to them. Who's the marksman who drilled this guy?"

"That's me, sir," admitted Bert. "He came off Archer onto 83, running a red light, almost hitting an ambulance I was escorting. I chased him down here and trapped him in this dead-end. He came at me waving that damned gun and I got real scared. I prayed, shot, and got him. That's all I know."

"Your lucky day, Bert, twice over," remarked Willy. "He didn't kill you and you might get a reward for bagging him."

***

"It's all over, Chief," reported Mahoney when he and Saunders returned to the station house. "Everyone of the Somalis is accounted for, except one. He's got a sub-machine gun, but he's also on his own and a long way from home. No raid tonight, or ever, probably. Bill did a great job as chief spy. Did you see his video of the bust? Steady hand through it all."

"Geez, Sam, you've been acting like I did something fantastic all the way back. Chief, I did my duty. They gave me a job I didn't really want, but I did it. That's what we're supposed to do, isn't it?"

"Yes, it is. But we can still make a fuss over really good 'doing your duty.' We can't give you a medal for today, but we can pat the hell out of your back. Accept it with grace, Bill, it doesn't happen all that often."

"I don't know if they told you yet, but Captain Olivera said the prisoners are all going to County. Yahye, Hamza, and Bashiir tried escaping with another guy. One got away, one was killed, the other two were cuffed. I don't know who was which, though."

"I got a call from Olivera just a little bit ago," mentioned Paul Radcliffe, coming into the Chief's office. "Yahye is dead, and Hamza and Bashiir were badly wounded, but will survive long enough for trial. I still haven't heard about the fourth man. I think we'll get him soon enough."

"That wraps up the whole case then," declared Mahoney. "We have the killers and we have the witnesses to convict them."

"Yeah, but we still don't have the money," countered Radcliffe. "Here's a funny thing too. This morning we were all so worked up by Abdullah's email that we ignored Mike. He came into the Chief's office with that bit about the campground, remember? He had been looking for me and had seen my email. But he wanted to talk to me about *his* email, or, rather, voicemail.

"After you went off he finally got his chance to talk to me. He had a voicemail from Angela Maguire, from the end of last week. She thinks she had seen Zahi, by himself, coming out of a building on Stanley and Oak Park Avenue in early June. I sent Gomez over to check it out and he came back empty handed. No obvious clues of any sort. No one there knows anything about Zahi, or even Somalia."

"Hmmm, three weeks ago," mused Mahoney. "Was that right before he was killed, or earlier in that week? Could he have gone there to hide the money?"

"Damn you, Sam!" growled Mike Feltz. "I should have thought of that. My brain is getting rusty sitting at home so long."

"No, Mike, you just haven't been thinking about nothing but millions of dollars for the last month. You hear Zahi went somewhere, and you're thinking about his social life. I hear he went somewhere and I wonder if he could have hid the money there. I'm in a rut."

"I'll call her in the morning and see what else she remembers about the incident," offered Feltz. "It's probably nothing, but I'll feel better if I follow this mini-clue up myself."

***

"Yes, I'm Angela Maguire. Who is this?"

"I'm Sergeant Mike Feltz of the Berwyn Police Department. You left a message for me last week. I've been out of the office for a few weeks with a broken leg. I'm only now getting back to light work, so I didn't get your message until yesterday. If you've seen the news today, you know we were pretty busy yesterday. But I would like to talk to you about your call. Can you come into the office here for a short talk later in the day? Eleven would be fine. I'll see you then. Thank you."

Angela walked into the Homicide unit area, and was waved into Radcliffe's office. She looked from Radcliffe, to Mahoney, and then to Feltz in his wheelchair. And there was Officer Durkin, who took notes for the police. They looked all set for a serious discussion.

"I wasn't expecting the ..." began Angela. "Never mind, that joke gets overused anyway. But all three of you. I don't think I have enough of a clue for even one of you."

"We're bored today," explained Mahoney. "The men who killed Zahi and Bilan were killed or captured yesterday. The captured ones are too badly wounded to be questioned today, so we have nothing to do."

"And I had forgotten what your clue might be a clue to," confessed Feltz. "We have the killers, but we are still looking for the money they were after. Sam reminded me last night that you might have a clue to where the money is. Do you?"

"Really? I think I saw Zahi on the street almost a month ago. Inspector Radcliffe showed me his picture after you finally identified him. It looked like him, I guess. Not like most of the black people I see every day in town. I didn't connect the face and the memory until the other day. That's it. That's all I know."

"You say you saw him leaving a building at Oak Park and Stanley," asked Radcliffe. "Which corner was it?"

"She said it was the northeast corner, Paul," interjected Feltz.

"That's right, thanks for reminding me. Gomez checked it out and couldn't learn anything. He *is* a rookie cop and maybe didn't ask the right questions, or the right person. I drove past there this morning. There's a cafe right on the corner, a barber shop just north on Oak Park, and a tavern and a dentist just east on Stanley. Which one was he coming out of?"

"None of them, Inspector. He was coming out of a door on the Stanley Avenue side. I don't know the number, but it wasn't one of the businesses."

"Sam, see if Gomez checked for apartments there. Are you sure it wasn't the cafe or the tavern?"

"Yes, the cafe is right on the corner. The tavern door is on the end of the building. It's right next to the next building which has the dentist. I've lived in Berwyn all my life, so I know the town inside out. What made this stick in my mind was that an old family friend, Jack Sorenson, used to have an apartment there."

"Sorenson again. Mike, if I never hear that name again, I'll be ever so happy," grumbled Radcliffe.

"Oh, you must be talking about Sorenson," commented Mahoney coming back in. "Gomez says he checked all the businesses and there are two doors, one on each side, which may go up to apartments, but they were locked. No one answered when he knocked. And he says he knocked a lot. What's Sorenson doing in this story?"

"A few years ago I had the flu, so did the whole family, but I had it worst," explained Angela. "He was giving me a ride to the hospital and stopped at that corner to pick something up. He went in on the Stanley Avenue side and came right back out. He called it his 'secret lair.' He likes being melodramatic sometimes."

"Okay, Sam, still think Sorenson isn't holding out on us?" asked Radcliffe.

"I know where Sorenson lives. That's where we arrested one of the thieves in May and where Yahye tortured him. And that's not this address. He does have other apartments; he's told us so. I know of only one other address, and this isn't it either. And he's told us he doesn't like his clients to know where he lives. Coincidence?"

"Since when have you started to believe in coincidence? Should we bring him in for another talk?"

"That's going to be difficult," revealed Mahoney. "You were at the wedding, too. He's gone off to Paris and won't be home for another couple of weeks. Nice for him, not so much for us. Mike, I'm going to be back working with Phyllis next week, so you'll have to remember to give him a call."

"Thank you, Ms. Maguire, for your information," declared Radcliffe. "I would appreciate it if you would sign your statement when Officer Durkin has printed it out."

"If Sorenson is involved somehow, why didn't she see him at the same time?" asked Feltz after Angela left. "We're supposing Zahi gives him the money to hide there. But it's not Sorenson's regular home. So if he stashes the money there, why doesn't he come out at the same time as Zahi? If I gave somebody ten million bucks to hold for me, I'd prefer he left when I did. I have to trust him, but it'd be easier to trust him if he wasn't lingering behind."

"That's a good point, Mike," agreed Radcliffe. "I've had my doubts about Sorenson's honesty, but Sam thinks he's mostly trustworthy. And I've been moving that way myself. And Ms. Maguire said he stopped there with her a few years ago. What if he gave up that apartment? No, we're just guessing now. We'll have to wait until he comes home to talk to him. Make a note on your calendar, Mike."

Chapter Seventeen

What's Behind the Door?

"I loved the Bastille Day parade yesterday," commented Jack. "Everyone waving tricolors, singing *La Marseillaise*, passing bottles of wine around. And fireworks as good as we'd have seen in Chicago for the fourth, if we'd stayed home. A very pleasant way to end our honeymoon."

"We took off late this morning, flew for more than eight hours, and it's still just the middle of the afternoon," sighed Marcy tiredly. "I love to travel, but the disconnect between body time and local time is always hard on me."

"I agree, darling, but the alternatives are to stay home (which I don't want to do) or take a ship," Jack pointed out. "I've never done an Atlantic crossing by ship. Might be fun, but there's no sight-seeing for the week it takes to cross, or the week coming back. Nothing but ocean. Seems to be a waste of time."

"It wouldn't be a waste of time to spend two weeks just with you, dear. That would be rather enjoyable, in fact."

"Oh, yes! Two weeks alone with you. We should have thought about that for our honeymoon. But we're closing on our house in two days, which means a sea-going honeymoon would have left us no time for Paris. That would have been horrid. We can always do an oceanic second honeymoon."

"Oh, how long do we have to wait for a second honeymoon, Jack?"

"I checked the rule book, The Official Rules of Everything, and it says there is no minimum time required between first and second honeymoons. The only requirement is that there must have been a first honeymoon."

"Silly man!"

***

"I wish we could have had the house ready to move into when we came home from Paris," confessed Marcy as they maneuvered around each other in her cluttered apartment.

"It's just five weeks since our offer was accepted," Sorenson reminded her. "That's fast in the realty world. It was only three weeks from our offer on the house until our wedding. Three weeks would have been incredibly fast. We could have had the closing sooner, but we were in Paris, and you didn't want to leave. Nor did I. We can survive being cramped in your apartment for a week."

"That's true, and I still have knick-knacks and clothes and I-don't-know-what-all to finish packing. You have to move some stuff, too, you said. A week, though. I just want it to be over and have us all moved in. It's silly, I know. Things won't happen sooner just because we want them to. What's the schedule? We close late tomorrow. By then we should be finished with all our last minute packing."

"The painters take possession on Thursday," revealed Jack. "They've told us it should take two days to paint everything except the basement rooms. That's Thursday and Friday, with the basement next Monday."

"Which means we can start moving in Saturday. The furniture store can deliver the bed and dressers then, and we can take residence. Oooh, it's so close after all! Darling, once we've finished packing and can't get at anything anymore, do you want to go to a hotel for the rest of the week?"

"Yes, that's a good idea. Some of our friends have been offering to put us up, but most of a week is a long visit, even for close friends. While you gather your belongings today, I will go take care of my various outposts. I don't have a lot of furnishings worth keeping in them, but I need to mark the few pieces I want to keep and the ones for the Salvation Army. I should be back by one."

***

Sorenson dropped the two large boxes in his arms on top of a pile of boxes already crowding Marcy's living room floor. He looked around and found her on the floor of her studio, folding a new box into shape and taping it. The table was already covered in boxes and offered no space for making a new box.

"I have labeled everything in my apartments for the movers," he reported. "All except my little office, which came furnished with a desk and chair. I added a cot and a hot plate just in case I had to hole up there, and they are now in a resale shop. The only things I needed from there are my ledgers and tax records: two boxes, now on top of your big stack in the other room. Some of the older items went into my safe deposit box.

"Do you need any help from me here? I notice you are still building boxes. Do you want me to help gather things to fill them?"

"Yes, that would let me finish ever so much sooner. Everything in that closet in the left corner. Lots of books, some CDs and DVDs. I've already gotten most of it put away, but I think two more loads should take care of it all. And then I'll be done, too."

Jack helped her empty shelves and fill boxes, and they chatted while they worked. Newlyweds, but old friends, they didn't have a lot of personal discovery to do. They each knew there would need to be adjustments to the way they lived. Permanently together, rather than only for a short time. What habits would have to change? And how?

"I have a standing appointment tonight to chauffeur my gamblers," mentioned Jack. "I'll have to leave about seven to pick them up. I'll be back a little after eight, and we can do dinner then. I won't have to drive them home until around midnight. Is this going to be an inconvenience for you? Now or in the future? Most of my work is done in the daytime, but this is an exception."

"No. I've told you I would *not* interfere with your work. One night a week that's a little interrupted, I can live with that. And you get paid, don't you?"

"Naturally. I'm a nice guy, but not so nice I work for nothing. Hang on, there's the phone. It's them. Hello, Mr. Eden. Yes, I'm back from Paris. It was very nice, thank you for asking. Yes, I was expecting to drive you tonight. Seven-thirty as usual? Good, see you then. Goodbye.

"I really like these men. Two thousand dollars every week for an hour's worth of driving, counting both ways. And they think it's a bargain. Best kind of clients for me, high pay that they think is low, and low risk, which they think is high."

"Is it really low risk, Jack? I said I wouldn't complain about your work, but I did claim the right to worry about your safety."

"You did, rightly so, and I approve of that. But this is truly safe. I drive them to the door and pick them up at the door. And the door is guarded by friendly thugs. Cab drivers might deliver these guys to the door, but they won't come back to pick them up. Cabbies don't like going into bad neighborhoods because they might get robbed. A sensible decision on their part, but not one these men like. I get to profit from the cabbies' caution."

"Well, then, look. I'm all packed now and so are you. Can you pick these men up if we go to a hotel tonight?"

"Certainly. They don't know where I live anyway. As long as I show up on time, they don't care where I came from. How about the Drake?"

"Not the Palmer House? I thought that was your favorite."

"It is, but I like to check out the other hotels too. And the Drake is quite good too."

"It's two o'clock now, let's get our bags and head out right away. Darn, your phone again!"

"Hello, may I help you? Oh, hello, Sergeant Feltz. Glad to hear you're back at work. Do I have time to see you? Yes. Will it take long? All right, I'll be there in fifteen minutes.

"That was Detective Sergeant Michael Feltz, Mr. Inspector Radcliffe's assistant. He missed most of the murder case with a broken leg, poor man. But he's back on the job now, and wants me to help him follow up a clue they got about the money. Do you want to wait for me to return, or go get the hotel room now?"

"I'd like to check in together. It still gives me a thrill to hear you say 'Mr. and Mrs. Sorenson' to the clerk. If it's not going to take too long, I'll wait.'

'Okay, love. I'll be back soon."

***

"Good afternoon, Mr. Sorenson," said Mike Feltz. "Thank you for coming in. You know Inspector Radcliffe, and Mahoney. He's here to do the leg work if there is any. I'm up to asking questions, but I can't get around too well.

"Here's the reason for my call. After the murders, we got pictures of the victims from the immigration people. We showed them to Angela Maguire, who found the bodies, but she didn't recognize them. But some time later, she recalled seeing Zahi Smith coming out of a building at the corner of Oak Park and Stanley a few days before he was killed. And she tells us that you once had an apartment there. Do you have an apartment at that address?"

"I do. Actually, it's a small office, where I keep my financial records and do my taxes. The last couple of months have been rather hectic for me, and I haven't been there in a while. I never brought Zahi there. I don't want my clients to know where I live or any of my other apartments. It has sometimes been safer to have my work life and my personal life separate."

"You didn't meet with him there around the fifth of June?" asked Radcliffe. "You have already admitted to meeting with him around that time at his hotel. Meeting with him is not a crime, you don't have to worry about that. We would just like to know if he was there with you."

"Paul is being delicate about this," explained Mahoney, "but he's suggesting that Zahi went there to give you the money, in preparation for their departure to wherever they were going. Did he?"

"I met him and his wife at their motels, only. Let me see, fifth of June? Ah, yes, that would have been the last time I met with them, at the Travel Inn on Roosevelt. I told them I would not take their job. And, … oh, my God! They clubbed me and doped me with chloroform or ether or something like that. When I got home later, I found my wallet in the wrong pocket. That wallet had an ID card with that office as my address. They could have taken my keys while I was out, and put keys and wallet back later.

"I haven't been there since, oh, early May, I guess, until today. If he took my keys and went there when I was knocked out to hide the money, it would still be there. But it's not. I was there today to pack up my ledgers and tax records, and didn't see any suitcases.

"Um, I suppose you want to go and check for yourselves. I don't mind, and won't make you get a warrant. But I will insist you bring a forensics man along to check for fingerprints on whatever you find. Because I don't think the money is there. The two big green suitcases were still in their motel room the whole time, even after I came to."

"We have the suitcases, empty," revealed Mahoney. "They were found in Zahi's car after a couple of his friends tried to take it out of the impound lot. We're still trying to find the money, and so were his friends and his enemies. That's why they called on you a couple of weeks ago. I don't know how they figured out Zahi might have given you the money, but we all seem to be on the same wavelength here."

***

As they went up the stairs to the small office, Sorenson explained his ground rules.

"You don't have a warrant, so you get to see only what is in plain sight, or what I offer to show you. If you don't like that, go get a warrant. I'm trying to be helpful, but I don't like being under suspicion of something.

If you want me to open something up, you have to ask. I get to decide if I open it or not. Are you okay with this?"

"Sam thinks you're a moderately fine, reasonably upstanding citizen," admitted Radcliffe. "Phyllis has been telling me similar things about you as well. I still have reservations about you. But I am willing to be persuaded otherwise. Let's see what's in here."

Sorenson opened the door and led them into the cramped office. They looked at the bare floor and the empty desk with dust marks where the ledgers had been. No sink, no toilet, not even a hotplate to cook on. No sign of any large amounts of money, either.

"What's through that door?" asked Radcliffe.

"That's just a closet," Sorenson informed them. "Nothing in it, not even a spare jacket. See?"

Saying that, he opened the door and they looked at four black suitcases stacked neatly on the closet's floor. They stared at them open-mouthed for some time.

"Well, I'll be damned!" exclaimed Sorenson. "Wait! Don't touch anything, Inspector! Sergeant Vlach, please do your fingerprint thing while we wait. I don't want anyone to think I've ever touched these suitcases."

"Yes, you're right," agreed Radcliffe. "I was so surprised after you said there was nothing here, I forgot about protocol. I still don't know what to make of you, Mr. Sorenson. I can usually read people pretty well, and you acted genuinely surprised when you opened that door."

"I just hope you have some fingerprints from Zahi to check those against," declared Sorenson. "You didn't get any from his body."

"No, but as a legal immigrant," Mahoney informed them, "especially one from a war zone, he was fingerprinted when he came to the U.S. We have copies of those from the Feds. All done, Otto? Okay let's get them out and see what's in them."

They put the first suitcase on the desk, the only raised flat surface in the office. Sorenson waved Radcliffe to go ahead and open the case. Money. Lots of money. Stacked neatly in wrapped bundles of hundred dollar bills. The second suitcase was the same. And the third. And the fourth.

"I guess you're pretty used to seeing this sort of money, Mr. Sorenson," observed Radcliffe, "but it's more than I've ever seen in my life. Do you think the whole ten million is here?"

"I've never seen this much before, either. My clients often like to think of themselves as big players, but they don't ever deal in such large amounts. But I do think this *is* very likely ten million.

"Now I know why he drugged me. He realized I wasn't going to help him, and wanted to hide the money with me anyway. He probably thought he could stick it under my bed or something. This place was even better for him because I rarely come here. You're lucky, Inspector, because I'm closing this office down, moving everything into my new house this week. If the landlord's office had been open today, I wouldn't even have the keys anymore."

***

"They found the money in your office?" exclaimed Marcy. "How utterly bizarre! You cleaned everything out today, how did you not find the money?"

"Mahoney and Paul Radcliffe were there with Feltz when I got to the station. They told me Angela had seen Zahi, shortly before his death, coming out of that place. I said he couldn't have known about it, and we went so I could prove it. Nothing in the place. It's really bare.

"And Radcliffe asks what's behind the door. A closet, empty, I say. I knew the closet was empty. I only used it to hang up a coat in cold or wet weather. I never left anything in it. Why would I check an empty closet? That's how I missed it earlier today. Wrong. Four suitcases full of money. They're still counting it at the station.

"So the damned money has been found at last. I'm not sure what it means that it was found in my office. I will have to talk to a good lawyer about whose property it might be. I don't want it in any case. It killed Zahi and Bilan. It almost killed me when Yahye and his boys came for me. Radcliffe said one of Zahi's friends, a guy named Abdullah, said it was cursed, and I think he's right."

"And if they hadn't called you, what would have happened?"

"The landlord would have checked the place out before renting it out again. So he would have found the money. Rather, he would have found four suitcases, thought I had forgotten them, and returned them to me. It's just as well this way. The police are happy. I'm happy this tragic story is over. The news media will let everyone know that the police now have the money, and we will finally be out of it."

"Thank God for that. I was truly worried about your safety, Jack. These men were killers, brutal ones at that. Your charm may have kept you alive in the past, but stone cold murderers don't usually fall for charm. It's almost five and we'll have to fight traffic to get to the hotel. If we leave now, we can be settled in before you run your 'errand' tonight. Let's go."

***

"If that money was found in your closet, and Zahi and his wife are dead, who does that money belong to?" asked Marcy as they sat in their hotel room after dinner, waiting for Jack's return trip for his gamblers.

"I don't know. I told you earlier I'll have to talk to a lawyer about that. I really don't want it. I have no claim on it. I'm not sure anyone really does. Radcliffe told me Yahye had accumulated most of it by robbery and extortion. Even if the law might say I have a legal claim to it, I have no *moral* claim to it. If I had any say in the matter, it should go back to the people it was taken from. They're probably innocent enough Somalis being robbed by one of their own."

"You don't want even a finder's fee?"

"No. Zahi's friend came to fear the money. It killed Zahi and Bilan, who only wanted to get away and live a quiet life away from all the thugs. It killed Yahye, who was no great loss, but who couldn't give it up either. It won't kill me, or you, if I kept some. Not any longer. But it *is* tainted. I don't worry too much about the history of the money I make, but this is different."

"Good for you, Jack. That's one reason I married you. You do have a strong moral sense, even if you do a lot of less than moral work."